RISE OF THE SANDSHADOW

For Sarah! ☺
The Sandshadow awaits.....

RISE OF THE SANDSHADOW

Kara B

Kara Bartley

Copyright © 2017 by Kara Bartley.

Library of Congress Control Number:		2017913557
ISBN:	Hardcover	978-1-5434-4877-1
	Softcover	978-1-5434-4878-8
	eBook	978-1-5434-4879-5

All rights reserved. No part of this book may be reproduced or transmitted in any form or by any means, electronic or mechanical, including photocopying, recording, or by any information storage and retrieval system, without permission in writing from the copyright owner.

This is a work of fiction. Names, characters, places and incidents either are the product of the author's imagination or are used fictitiously, and any resemblance to any actual persons, living or dead, events, or locales is entirely coincidental.

Any people depicted in stock imagery provided by Thinkstock are models, and such images are being used for illustrative purposes only.
Certain stock imagery © Thinkstock.

Print information available on the last page.

Rev. date: 09/26/2017

To order additional copies of this book, contact:
Xlibris
1-888-795-4274
www.Xlibris.com
Orders@Xlibris.com
761256

CONTENTS

Prologue ix
Run Quickly Or Stand Still! 1
Ruby Red 6
A Past Unknown 9
Wake Up! 12
You Are Not Alone 13
After Visiting Hours 19
Familiar Faces 21
Home Again 23
Something Taken 29
Back To The Books 33
Who's There? 36
Do I Know You? 41
Stay Safe 43
Is It Over? 46
Somewhere Out There 49
They All Fall Down 53
A Common Thread 59
Connecting Trains 64
Closer Than You Think 72
For Those Who Listen 76
Ripple Effect 81
Welcome Back 84
Family Ties 89
Journey To The Temple Of The King 91
Silently Waiting 96
Lessons Learned 102
To Be Determined 107
Change Of Setting 113

From Beneath The Surface	116
A New Permutation	119
A Change Underway	125
Treasure Seekers	129
Resounding Thoughts	133
Beyond The Reaches	136
A Vicious Triumph	145
Answers, Please!	147
History In The Making	154
A Change Is Necessary	163
Paper Trail	168
Picture Perfect	170
Shadow Of The Night	176
Dreams Be Told	179
Keepers Finders	187
Kindred Spirits	192
Unending Expectations	206
Falling Stars	211
Let The Darkness Decide	215
About The Author	219
About The Illustrator	221
The Paleo Twins	223

*For my father, Richard. Your love and support will never be forgotten.
When I see birds flying, I know that you are flying with them.
This one's for you, Dad.*

PROLOGUE

Wichita, Kansas
July 1992

Rain pounded the pavement as Jenna Matthews ran through the streets in search of refuge. Her shoes slammed against the puddles, splashing water all around. She was soaked to the bone, but still she ran. Behind her, a predator followed. One with deadly intentions. Jenna didn't dare look back.

Up ahead, she saw houses not far in the distance. Just a few minutes more and she would be home. Ignoring the pain in her legs, she sprinted through the downpour. She'd been running for nearly ten minutes without stopping, but knowing what was behind her, she didn't once think to rest.

Had she only stayed in the museum, this pursuit would never of happened. But after her disturbing discovery only twenty minutes earlier of an exhibit gone awry, the museum was the last place she wanted to be. Thinking only of her safety, she'd darted out of there without considering the consequences. Having known there'd be a chase, she would have stayed at the museum.

Lightning now rocketed across the thick, black sky, lighting the world above her. Jenna peered up as she ran. The storm was raging overhead. She pushed herself on, telling herself that she could make it if she hurried. In her heart, she truly believed it.

Thunder rumbled near the ground but Jenna was not fooled by the sound. The noise she heard was animalistic. The creature behind her was on a warpath, and her blood was what it was after.

Another surge of lightning blasted through the sky, this time reaching down to the road in front of her like a forked tongue. She screamed and came to an immediate stop. Sparks jumped off the lamppost as flashes of electricity showered onto the street by her feet. Jenna was terrified; now she was trapped. She felt like an animal being herded by the storm. There was no going forward, there was no going back.

Jenna slowly turned when she heard the predator approaching from behind. Frozen in fear, she watched its jaws open. Was this the end for her? She didn't know. But one thing was for sure. Her nightmare was truly about to begin.

RUN QUICKLY OR STAND STILL!

Wichita, Kansas
August 1992

The soft wind pushed through the night air as it brushed Jenna Matthews' auburn hair over her shoulders. She stood with her head tilted to the sky, staring up at the stars. Although her eyes were lifted, her mind was focused on the field of cornstalks that stood before her. Back and forth they swayed as if to welcome her back into their world.

Jenna was alone for the night with the house to herself. Her parents had gone to see a movie and had left her in the company of the family pets, all of which were sleeping inside. She'd been drinking a glass of lemonade in the kitchen, when something in the backyard caught her eye through the window. A mysterious light had been creeping through the cornstalks towards the house. It had her full attention.

But now that she was outside, the light had disappeared, leaving Jenna trapped within her own thoughts. Strange images were coming in and out of view as they flashed in her mind. First was a road. A dark and lonely road. Jenna saw herself running down it, frantically searching for a place to hide. Behind her, a faceless beast was in pursuit. The snarling and clashing of its teeth frightened her even more. For a second she turned to see her attacker, but as she did the image dissolved completely. She stood alone on the road staring off into the darkness, praying for sanctuary, hoping it was only a dream.

Just as her nerves began to calm, her body was swept away to a cold, lifeless desert filled with nothing but white sand. Surrounded by night sky, she watched as the sand rose in front of her to take the form of a terrifying monster. The creature reached for her. Screaming into the night, Jenna cowered as it smiled with deadly intention. It hovered over her, edging closer. Its smell made Jenna sick. She couldn't get away from it. But then the image turned to black and she was left standing alone in the darkness.

Jenna's next vision struck her with the deepest dread yet. She was imprisoned within a dark glass pyramid, fighting to get out. She pounded her fists against the walls as something predatory stalked her from the outside. Its claws etched along the glass, slowly, deliberately. And then she heard the noise.

"No, NO!" She closed her eyes and screamed. Then there was silence. And nothing else.

The visions faded.

Hearing only the breeze of the soft wind around her, Jenna opened her eyes. She was once again standing outside her house. Her fingers were wound tightly around a baseball bat that she held securely in front of her. It was her most trusted weapon, and right now she needed it.

With the bat ready for action, she tried to rationalize the bizarre visions. "It was just a dream…" The frenzied beats of her heart then began to subside. She lowered the bat and took a deep breath. "Oh thank God!"

Jenna was not one to let her emotions navigate. She was a confident, strong-willed sixteen-year-old. But after recent events, her mind was in upheaval. Her unfaltering foundation had undergone a seismic rumble, leaving her questioning everything around her. She hadn't left the house in weeks. Her safety net was her home and family. And she was not about to leave either one.

Her focus then turned to her parents. *Where were Mom and Dad anyway? They should've been home by now!*

As if she had willed it, the telephone rang inside the house. *That better be them!* Jenna ran up the back porch stairs and into the kitchen, towards the ringing phone on the wall.

"Hello?" she said, lifting the receiver.

"Hi Hon, it's Mom."

The ripples in Jenna's veins were soothed at the sound of her mother's voice. "Hi, Mom. How was the movie?" But she cringed after she said the words. Her tone was much too earnest and she knew that her mother would pick up on it.

"Hon—are you okay? Is something wrong?"

An awkward silence ensued. Jenna was hesitant to tell her mother about her visions. Her parents already thought she was a basket case. After a moment's pause, she decided not to. Quietly, she leaned the bat against the wall.

"Jenna—talk to me," her mother said.

"It's okay, Mom. I'm fine. Everything's fine. Where are you?"

"Your father and I had to stop at the grocery store to pick up some things and we were just walking past the ice cream section…"

"Stop right there—" Jenna grinned, "double chocolate."

"Anything else?"

"Nope, just that. Thanks, Mom."

"Okay, we'll be home in about twenty minutes. Where are the boys?" her mother asked.

Jenna walked down the hallway into the sitting room. Peeking through the doorway, she smiled. The extended family was all asleep. Max, the golden retriever, was tucked away in one of the corners with Sam, the black Labrador lying next to him. To Jenna, they looked like two giant salt and pepper shakers that had escaped from the spice rack. Charlie, the German shepherd, was curled up under the coffee table licking his stuffed toy turtle. And stretched out on top of the couch were Ted and Tony, Jenna's two fat red tabby cats.

"They're all good, everyone's inside. It's a picture in here," Jenna said, trying not to disturb the serenity of the room. She then headed back down the hallway into the kitchen.

"Your father and I will be back soon."

"Okay, Mom, and don't forget the ice cream!" Jenna hung up the phone. She stared blankly at the wall for a moment. "I'm just imagining things," she said aloud. But glancing back at the window, her eyes were drawn to the glass where outside the light reappeared in the cornfield. "Oh, great. Not this again!"

Quickly, she reached for the bat. "Get a grip, Jenna!" she scolded herself. There was no sense in hiding indoors. Better to find out what was out there. With the bat gripped in one hand, she opened the door with the other. "Breathe, just breathe…"

As she stepped out into the evening air, a sharp shiver tingled up her body. She rubbed her arms in an attempt to warm herself and calm her growing anxiety. Although it was summer, the temperature was oddly cool for an August night in Wichita.

Goosebumps formed on her arms as she moved. Slowly, she stepped down the porch stairs towards the army of cornstalks.

The light was gone again. She had no idea where it went but with the bat pasted to her fingers, she felt safer.

A weird sensation had begun to coat her skin. A feeling stirred inside of her, like a cauldron brew being summoned to a boil. Jenna was torn between two places: the safety of her house and the sanctity of her mind. If the haven inside her head was breached then nothing would ever be safe. And that just made her angry. She was stronger than that, and now more than ever, she wanted to prove it to herself. She shook off her insecurities the best she could and stationed herself firmly on the ground, using her legs as weighted courage.

"You will not defeat me!" she said with resolution.

A faint chirping appeared in the grass as if to answer. Jenna was surprised by the sound. She listened as something small landed by her feet. Bending down, she came upon the large eyes of a grasshopper. Its emerald body was slightly concealed by the grass. The insect sat poised in position, ready for its next leap.

Jenna placed the bat gently on the ground, and with a steady arm reached out her hand. The grasshopper did not jump away. Instead, it stepped onto her palm. It appeared to be interested in her.

"Well, hello there, little guy. What are you doing out so late?" Jenna leaned her head to one side and looked inquisitively at it. The grasshopper just sat in the center of her hand, quiet and still.

"Where's the rest of your family?" She gazed out into the yard. "Now that I think of it, I haven't seen many of you around. Where've you been hiding?"

The grasshopper did not chirp, nor did it try to leave. There was something peculiar about the animal. Jenna was drawn to its big, black, oval eyes. It was as if they were trying to tell her something.

Then, out of nowhere, a loud sound blasted through the air. "What was that?" Jenna lowered her hand to the ground, but the grasshopper did not hop away. Its legs remained firmly tethered to her skin.

"Where did that come from?" It had sounded like a cross between a gunshot and a grandfather clock.

The noise came again, but this time it was closer, louder. Jenna's ears were starting to sting. She could feel the weight of the grasshopper as it remained on her palm. It would not leave her. She used her index finger to softly push the animal onto the ground. But even then, it did not hop away. It sat amongst the blades of grass and began to chirp. Jenna covered her ears with her hands. The noise it was making was strange, unnatural. It was like a panic-stricken alarm clock that had no 'off' button.

Jenna stood; her eyes fastened to the animal below her. "What's happening?"

Another gunshot-like sound punctured the air. And another. And another. Each sound that followed was louder than the first.

Jenna spun around in all directions, searching for the source of the sound. But then her eyes were lured back to the rows of corn where the light she had seen earlier suddenly reappeared. It was coming towards her.

"Oh my God!" She was frightened, but remained frozen in place.

This property was the source of many fears for Jenna, and now she was starting to feel helpless being out there alone. She searched the ground for her baseball bat but was shocked to see that it was gone. "No!" she cried.

The grasshopper continued to chirp in the grass by her feet. Jenna peered down at the insect and watched as its mouth began to move. She shook her head in disbelief as the animal looked up at her and spoke.

"Run quickly or stand still," it mouthed.

With great force, the light broke through the cornfield and raced into the backyard. The colour drained from Jenna's face. "Oh…God—"

A terrifying noise then ripped through the air. Her heart leapt into her mouth as the fears she had buried suddenly resurfaced. She was no longer able to cope with her surroundings. She struggled to stay on her feet without success. She collapsed onto the ground, and finally succumbed to the pain.

As she drifted into unconsciousness, a flicker of hope remained—that somehow she would find her family and warn them of what was to come.

RUBY RED

"This piece is of extraordinary value," Maggie Secord declared to the old man standing in front of her. "It's a rare ruby." With meticulous scrutiny, she looked through her glasses at the object in her hands. It was heavy but small, roughly the size of a golf ball. The round cut gem glistened under the lamp on the table. Maggie's eyes were drawn to the center of the red glass. "How did you get this?"

The old man fidgeted in place, giving Maggie the impression that he was uncomfortable being there. He began to pace across the floor to the other side of the mahogany-coloured room.

"I found it here in Wichita," he said.

"Really? Here? That seems a little strange."

"Why do you say that?" he asked.

Without lifting her head, she gazed up at the old man. "Because this jewel isn't from here."

The old man said nothing.

As an archaeology professor at Brockfield University in Wichita, Maggie had become accustomed to people wandering into her office, asking for her assessment. She was cross-appointed with the Lionhead Museum and had spent endless hours working with their collections. In her field she'd met many wild and flamboyant characters; from the amateur enthusiasts who swore they had found Cleopatra's misplaced jewellery to the retired widows who needed to sell their Ming vases to pay for their next cruise vacation.

Maggie's personal favourite was the man who called to say that he had found the Sphinx's nose. He was holding it for ransom in his mother's basement somewhere in North Dakota. That, without a doubt was the most interesting story Maggie had ever heard.

Until now, when this old man walked into her office. Though perhaps he seemed more dodgy than interesting.

"It's a Siamese medallion, hardly something you'd find in Kansas," she said. "It's been taken care of, though. So, in my expert opinion it belonged to either a museum or a private collector."

"Oh, I see," he said, turning away.

Maggie was sceptical of the old man. He'd shown up unannounced twenty minutes earlier begging for an appraisal on a jewel that he had with him. She'd explained that her calendar was quite full but that she could fit him in on the following week. But the old man was impatient. He'd insisted that Maggie see him, informed her that time was running out and that he could not wait. And just when she was about to call security, he'd pulled out an ace—he told her that he knew Barbara Matthews, curator of the Lionhead Museum.

Maggie's interest was then piqued and she'd agreed to examine the object, if only to learn how the old man acquired it.

He stood now, watching carefully as she studied the jewel. Her fingers slipped over every facet, every crimson angle. An odd smile crept along her face.

"Do you see this insignia here?" she said. "That's a royal branding, from Siam."

"You don't say." The old man leaned his head and looked.

"Hmm, that's interesting…"

"What's interesting?" he said.

"There's another symbol here."

"Oh?" he grinned.

Maggie examined the markings underneath the light. "Well, this is odd. This symbol looks Egyptian…"

"Oh, it might be, yes," he said. "You're very wise. It's the reason I chose to come to you, you know."

"That's very kind of you to say, thank you," Maggie smiled. "So, how long have you had this for?" This time she didn't look up.

The old man didn't answer. Instead, he looked away.

Maggie's trance was broken when she realized that she was talking to herself. "Sir, are you okay?" she said, peering up at him.

With his head turned, he waved away her kindness. "I'm fine, yes. Please don't dote on me," he said. "I'm just curious as to what your findings are."

"Well, I'm not sure yet, I'll need some more time."

"Time *is* crucial," he said. "But not for you."

As he turned back, Maggie jumped from her seat. The man's eyes had glazed over in a harsh yellow stare. He looked almost reptilian.

"Oh my God!" she said in a state of shock.

"Give me the ruby," he glared at her. His manner had completely changed.

Maggie watched as he unravelled in front of her. "What's wrong with your eyes?"

"There is no time for this—give me the jewel!"

"But…I'm not finished yet…" her voice cracked.

The man was frantic. He reached across the desk and plucked the ruby from her hands. He grimaced and scurried out of the room.

"Wait!" Maggie yelled. She chased after him. Running into the hallway, she searched all around. She was surprised to see that the old man was nowhere in sight. Judging by his mobility, he couldn't have gone very far.

With no name or contact information, Maggie had very little to go on but the memory of their meeting. The mere mention of Barbara Matthews at the Lionhead Museum was the only bit of information that she had. And for Maggie, it would have to do.

A PAST UNKNOWN

Beneath closed eyes, Jenna's mind was alive. Anyone walking past the hospital room might have mistaken her restful state for peaceful slumber, but on the contrary, her mind had been very active since her body collapsed. It had taken her on a whirlwind trip through time, whisking her away to a path littered with memories. Some of which were not hers.

The clicking of the clock on the wall was so loud, that to Jenna it felt like a stampede of elephants heading her way. In a passive voice, she uttered, "The elephants...are...com...the ele...are...co..." Then she heard something small, buzzing in her ear.

Beside her on the pillow was a bright yellow bumblebee. The words she muttered were gibberish as her mind registered the bizarre image. "Oh hello, bee...you look like a nugget. Yes, that's it, a little nugget," she laughed. "There's a nugget in my cereal—help!" She smiled.

But a quick prick of its stinger took Jenna to a very different place.

Grey cloud filled the air as a cool wind whistled all around her. For this, she was awake. Jenna rubbed her eyes and looked around. "Where am I?"

There was no answer, just a whisper from the leaves drifting past her. Her pulse began to accelerate when she realized that she was all alone in a place that was unfamiliar.

A noise came from ahead of her. Although partly masked by the cloud, Jenna believed that it was the sound of a child's cry. With unsure steps, she moved towards the sound, slowly, carefully. The crying stopped for a moment and all she heard was the sound of leaves crushing beneath her feet. Then she paused. The child's cries were now coming from behind her. She turned to listen. "What is going on?"

Another voice chimed in, an echo in the trees. It was the sound of a woman, sobbing. Jenna pivoted toward the sound. Her legs began to move on their own, an unforeseen force was pushing her onward. "Wait, stop. I don't know what's out there. I want to go back."

Her legs kept moving.

A moment later, her feet slid over something hard, stone-like. She tried to stop moving, but it was useless; her body was on autopilot.

A few steps further took her over another stony surface. Small. Flat. Rectangular. Jenna had no idea what it was. Her vision still clouded, she bent down and felt the object with her fingers. "Oh God—"

The chiselled markings on the stone painted a horrifying picture. Death. She was in a cemetery.

The air was now still. No cries, no sobs.

"Why am I here?" Jenna called out. The cloud began to disappear, and within seconds, she had her answer.

Standing before her was a pink granite headstone with a marble lamb carved on top of it. It looked like a child's grave but there was no name on it. Jenna examined the stone carefully and saw the dates, 'April 14, 1933—November 25, 1939', chiselled into the granite. The child was only six years old when he or she died.

A wave of sympathy replaced Jenna's fears for the moment. She pressed her hand up against the stone and shook her head. A few scattered leaves covered the remaining words on the headstone. As she removed them, she was struck with an ill twist in her stomach. Written beneath the dates were the words: '*Up In Heaven Where The Flowers Never Fade.*'

Jenna stood slowly and backed away from the grave. "Why did I need to see this?" Her mind filled with morbid thoughts as the cloud moved back in. Her vision grew blurry and she began to feel tired. All Jenna wanted now was to get out of the cemetery.

With her body no longer being controlled by outside forces, she turned from the grave and ran. She stumbled past the surrounding headstones while desperately searching the area for a way out. But there was no visible exit.

Jenna watched with drowsy eyes as the cloud began to take form ahead of her. Thin, billowing fog-like fingers wound their way through the cemetery, creeping like a serpent towards her. The sight of it made her anxious but the drowsiness was taking over. She was losing strength by the minute.

It wasn't until she heard a low growl that she realized she'd been caught. Standing behind her, was her most dreaded enemy.

As the creeping fog approached, Jenna stopped dead in her tracks. She couldn't move on, she couldn't go back. She was trapped.

As she turned back to look, she saw a large animal pacing behind the child's headstone. Its bulky paws grazed over the grass as it scoured the cemetery with crimson eyes.

Get out! Get out! GET OUT! Jenna silently told herself, hoping to remain inconspicuous.

A twig crackled beneath her foot as she backed away. But it was too late, the animal had spotted her. There was no place to run.

Suddenly, something wound around her torso. Looking down, she saw the fingers of cloud wrapped around her; they were preventing her from leaving. She screamed as the sounds of her enemy crept in closer. Even in her daze, Jenna could tell that her world was about to change. After trying so hard to block out the terrorizing events that haunted her these last few weeks, she was now in the presence of the Siamese Mummy—with no allowable escape. Her past actions had led her right to this moment. Why it had brought her to the cemetery, to a child's gravestone was beyond her thinking.

The band of fingers began to tighten; Jenna could feel her breath being squeezed right out of her. There was no escape from their grasp. Fearing her ultimate doom, she took one last look at the lion-sized feline that paced behind her. "Why are you doing this? Why won't you leave me alone?"

For some reason however, the cat did not leave the child's grave. It appeared as though it was protecting it.

Jenna choked on her lack of breath. With thoughts of imminent death looming above her, she heard an odd buzzing in her ears. The bumblebee had returned. With one sharp stab, it forced its stinger into her arm.

Jenna howled in agony as her head flopped from side to side. The pain was excruciating. In an instant, everything disappeared out of view—the cloud, the entrapment, the predator itself.

All that was left, was fear.

WAKE UP!

Like a flash of white lightning born from the sky, Jenna's body came to life. Panic-stricken and terrified, she awoke to the sound of her own screams.

"NO NO NO!" She wailed as her body jolted upright.

A multitude of arms immediately encircled her body, pushing her back down. She grimaced as something sharp pricked her arm.

"NO—please stop! Get away from me! Get away!"

The room was filled with nurses tapping machines, yelling out orders and shining bright lights into her eyes.

"It's out there waiting for me—and you're all next! Don't you see? It's coming!" Jenna hollered.

Around her, the doctors and nurses just looked bewildered. Her parents, who were standing on the other side of the room, looked horrified. Jenna couldn't understand why they were all just watching her, rather than running. She was trying to warn them that danger was imminent. Why weren't they listening?

Her speech began to slur as she consciously let her body fall back onto the bed. Within a matter of minutes she was fully asleep. Physically, she was now at peace. Mentally, she was somewhere darker. And for the time being, that is where she would remain.

YOU ARE NOT ALONE

Jenna heard voices all around her. Some were familiar, some were not. It didn't matter, though. Everything was copasetic. She felt relaxed, as if she were at home, lying on the sofa watching the television.

She heard a woman say, "I think she's awake—get Dr. Roberts."

Casually, Jenna opened her eyes. The light in the room was dim. She turned her head to look out the window and saw only darkness. It was night time. Her father stood next to the window, looking down at her.

As Jenna attempted to verbalize her first thoughts, she laughed. "Da...Dar..." Her speech was slightly slurred. She rested a moment and then started again. "Dad...is that you?"

Her father moved to the side of the bed and leaned over. "Yeah, kiddo, it's me. Your mom and I are both here," he said, gazing across the bed.

"Mom—you're here," Jenna said, flopping her head to the other side. "You're not missing anymore!"

"Missing? No, Jenna. I'm here," her mother said, taking a hold of her hand. With a confused expression, she looked up at Jenna's father. "What is she talking about?"

"Tooftons and merriment...that's what I'm talking about! Heed my cry, I called to the garden!" Jenna trumpeted.

Her parents shook their heads in disbelief.

"Red interlaced with white goes the other half...find it I must! Then phew—into the harvest of the tweeds!" The corners of Jenna's mouth twisted upward and she released a hearty cackle.

The door to the room opened and in walked Dr. Roberts followed by another nurse. Their appearance momentarily broke Jenna's chain of babbling.

"There's our girl," Dr. Roberts said, walking up alongside the bed. Jenna's father moved aside as the doctor examined her. "It's good to see you awake, Jenna. I'm afraid you've given us quite a scare. How are you feeling now?"

Jenna was absolutely giddy. "I'm just perfect as pie, peach I think or maybe lemon cobbler, with toad stools and wicker baskets," she laughed. "And we mustn't forget the spider monkeys and talismans…"

"She's been saying all sorts of strange things," her mother said. "I've seen high temperatures before but I've never heard anyone talk like that. Is that normal?"

"It's nothing to worry about, Mrs. Matthews. A high temperature like Jenna's can cause many things—hallucinations, dreams, fantasies, aberrations." He lifted his head and inspected the intravenous line. "She's no longer dehydrated. We can probably take her off the saline solution and start her with regular fluids," he said to one of the nurses. "The medicine is bringing her temperature down, although it's working a little slower than I expected."

"What do you mean it's nothing to worry about?" Jenna's mother said, with a look of horror on her face. "She sounds absolutely crazy!"

"Barbara's right. We've never seen Jenna like this before," her father added.

"Hey—it's all right, I'm totally fine!" Jenna said, looking up at them. She couldn't understand why everyone was so worried. To her, the giant bed of cotton balls she was lying on was the best thing ever. "So, if you could all just keep it down…I can't hear the movie."

"Okay, Jenna," her mother said with a forced smile.

"Look, I understand your concern and we will get to the bottom of this, I promise," Dr. Roberts said. "As for Jenna's gibberish, that's the temperature doing that, and the medicine. At least let that be a comfort to you now."

"Gibberish? Whose gibberish? Better not be mine…I just put mine away an hour ago. Locked it up and threw away the key, I did!" Jenna laughed.

"What we need to focus on are the injuries on her hands," Dr. Roberts continued. He turned Jenna's right palm upward and removed the bandage to view the cuts.

When she was first admitted, her temperature was 106 degrees. Other than that, she exhibited no other signs of distress. No pain, no illness. No injuries—until they looked at her hands. Both were covered in cuts. The short pattern of slashes indicated some sort of attack. In addition to the cuts were several bite marks. Jenna had held up her hands to protect herself against something.

"This is the part that concerns me," Dr. Roberts said. He looked over at Jenna's father. "You said that you saw nothing when you arrived home?"

"No, nothing. But those aren't from our pets. Our dogs would never do that, they would never harm Jenna. And they were all sleeping inside the house when we got home. Jenna was outside when this happened. It had to be something else."

"I agree. These puncture wounds—the distance between the canine impressions is too wide. This was done by a much larger animal."

"Oh God..." Jenna's mother gasped. "You mean like a bobcat or something?"

"Perhaps," Dr. Roberts said. "You live in a somewhat rural area, it's possible that Jenna encountered some sort of wild animal out there."

Jenna listened as they spoke. "I love cats. Big ones, small ones, mummified ones."

Her father touched her shoulder, gently. "Jenna's pretty brave with animals, she's always helping me out at my clinic. I'd hate to think that she came across something dangerous in the yard, although obviously she did."

Dr. Roberts nodded. "I'm afraid so." He examined Jenna's hand again. "Your wife told me that you're a veterinarian, and that you operate a clinic next to your house."

"Yes, that's right," her father said. "When we moved here from Niagara Falls, I decided to open my own practice. I built the clinic next to our house. It's been a little over a year now, but we're all settled in."

"Well, that's a big undertaking, building your own business. Tell me, do you ever get stray animals, or anything unusual near your clinic?" Dr. Roberts asked.

"Sometimes we get stray cats, coyotes, that sort of thing. But nothing that would ever do this."

Dr. Roberts replaced Jenna's bandage. "I see. Well, the blood tests should be back soon. We'll have more to go on then. You said that you were speaking to Jenna shortly before this happened?"

"Yes, Barbara spoke to her on the phone twenty minutes before we arrived home. She was fine then. But when we got there, Jenna was lying unconscious in the backyard with those cuts on her hands. We called an ambulance and they brought her here."

"I understand that she regained consciousness on the ride over," Dr. Roberts said.

"Yes, that's right," her mother said. "She was terrified—she thought that something was following her. We figured it was one of her nightmares."

Dr. Roberts had a strange expression on his face. "One of her *nightmares?*" he asked.

"Yes, Jenna had been experiencing severe nightmares, stemming from a museum visit about a month ago."

Jenna's eyes lit up like lamps. "The museum—let's go to Lionhead! Can we go? Can we go? I haven't been there in years!" she spurted. "I love the hall of African mammals!"

"Sure, kiddo," her father said. "As soon as you're better."

"Thanks, cause I really need to visit Egypt and Thailand. Oh, and also the land of cat kings and warriors and giant bugs," she said, listing the places on her fingers. "We're gonna have a hootenanny! Wanna come?"

Dr. Roberts watched her behaviour, carefully. "What exactly were these nightmares about?"

"Jenna was scared that something had come alive in the museum where I work, and had followed her home," her mother said.

The conversation was severed when a little girl wandered into the room looking lost. She was dressed beautifully, wearing a black velvet dress and red patent shoes. The tight curls of her honeysuckle hair clung to the air as she bounded towards them.

"Little girl, you can't be in here!" Dr. Roberts yelled.

One of the nurses rushed over as the girl turned and wiggled her fingers at Jenna.

Jenna responded with a wave and a smile. "Are you part of the movie?" she said.

The nurse quickly hustled the little girl towards the door. "Come on, sweetie, let's go."

The little girl said nothing. Instead, a devious smile blossomed towards her cherry-white cheeks. Then with a childish dash, she darted out of the room before anyone could catch her.

"Boy, she was nice." Jenna grinned. "Black is definitely her colour."

Dr. Roberts shook his head. "Where are her parents? Nurse, would you please go and make sure that that little girl isn't lost. Find her family, will you? Thanks."

The nurse nodded and left the room.

"Sorry about that," Dr. Roberts said. "Well, your daughter appears to be improving but I'm afraid we're going to have to keep her in the intensive care unit. Her vitals are stable, though. That's very good."

"And the mummies were very tall beneath the sand, very tall," Jenna said, making perfect sense, but only to herself. "I like sand. It's soft on your feet and good for hiding things." She glanced around the room at all the faces staring back at her. "That's my mom and that's my dad. Where's Scotty dog and Grandma Abby? Shouldn't they be here for the party? They're missing out!" Jenna wanted her brother and grandmother in the room, too, so that she could whisper secrets and talk about cornstalks with them.

"Scott's away at university, remember Jenna?" her father said. "And your grandmother is visiting family, but don't you worry—we'll let them know."

"Oh, okay, as long as they know," Jenna giggled. Her amusement turned serious when she looked at Dr. Roberts. "Say, you look like my doctor. It's probably because of the coat...and the glasses. Yes, definitely because of the glasses. But who are all these other people?"

One quick scan around the room and her father answered. "Jenna, that's your nurse."

Jenna closed her eyes, scrunched her nose and smirked. "She's not my nurse...she's a mummy. And so are all the rest."

The unspoken feeling in the room was now unanimous amongst the visitors. Jenna Matthews was delirious.

"Sweetie," her mother said, gently tapping her hand, "you're in the hospital, and that's your nurse."

"Oh, okay, but she still looks like a mummy." Jenna cupped her hand around her mouth and whispered, "Someone should tell her, it's embarrassing."

"Okay, kiddo. We'll do that," her father said. He turned from the bed to speak to Dr. Roberts. "Is there something you're not telling us?"

The doctor paused. "No, but like I said, the test results should be back shortly. We'll know more then." He patted Jenna's father on the shoulder. "Why don't we leave you alone with your daughter for a little while. I'll be back later to check on her." With that, Dr. Roberts and the nurse left the room.

Jenna sulked. "Is the party over? Was it something I said?"

"No, sweetie," her mother consoled her. "Your father and I are going to spend some time with you alone."

"Well, then you should tell the mummies to leave, too."

Her mother's eyes skirted around the room. "Jenna, everyone's gone. It's just the three of us now."

"Not the mummies, they didn't leave. Maybe if you asked them nicely they might."

"Jenna—what are you talking about?" her father said.

Jenna lifted her arm and pointed to the back wall. "The mummies—they're all watching us."

Her father stared at the back of the room. "Can you see the mummies right now?"

"Yes, they're standing right behind you. Can't you see them, Dad?" she yawned. "They're right over there. They're talking to me...saying things I can't repeat. I can hear their cries."

"It's probably from all the time she spent at the museum," her father suggested.

Her mother gave a reluctant, tearful nod.

"Hey, can we talk later? I'm so tired from all the running. Tell King Odon that I named every cornstalk." With those final words, she fell fast asleep, leaving nothing but silence in the room around her.

AFTER VISITING HOURS

As the clock on the wall approached two-thirty, something foreign entered the hospital. Lying in her room, Jenna's eyes slowly opened. She began to speak. "It's coming for me...it wants me."

Dr. Roberts stood inside the darkened room watching her. He walked alongside her bed and gazed down. "Jenna—what's coming?"

Jenna stared at the ceiling. "It wants me..."

The visitor moved through the halls with ease, indiscernible to the naked eye. Quietly, it made its way to the intensive care unit. Through the doors, it slithered, passing by desks, people and air. Its cryptic body curved and slinked down the hallway, making its way towards Jenna's room.

No one took notice as it hissed by them.

Dr. Roberts looked up when something unseen whispered into the room, and suddenly, unexpectedly, he felt incredibly tired. He took off his glasses and rubbed his eyes.

"It's here," Jenna said.

Failing to keep his eyes open, Dr. Roberts walked over to the chair in the corner and sat down. Seconds later, his body slumped over.

The hallway light outside the room began to flicker. Jenna felt the arrival of something unnatural. She remained in place as her door slowly opened. A gentle breeze came from the open window next to her, but it couldn't distract her from the uninvited presence now inside her room.

"I know you've come for me," she mouthed.

A ghostly shadow moved through the space as it approached the bed.

"Why are you doing this?" Jenna said, her body still as a board.

"T...a...l...i...s...m...a...n..." the creature replied.

Jenna felt something moving up the sheets towards her head. Her torso buckled beneath the weight of something heavy. She exhaled and began to cough.

"Give me the…t…a…l…i…s…m…a…n…" the voice whispered. Its tone was sharp and bitter.

"I don't have it," she coughed again. Her limbs were fastened to the bed; she was unable to move. Her body craved freedom as the air escaped from her lungs.

Then in a flash, the intruder turned towards the door and let out a piercing scream.

Jenna's ears burned from the sound. "Ahhh!" she screeched.

The prowler then disappeared into the night as its trailing shadow slid through the open window, leaving behind a path of sand.

A silent visitor stood in the doorway, watching the prowler leave. Disguised and concealed in a shroud of protective darkness, the visitor waited.

FAMILIAR FACES

With both hands pressed against her ears, Jenna cried out, "I don't have the talisman!" Slowly, she opened her eyes and looked around the room. The sun now beamed through the window, scaring away any thoughts of darkness. She lowered her hands when she saw her family staring at her.

Her parents were at the foot of her bed. Dr. Roberts was examining one of the machines next to her. And standing at the entrance of the door, wearing a very sly grin, was her grandmother.

"Grandma!" Jenna squealed in excitement.

"Well, I don't have the talisman either!" She smiled and crossed the room with arms extended. Leaning over, she hugged Jenna tightly.

"I've missed you so much!" Jenna wrapped her arms around her and squeezed. "That's it—you're never allowed to leave again!"

"Apparently," she laughed. "Is this what happens when I'm away—you end up in the hospital?" Her grandmother then turned to the stunned faces in the room. "Well, don't look at me like that. I decided to come home a little early is all." She smiled at Jenna's parents. "Aren't you happy to see me?"

"Of course, Mom, it's great to see you!" Jenna's mother said, reaching out to embrace her. "We just weren't expecting you home until tomorrow."

"And Reid—how are you?" Jenna's grandmother asked.

Jenna's father leaned over and hugged her. "Abby—you have no idea how good it is to see you. We've been better as you can probably tell."

"That's all right, my dear. I'm here now."

"Mom, how did you get home from the airport?" Jenna's mother asked.

"Well," she said, "I decided to surprise all of you and find my own way back. You know, I'm not *that* old. I do travel alone, if you remember."

Jenna's mother laughed. "Of course, we know that. But how did you know that we were here? We called but we weren't able to reach you."

At that moment, Dr. Roberts broke into the conversation. "I'm sorry to interrupt but I thought you'd like to know that Jenna has made an incredible recovery." He now sat on the bed beside her. "Your vitals are strong. Your cuts will take some time to heal but keep the bandages on. The ointments I'm prescribing will help. I'd like to do a few more tests to be sure but at this rate, your family can take you home this afternoon."

"Are you sure?" her father said. "I mean...she was so sick yesterday."

"I know," Dr. Roberts said. "It doesn't make any sense, medically, but there's no arguing with facts. Jenna is ready to go home."

Jenna's mother smiled with guarded lips. "I can't believe it."

"Oh—pish posh!" Grandma Abby's voice resounded. "You all look like you've never seen a miracle. Jenna's health has returned and so have I. The time has come for us to go home."

HOME AGAIN

Jenna finished off the last lemon square and placed the plate back on the bedside table. "Thank you, Grandma, those were delicious."

Her grandmother stood by the window watching the colours of the day fade into darkness. She was dressed in black flowing linens, typical of her whimsical gypsy flare. Her silver lengthy curls coiled down her back, providing a stunning contrast to her dark dress. "Well, how does it feel to be back in your own bed, my dear?"

"It feels good. I'm so glad to be out of that hospital. I know it's only been a few hours since I left but thank God I'm home!" Jenna reached towards the foot of the bed and pulled her two sleeping cats over. "I missed you guys." They meowed in response as she squeezed them.

"I'm sure they missed you, too. Cats are such welcome reminders of strength, aren't they?" Her grandmother turned to face her. "So, tell me...how is school?"

Jenna paused. "Oh, I guess you didn't hear. I haven't been back yet. I'm just not ready to leave the house."

Her grandmother's reaction was immediate. "Oh, sweetie," she said, sitting down on the edge of the bed. "Why didn't you say something earlier? Let's talk about this."

Jenna's grandmother had been away for nearly a month, visiting family back in Salem, Massachusetts. While away, she'd been in contact with Jenna's parents but not with Jenna, which was unusual. Under normal circumstances, Jenna would have been on the phone with her every night, giving her the daily run-down of teen life in Wichita. But after her last visit to the Lionhead Museum about a month ago, Jenna's world had been turned upside down. No one understood why, except for Jenna who refused to talk about it. She had become completely despondent, and hadn't left the house since the incident.

Jenna's parents hadn't mentioned anything to Jenna's grandmother about what had happened, as they didn't want to worry her while she was away. They hadn't told her that Jenna had missed all of her baseball games, summer parties, movie nights at the drive-in and her first week of school. It wasn't the typical lifestyle of a teenage girl, and Jenna didn't give her parents much to go on. She simply closed herself off from the world around her and remained hopelessly devoted to the television. Day after day, she would lie on the couch attached to the cats, watching program after program.

Her parents tried to get her to see a specialist but Jenna refused. She wouldn't discuss her problems or let anyone else hear about them. The only signs of stress she displayed were her nightmares. She frequently woke her parents by screaming in the middle of the night with horrid dreams of darkness stalking.

Now Jenna's grandmother looked at her with great concern. "Why haven't you been out?" she asked.

"I don't know," Jenna said from behind the orange fur. "I just feel safer here. The night I went to the hospital...that was the first time Mom and Dad had left me alone with the house. I guess they won't be doing that again."

"Jenna, your mother told me today that something happened to you at the museum, around the same time I left for my trip. Why don't you tell me what happened that day. Maybe we should start there."

The colour in Jenna's face slowly drained. She placed the cats down, stood from the bed and wandered over to the other side of the room. She fiddled with some of the books on her desk. "I don't want to talk about it."

"Sweetie, your parents told me that your nightmares started after that museum visit. I understand how hard it is sometimes to talk about problems but maybe I can help. We've always talked through our issues before."

Jenna pouted. "You won't believe me, no one will. It doesn't sound real to anyone but me. But it *was* real. It *did* happen!"

Her grandmother shifted on the bed. "*What* happened?"

Jenna shook her head and looked around the room. "I was followed."

"Followed?"

"Yes, by something really bad. It was watching me inside the museum...an artifact. I ran out of there as fast as I could but I was followed."

Jenna's grandmother crossed her arms. "By the artifact?"

Jenna picked up on her grandmother's tone. "You don't believe me...do you?"

"I didn't say that, I'm just listening is all. Please, keep going."

Jenna gazed off across the room. "It was an animal, the restless spirit of the artifact. It chased me out of the museum and followed me home. And now it's out there." She walked over to the window and looked out. "It's waiting for me."

"Waiting for you...outside?"

"Yes, except it already found me. This animal put me in the hospital. It's dangerous—it attacked me!"

Jenna's grandmother stood from the bed and walked over to where she was standing. "Are you sure this was the animal that harmed you?"

Again, Jenna could sense the doubt in her grandmother's voice. "What do you mean—of course I'm sure!"

"It's just that...you were attacked in the dark. Perhaps you were too shocked to see what was *really* attacking you."

Jenna looked at her suspiciously. "How did you know that it was dark out? I never told you that."

Her grandmother smiled. "Your parents told me this morning when I arrived at the hospital."

Jenna grunted. "Oh."

Another reason Jenna was hesitant to speak with her grandmother about the topic was because she believed that her grandmother was in fact, the animal in question. Or at least that's what she had originally thought when she first encountered it weeks ago. But that theory had been put to rest upon realizing how ridiculous it was.

A few days prior to Jenna's meltdown, the corpse of a large mummified cat had been put on display at the Lionhead Museum in Wichita. Along with it was a book entitled, *A City Lost*, which referenced the cat and the history of its life. Within a few hours of its unveiling, the Mummy was wreaking havoc on the city. Its restless soul—a lion-sized wild cat—had returned to the land of the living and had possessed Jenna's grandmother, or so she had believed at the time. It then began its hunt for a precious jewel, which happened to be hidden on Jenna's property. It had zeroed in on Jenna, specifically, and had chased her down until she was mentally exasperated.

The disturbing discovery that her grandmother was the trapped soul of the mummy had sent Jenna's mind into a tailspin. She was desperate to do anything that would dispel the theory. For her, it meant that she had to help find the jewel and end the Mummy's curse.

Through puzzles, near escapes and terrifying experiences, Jenna ultimately found the small, red ruby severed in three pieces. She'd reconnected it, just in time for the animal to disappear, and for life to return to normal. Or so she had thought. Her last visit to the Lionhead Museum was supposed to have confirmed that, as well as put an end to her grandmother/Mummy shape-shifting theory. But after her fateful run-in with the animal that day, Jenna realized that life would never be the same.

Time had taken her sanity. Doubt was what replaced it. Remaining silently closed off from the world was the only trait that she treasured. Until now. With her grandmother standing next to her, looking as normal as ever with no signs of claws, whiskers or fur, Jenna sighed. There was no more hiding. She was forced to deal with her problems—that was the hold her grandmother had on her.

"Jenna, talk to me," her grandmother said.

"I'm sorry, Grandma…I'm just a mess," Jenna said, as the tears trickled down her cheeks. "I know it sounds crazy, and you probably think I'm delusional. Maybe it *is* all in my head—I can't tell anymore."

Her grandmother gave a sympathetic look. She then reached out and lifted Jenna's hands up. "These cuts, these wounds—they weren't made by ghosts." She gently stroked the bandages. "Something did attack you, Jenna, I believe you. But it might not be what you think."

Jenna shook her head. "What else could it be? What else do I have to be afraid of?"

"There are a lot of evils in this world, my dear. Living on a farm, outside the city limits, can bring different challenges. But don't let that be a burden to you now. You must rest. Besides, I am here."

"And I'm really grateful for that," Jenna said.

"Well, believe it or not, I think we made some progress," her grandmother said. She turned and headed for the bedroom door.

Jenna looked on with a confounded gaze. "Where are you going?"

"I'll be right back. I'm going to make you some hot chocolate... with a special twist," she winked. With a snake-like slither, she exited the room.

Jenna knew what that meant. She was about to endure one of her grandmother's special herbal concoctions. But if it were mixed with chocolate, she would eat or drink anything, just as long as she didn't have to leave the house to do it.

Jenna leaned towards the window. Staring out, she looked up at the night sky. It was peaceful. No wind. No noise. It was just what she needed. Minutes passed by with no disturbance. But then Jenna saw the first strike of lightning in the distance. With the land being so flat she was able to see quite far. Her eyes ignited with a pleasant thrill. Jenna loved storms. To watch Nature come alive in front of her was absolutely amazing. At any other given time, she would've propped herself up on the swing set or the back porch stairs to watch the weather go by. But this was no normal day.

Immersed in the evening's electrical show, Jenna didn't hear her grandmother re-enter the room. "You long to go out there, don't you?" her voice came from behind.

Jenna spun around, startled. "Grandma, you scared me. You're so quiet," she grinned.

"See, there is a part of you still inside. It's nice to see you smile, dear." Cupped within her hands was a hot, steaming mug. "Take this, Jenna. You'll feel better in the morning. Maybe you'll even want to venture outside again."

Jenna replied with a confident headshake. "I don't think so, but thank you, Grandma." She took a few sips of the drink and made her way towards the bed. "But if it'll help me sleep, that would be great." Her eyelids slowly began to close as she slipped beneath the covers. The drink was making her drowsy. Her words began to slur. "Thank you, Granndmaaa. This was delicioussss..."

"That's right, Jenna, drink up. Drink until the end."

Jenna took a few more sips and then drifted off completely.

Her grandmother removed the mug from her hands and smiled. "Sleep well, my dear, and dream lightly."

*****

Jenna stirred in her sleep only once that night. She opened her eyes and saw her grandmother standing guard by the window, keeping a watchful eye on the cornfield.

"Grandma…you're still here?" she said in a lazy voice.

"Yes, Jenna. Everything is fine. Go back to sleep."

"Okay, Grandma. See you in the morning."

"Yes, my dear. You will."

SOMETHING TAKEN

Jenna awoke to a familiar buzzing in the air. The sound stirred her as she lifted her head from the pillow. Ears alert and eyes still closed, she listened. Then with a hearty thunk, she fell back down. She was too tired to get up.

The sound persisted; it came from the kitchen downstairs. The noise subsided when she heard her mother's voice below. "Hello? Oh, hi Maggie. I'm so sorry I didn't get back to you. Yes, she's home now. I know, thank goodness..."

Jenna's ears perked. Her mother was talking about her with someone on the telephone.

"Really? I don't know anyone like that. What did he say?" Her mother paused and then continued. "That's interesting, what did he want? Really? Well, it's not from our collections. Describe the insignia..."

The remainder of the conversation was lost to Jenna when she sat up and opened her eyes. She yawned, stretched and glanced around the room. The cats were gone and so was her grandmother. She took a moment to gather her strength. Then with one foot in front of the other, she dragged herself out of bed and headed downstairs to the kitchen.

Jenna was looking forward to a new day, especially one that didn't involve wearing a backless hospital gown. She was extremely happy to be out of that God forsaken patient factory. All that poking and probing. All that drilling for blood. Jenna felt like a large, fleshy pin cushion. Thankfully, she didn't remember the entire experience. The only memories that lingered were the coloured bruises that now graced her arms, and the bandages on her hands.

As Jenna entered the kitchen, her mother hung up the telephone. "Well, look who's up! How are you feeling?" she said, walking over to her.

Jenna smiled. "Actually, I'm feeling pretty good, Mom. Definitely better than yesterday."

"Oh, that's wonderful. How about some breakfast—are you hungry? Why don't I make you something," her mother said, sitting Jenna down at the kitchen table. "Pancakes...scrambled eggs...gypsy toast?"

Jenna marvelled at the thought of breakfast. She craved it after being in the hospital. "I'd love some gypsy toast, Mom, but only if you have time."

"I have lots of time. I took the day off of work." She placed a glass of orange juice on the table. "This'll get you started." She then moved about the kitchen preparing the meal.

"Actually, Mom...I think I'd like to go to school today."

Her mother nearly dropped the frying pan she was holding. "What?"

"Yeah, I mean...I feel really good." Jenna took a sip of her juice.

"Jenna, you know you can stay home a few more days if you need to. Your father and I don't want you rushing back into things if you're not up to it."

"Mom, I'm fine. I feel great. All I want is for things to get back to normal."

Her mother stared at her for a moment. She then walked over and felt Jenna's forehead. "Are you sure?"

Jenna nodded, pushing her mother's hand away. "It's okay—really. I mean it."

"Well...I guess if you're up for it, you can go. But if you feel sick at school at any point, I want you to come home right away."

"Okay, I will. Now stop worrying, you're gonna get wrinkles."

"Wow, you *must* be feeling better," she laughed. "Your attitude is definitely back."

"Ha ha...so where is Grandma?"

Her mother returned to the stove to finish cooking. "She went into town to visit a friend."

Jenna yawned. "At seven-thirty in the morning?"

"You know your grandmother, she does things differently. Okay, look—if you think you're ready to go back to school, then I'll drive you there."

"Okay, great." Jenna's fingers played along her needle-pricked skin as she scratched her bruises.

Her mother shook her head while flipping the toast in the frying pan. "I don't know, Jenna. Maybe you should stay at home just a few more days. At least until your cuts heal."

Jenna frowned. "Mom, seriously, I'm fine!" As she spoke, she unravelled the bandages on her hands.

"Jenna, wait…let me get the ointment. I'll help you—" Looking back, her mother gasped. "Oh my God—your cuts are gone!"

Jenna was just as surprised. Not a single scratch was visible on her palms. No torn skin, no slashes. Nothing. She didn't know what to say.

"I don't believe it! How do your hands feel?" her mother said, rushing over.

Jenna touched them. "Wow—they don't hurt at all. I guess I'm a quick healer."

"That's incredible! Did you put something on them? Did Grandma give you something?"

"No, I don't think so. But she was in my room last night, maybe she did and I just don't remember. Doesn't matter now, I guess." Jenna smiled. "I feel really good, Mom. I think today's the perfect day for me to go back to school."

Her mother was silent. She just stared at Jenna.

"Mom—are you okay?"

She nodded. "Yes, it's just that…you've only been out of the hospital one day and your cuts are gone."

Jenna didn't want her mother worrying any more than she had to. "I guess they weren't as bad as everyone thought they were. Look, Mom—this is a good thing. You don't have to worry now. But I *am* hungry, do you need help with breakfast?" She pointed to the frying pan in her hand.

"Ahh…no. It's done." Her mother turned and reached for a plate from the cupboard. She scraped Jenna's breakfast onto the plate and sat the frying pan in the sink. To Jenna, it seemed like she was hesitating. Turning off the stove, her mother then handed her the plate and sat down across from her. "You go ahead and eat."

"Geez, Mom—you look like you've seen a ghost," Jenna said, digging into her breakfast.

Her mother said nothing.

"Well, I for one, am looking forward to school today."

"That's great, Jenna," her mother said, staring at her hands. "I guess when you're done eating, we'll get you on your way."

Jenna smiled back at her. "Perfect. I can't wait!"

BACK TO THE BOOKS

The day went surprisingly well. Jenna reunited with her friends and teachers. Her backpack and locker were leaden with friends' notes, new reading material and homework assignments. It was as if she had never missed a day. And she felt wonderful through it all. No one would have ever guessed by looking at her that she'd spent the last few days in the intensive care unit at the hospital.

History was her last class of the day. The history room was without a doubt, her favourite place to be in the school. It warmed her mind every time she entered it.

Stepping inside the room, she took a deep breath. Jenna quickly coalesced with the students she'd not yet seen as each one acknowledged her return in some form or another. Whether it was making eye contact, or whispering to the next person, she was amazed by the degree of recognition.

"It's nice to see you, Jenna. We're glad you're back," Mrs. Wallace said.

"Thanks," Jenna smiled. She really wasn't one for making waves or grabbing attention, unless it was on the baseball diamond. In class, she preferred to remain anonymous. Her recent bout in the hospital however, had everyone talking.

As she slid into an empty desk in the far corner of the room, she began to relax. Jenna was happy to finally have some normalcy in her life. Just being amongst the desks invoked a sense of belonging.

She scanned the room, examining the relics, models and displays that adorned the walls. For her, this was definitely the most interesting place in the school. And it was a perfect fit too, room and teacher. Mrs.

Wallace brought a sense of whimsical factuality to the subject matter. She was theatrical enough to keep the students engaged, without scaring them into another dimension.

Jenna listened as Mrs. Wallace began to speak about the configuration of cosmic entities and their relevance to historical cultures. Jenna was utterly captivated.

She was pulled from her trance momentarily when a tingle on her upper left arm required her immediate attention. Her nails breezed over the fabric as she scratched the spot. It was then that she lost her concentration.

She took note of the time; the clock on the wall read one-thirty. Glancing around the room, she watched the other students. Most of the class was staring at the teacher; only a couple girls were writing notes and passing them to their friends. With everything so seemingly normal, Jenna couldn't understand why she was distracted. When she stopped to think about it, she heard a noise outside the classroom windows. The wind was picking up speed.

She looked over and saw the leaves on the oak tree beside the window lift dramatically onto their sides. *That's not good,* Jenna thought.

The wind howled as it pushed against the walls of the classroom. A large branch thrust against the window, making everyone inside the room jump.

"My goodness, the wind has certainly picked up," Mrs. Wallace said.

Jenna could feel the movement of air, as if she were a part of it herself. In her gut, she understood the sensation—something was coming.

"Jenna, are you all right?" she heard from the front of the room.

Jenna turned her head. Everyone in the class was watching her. "I'm...fine. Sorry, I was just watching the wind."

"Okay," Mrs. Wallace said. "I just wanted to make sure. So, for tomorrow..." she continued.

Jenna sank back in her chair. *Great—now everyone thinks I'm nuts.* She looked up at the clock; the hands now read five minutes to three. Jenna stared in disbelief. The school day was almost over; the final bell was about to ring. *What the...* She couldn't figure out where the time had gone.

Mrs. Wallace started down the rows to hand out the homework assignments but when she arrived at Jenna's desk, she stopped. Her high heels tapped on the ground impatiently as Jenna packed away her things.

"The day is over, but you can never leave," Mrs. Wallace said with a stern tone.

"What?" Jenna said, looking up. She was caught off guard by her teacher's comment. Jenna was surprised however, when she saw Mrs. Wallace standing at the front of the room erasing the chalkboard. The room was now empty; all the students had left.

What is going on? she asked herself.

"We'll see you tomorrow, Jenna. Remember—pages twenty through forty of the manual. There might be a pop quiz," Mrs. Wallace said with her back turned.

"Oh, okay…thanks," Jenna said. She hadn't heard a word of anything after losing her concentration in class, not even the homework assignment. Everything was pretty much a blur. What she *had* heard, was the wind outside, and the foreshadowing of danger that the wind brought with it.

WHO'S THERE?

Jenna hurried towards her locker. The last class of the day was over and practice for the school's baseball team was about to begin. She had only a few minutes to get to the gym.

"Matthews—there you are! Stop stallin', unless your throwin' arm is weak," someone said from behind her.

Jenna primped her hair in the mirror. "At least my arms don't drag, caveman!" She smiled and turned around.

Her best friend Jason was standing behind her with his arms crossed. "Be still my heart—a girl after my own insults."

"Jason—" she walked up and hugged him. "It's so good to see you. How was Arizona?"

"I just got back this morning. It was great, cactus galore, but more importantly—how are you? I just heard that you were in the hospital. What happened?"

Jenna had no intention of sharing any news of her hospital visit with him or anyone at school for that matter. "It's a long story, I'll tell you later. But I'm back now and I'm feeling great! Don't I look great?" she said, posing for him. "And better yet, my throwing arm is gonna toss you into the dirt, my friend."

"Well, you might've come back full throttle, but forget that arm business because you're goin' down!" he joked.

"Jason—we're on the same team," she said, with her hands on her hips.

"Oh, right." He smiled. "Look, there's something I've got to get from my locker. I'll meet you in the gym in five minutes."

"Okay, Rookie," she yelled, as he ran down the hallway.

He winked, and then kept on running.

Jenna watched as the student populace thinned from the hallway. Doors slammed all around her until she was alone with the silence.

She looked back at the mirror hanging from her locker door. As she maneuvered the elastic band of her ponytail, she was startled to see a little girl standing directly behind her.

She spun around, but the girl was gone. Jenna looked up and down the hallway but saw no one there.

"Hello?" she called out.

There was no answer.

Jenna was worried, now she was seeing things. If Dr. Roberts heard about this, he'd put her right back in the hospital.

As she contemplated her mental state, something down the hallway shifted. A shadow stood by one of the classroom doors.

Squinting, Jenna saw the outline of the little girl. She was holding something in her hands.

Jenna closed her locker door and began to walk towards the girl. She felt inexplicably drawn to her. "Can I help you—are you lost?" Jenna asked.

The girl didn't respond. Her glassy eyes and buoyant smile came into view as Jenna stepped closer. Her blonde ringlets bounced in the air as she nodded her head up and down, playfully. She looked no older than six or seven.

Tucked within her hands, was a thin, pointed object. As Jenna approached, she realized that the little girl was holding an oak leaf. Gently, she twirled it between her fingers. Her eyes had an unmistakably innocent feel to them, like a sweet little deer. Jenna couldn't turn away. Instead, the girl disappeared right in front of her.

Jenna turned in all directions; the girl hadn't just ducked away somewhere, she'd vanished completely. She wasn't just quick, she was magical.

Jenna was stupefied. "Hello?" She looked in all directions.

A noise like someone drawing on the chalkboard drew Jenna's attention to the classroom she was standing outside of. Through the window in the door she saw that the room was dark. What was going on here?

Slowly, she turned the handle and pushed the door open. Peeking her head inside, she frowned. The room was empty. "Okay—that's weird," she said aloud.

All the chairs were pushed under the desks and the lights were off. But something was out of place. The date on the board read, 'August 22nd, 1939', and printed above it was the name, Hanover Elementary School.

"Hanover?" Jenna said. She stepped over the threshold and entered the room. Immediately, she scanned the open space. Her surroundings were unrecognizable. Pictures were strewn across the walls, unfamiliar pictures. Babe Ruth swinging his bat in 1932. Photographs of the "Black Sunday" dust storm as it rolled through Texas in 1935. The collapse of the Honeymoon Bridge at Niagara Falls in 1938. John Steinbeck with his novel, *The Grapes of Wrath* in 1939.

"These weren't here when I left..." Jenna doubted her own vision, but she couldn't ignore what she was seeing.

Various newspaper clippings lined the walls of the room. There were several pictures of Amelia Earhart posing with her airplanes, as well as articles pertaining to her disappearance in 1937 over the Pacific. One clipping was an advertisement for the original 1933 film *King Kong*, when it premiered at Radio City Music Hall and the RKO Roxy Theatre in New York City.

Slowly, Jenna walked along the walls as her fingers traced the lines of each paper that she passed.

On the other side of the room were several articles describing maritime disasters during the 1930's. Jenna read them carefully, giving her full attention to each and every printed word.

"This is unbelievable!" she said, touching the newsprint. She wanted to be sure that she wasn't dreaming.

Jenna didn't realize that something was approaching until a sharp crack from the floor jolted her from her trance. Her head jerked from side to side. "Is someone there?"

No answer. Only silence.

"Don't be silly, Jenna," she scolded herself. "There must be a logical explanation for all of this."

With that little surge of confidence, she returned to the plethora of papers attached to the walls. There were pictures of Franklin D. Roosevelt being sworn in for his second term as President of the United

States, photographs of the *Hindenburg* crashing in New Jersey, and images of the racehorse, Omaha, winning the Triple Crown.

"Wow…" Jenna stopped. The room didn't look anything like the present state of the one she'd just been in. None of the pictures, articles or clippings were recent; they all referenced events that occurred in the 1930's. This definitely wasn't her room, or her school.

Jenna frowned when she saw the next article. *'Community Mourns Life of Child.'* But before she had a chance to read it, the door to the room slammed shut behind her. Jenna's heart practically jumped out of her body and ran down her sleeve. She raced across the room to get out but the door wouldn't open.

"Let me out of here!" she yelled. "Someone help me—I'm locked in!"

A faint whisper came from somewhere behind her. "Jennnaaaaaa…" it called out.

Her body catapulted into the air as she turned to face the sound. "Who's there?" She searched the room, her eyes ready for anything. "WHO'S THERE?"

In the far corner of the room, a shadow appeared. It began to slither across the floor to where she was standing.

Cautiously, Jenna backed away from it; every bit of her intuition was telling her to hide.

A flash of light came from outside one of the windows and Jenna looked over. Outside, was the little girl.

The shadow ceased all movement and let out a terrifying screech. Its pain echoed through the room as Jenna covered her ears in fright. She crouched behind a desk and watched as the shadow disappeared into the wall forming a shapeless bulge behind it. The bulge flowed along the walls of the classroom.

"Oh my God!"

The classroom door suddenly opened and Jenna lurched towards it. Her heart beating erratically, she flew out into the hallway holding her chest. She leaned against the wall as she desperately tried to catch her breath.

"It's okay, calm down," she told herself.

Somehow Jenna knew that the thing in the classroom behind the walls could not fully burst into her world. Not yet, at least.

The familiar state of the hallway helped to soothe her nerves. But then the howl of the wind outside the school caught her attention. She could hear it through the walls of the building. Looking back into the classroom, she sighed. The room was just as she had left it, at three o'clock that afternoon.

There were no papers lining the walls, no pictures, no photographs. Just a dark, vacant room. Jenna gazed at the chalkboard but saw nothing written on it. Everything had been erased. It was definitely her school now.

Outside, the wind was forcibly strong. With one glance through the window, Jenna's eyes widened, because there, beneath the oak tree, stood the little girl looking back at her.

DO I KNOW YOU?

Jenna bounded through the hallway towards the front door. Her feet were racing, her pulse was surging. What she wanted was answers.

She pushed the door open and ran outside. She gulped when she saw her surroundings. The sky was a sickening shade of green. Grape-like ominous clouds dangled from the sky above the school. "Oh no!" Jenna felt the weight of something perilous coming her way. The winds whipped her hair all over, but still she wanted to see the girl.

As her eyes came across the oak tree, she saw the figure of the little girl behind the trunk. Her black dress twirled on the spot giving Jenna the impression that she wanted to be found.

Jenna slowly walked towards her. She had no idea what to say. Ideas scrambled through her mind as she tried to form the right words.

With only a few feet between them, the girl stepped out from behind the tree. "I know who you are, Jenna."

Jenna stopped immediately. "Oh? And who are you?"

"I am a friend...of a friend...of a friend...of a friend..." The girl repeated the words as if they amused her.

Jenna shook her head. "I don't understand...how do you know me?"

"I know Abigail...your mother's mother...mother's mother...mother's mother..."

Her childish flare and repetitive jabber made Jenna take a step back. "How do you know my grandmother?"

"Through this and that...this and that...or that and this...that and this. I am a friend, a helper, but just a girl. That is how you see me."

Jenna was getting tired of the game the girl was playing. "Are you lost or something? Where's your family?"

The girl pointed a finger toward the sky then back down to the ground. "Up and down, up and down. Down and up, down and up. They're here and there...but here for now, remember that."

There was more to this girl than just her nonsense, Jenna was aware of that now. But getting a proper answer out of her was proving to be difficult. The fact that she was following Jenna around the school irked her to no end, especially since she didn't know who the little girl was or what she wanted. Jenna was done playing around.

"How do you know who I am? And how do you know my grandmother?"

The girl's demeanour turned serious. "You don't know who I am... yet. I am just a girl, but you will soon find out who I belong to. Don't stray too far, Jenna." Her head tilted to one side as a gust of swirling wind moved towards them. "Beware the storm that hunts."

The front door to the school blew open, and Jenna turned to look. Mr. Thompson, the math teacher, stood at the entrance. "You've got to get in here!" he hollered. "There's a tornado coming!"

"There's a little girl!" Jenna screamed. "I can't leave her!"

"Leave who? There's no one around. Everyone's inside already—hurry!"

It took one hectic glance for Jenna to realize that the girl was gone. But the winds were intensifying. Leaves tore from the trees behind her. Branches cracked from the pressure of the winds; it was time for her to go. The little girl had warned her, and now Jenna felt it in her bones. This wasn't just any storm, there was sorcery behind it.

"Get in here now!" Mr. Thompson yelled.

Jenna ran for the door. With one hearty leap, she vaulted inside. Her body was now safe, but her thoughts were trapped outside, struggling to escape the torrent of what was coming.

STAY SAFE

Students and teachers huddled together within the protective walls of the school's storm shelter, while the winds twisted viciously outside. Squealing. Screeching. Mad clawing at the air. The storm pummelled the building, searching for a way in.

Jenna sat with her legs tightly tucked within her arms as she rocked back and forth. She had experienced a tornado before, but not at the school.

The first time she saw a funnel cloud drop from the sky, she was at home with her family. It had raged past her house, lifting part of the roof and the cornfield out back. But her family was lucky, the damage had been minimal.

This storm however, was much fiercer. And to make matters worse, she hadn't seen Jason in the storm room. She hoped that he was safe somewhere inside the school.

Around her, she heard the frantic whispers and cries of terrified people. Teachers sat holding the hands of paralyzed students as unexpected bonds formed throughout the darkness. Jenna tried hard not to give into the fear. She wanted to tune it all out. Closing her eyes, she focused on the strength within.

Her lips jiggled as she mumbled one of her grandmother's poems to calm herself. "Spells are cast so minds can fly, cats can call and so can I…"

"Birds and beasts can soar through sky…" a voice murmured from somewhere in the room.

Jenna's eyes burst open. Someone was reciting the same poem, but the lights had gone out and she couldn't tell who it was. Quietly, she continued. "Toads and bats, stars can spy…low and high above the cry—"

Another voice chimed in. "See the rolling clouds move by…"

Jenna searched for the voice, this time she found it.

Off in the corner sat a figure by itself. Jenna couldn't make out who or what it was. But when one of the teachers turned on their flashlight, a silhouette of a small child jumped onto the wall.

Jenna, as surprised and cautious as she was, was compelled to talk to it. She now knew exactly who it was. It was the little girl.

No one seemed to notice when Jenna stood and left her spot; all the teachers were preoccupied with other students.

As Jenna approached, she could see the little girl beyond the glare of the teacher's flashlight.

Facing away, she spoke to Jenna. "Be safe as you can…safe as you can."

Jenna froze. "It's you, isn't it? You're the little girl I saw outside."

"Yes."

"Who are you? Tell me!"

"I already did, Jenna." When she turned around, she was holding a toy lamb in her arms. "This is Mia, she's my best friend."

"You said you know my grandmother. How?"

"You haven't figured it out yet, have you?"

Jenna shook her head. "No, I haven't."

"You need to figure it out. I can't tell you. I can only watch." The girl's tone was apocalyptic, malignant in many ways. It gave Jenna shivers.

"Why are you here?"

The girl ignored Jenna's question. Instead, she cradled the lamb and rocked it in her arms. "Mia and I will always be together."

Just watching the girl's mannerisms made Jenna uncomfortable. The feeling she was getting was oddly cadaverous. This girl was not from this world. It triggered a memory, from when she was in the hospital; one that she couldn't quite place.

A string of moving lights suddenly yanked Jenna's attention away from the girl. She closed her eyes to block out the brightness. When she opened them, she was sitting back on the floor with her arms wrapped around her body as if she had never stood.

The winds pounded against the walls and heavy metal doors, bringing more delirious shrieks.

"Oh my God!" several students screamed in unison.

"Try to stay calm," one of the teachers said.

"Are you okay, Jenna?" Mr. Thompson said, shining a light on her. "Are you all right?"

Jenna just stared blankly at him.

Then all of a sudden, the floor of the shelter shook with a grievous force. The tension broke into hysterics.

"Everyone down—NOW!" one of the teachers yelled.

Each person fell flat along the floor in utter panic.

A monstrous mechanical scraping tore through the air, filling Jenna's gut with queasiness. Peering through frazzled fingers, she watched as the room spun out of control. But in one darkened corner she saw the little girl standing still in place.

"Keep your heads down!" Mr. Thompson screamed. His words slid across the floor.

Jenna's eyes were glued to the girl. Not one part of her moved, not even her curls.

The power of the storm was at its highest peak. Human cries drowned in the mass of air disturbance. The walls shook. The ground quaked. The ceiling trembled. Jenna envisioned a large swirling hand reaching down from the sky to remove the top of their safe house. Any moment, the roof would lose its precious hold and soon they would all be lost to the heavens.

"We're going to be okay—just stay still!" Mr. Thompson shouted. "Nobody move!" His voice was commanding, a godsend to those around him.

The little girl began to twirl about, holding the toy lamb up in the air like a small child. "Spells are cast so minds can fly, cats can call and so can I."

The uneasiness in Jenna's stomach soon gave way to a feeling of unexpected morbidity. Something was horribly wrong and it wasn't just the tornado.

IS IT OVER?

The winds outside slowly began to weaken. Everyone listened as the storm loosened its hold on the school. The fear inside the room was still present but there was a release of human emotion as the winds died. One by one, the teachers regained composure and resumed their role of authority. Names were yelled out, panicked glances were exchanged and heavy sighs pressed against the air as each student slowly began to stir. Activity in the room was stifled by a frightened sense of caution, for no one really knew if the worst was over.

"Is everyone okay?" Mr. Thompson asked.

The responses came at staggered intervals. Voices shook and heads nodded in spastic jolts but everyone in the room was all right. It appeared that no one was hurt, not physically anyway.

Jenna got to her knees and gently lifted herself up. One of the teachers walked up behind her and helped her to her feet. "Jenna, are you okay?" It was Mrs. Wallace, her history teacher.

Jenna nodded in return. She was about to say she was fine but then stopped when she saw the little girl standing behind Mrs. Wallace, twirling in place. The girl was smiling, indifferent to the tension around her.

"Are you okay?" Mrs. Wallace said, concerned.

Jenna pointed to the space behind her. Reclaiming her voice, she shook her arm. "Look—look!"

Mrs. Wallace turned around. "What is it?"

"Don't you see her? It's the little girl. She's right there!" Other students now looked on as Jenna's meltdown took center stage.

"What little girl?" Turning back, Mrs. Wallace stared at her. "Are you hurt?"

"No—don't you see her? She's right there!"

"I don't know what to say, Jenna. But there's no little girl. Maybe you saw another student."

She looked over at Mr. Thompson and gestured for him to come over. "I think Jenna might need some medical attention."

Understanding that her sanity was now in question, Jenna retracted her statement. "Actually, I think it was another student, you're probably right. It was probably Sandy Markham—it looked a lot like her, actually. Forget I said anything."

The awkward moment was broken by a rumbling of infrastructure.

Mr. Thompson shouted, "Everyone—in the center of the room, NOW!"

Quickly, all the students and teachers crowded together in one large swarm. The walls around them trembled as tiny cracks formed down the sides. Jenna watched in fear as pieces of their storm room crumbled along the corners.

Contradicting his own words, Mr. Thompson immediately crossed the floor to the door that led outside. He pushed and pushed on the metal frame but the door remained sealed; it was jammed from the outside. "Probably a downed tree or something out there." Looking back at the frightened faces, he said, "It's okay...we'll find a way out."

Some of the other teachers began to chatter. "Maybe if a few of us pushed on it together it might budge."

"No," Mr. Thompson stopped them. "There could be live power lines down near the door. God knows what's forcing it shut. We'll find another way."

Jenna could sense the gravity in his voice. She watched as all the other teachers bowed to his knowledge.

"Look, I want everyone to stick together. Stay close, no drifters. Teachers—take the ends and the sides, and follow me. Everyone stay calm."

Like an army of ants, they marched into position as the group carefully moved towards the door that led back into the school.

"I don't know what condition the building is in, so let's be careful," Mr. Thompson said. "Don't touch anything or move anything. And remember, stay together."

Everyone nodded.

When Jenna turned to look for the little girl, she was surprised to see that she was gone. Feeling somewhat disheartened, she took a deep breath and exhaled a sigh of relief. Her emotions were mixed and confusing. She felt strangely attached to the ghostly image and yet was frightened of what the girl possibly represented. Shaking off her spiritual spider-sense, she delved into the moment.

The sounds of anxious breathing came from all around as the journey to safety began. Clinging to the group, Jenna moved ahead with the others. Then, with wide eyes, she watched as Mr. Thompson opened the door.

SOMEWHERE OUT THERE

Together, tightly knotted and woven within each other's arms, the group of students and teachers carefully trudged down the main hallway of the school. The area was dark, giving the corridor a cold, lifeless feel.

Mr. Thompson was leading the pack. He had lived through three tornados in his life. As a seasoned veteran of storm survival, he knew what to do. "Watch out for hanging wires and anything sharp. Everyone, stay close."

A worried hush fell over the group when they saw how damaged the school was. Walls were buckled. Locker doors dangled from the ceiling tiles. Gaping holes pierced through the roof. Pieces of paper floated mindlessly about as broken hallway lights lay on their sides, flickering. No one said a word. But there were many gasps.

Jenna shook her head when she passed by her locker. The door was gone and all the contents were missing. When she slowed down to look, one of the ceiling tiles gave way behind the group. It crashed onto the crumpled floor making many of the students scream.

"It's okay, it's okay!" Mr. Thompson shouted. "The door's not far. Just stay calm, everybody."

The rooms they passed looked like they had been through a war. The globes in the geography room were embedded in the walls. Half of the chalkboard from the math class was standing on its side; the other half was lying through the window. And the bicycle-sized, metal Eiffel tower from the French room was sticking out of the ceiling like a failed rocket.

Classroom doors were off their hinges and many of the walls had been breached. The only room that seemed to have escaped destruction completely was the history room. Quickly glancing at the state of the room, Jenna couldn't believe her eyes. Not a single item had been moved. There was no time for her to pause and think, though, she had to keep walking to get to safety.

Turning back to the group, she stopped when a light from the ceiling sparked above her. In the blink of an eye, she and another student were shoved to the side by Mrs. Wallace just as a large metal fixture crashed to the ground. Shards of glass skated across the floor and merged with scattered screams.

Mr. Thompson yelled, "Is everyone all right back there?"

Jenna, Mrs. Wallace and the other student all clung to each other, tightly. In a united panic, they answered, "Yes."

"Come on, let's get out of here!" Mr. Thompson said, waving them back into the group.

Jenna's heart was beating wildly out of control. Part of her believed that she would never see the light of day. In an attempt to suppress her fears, she closed her eyes and thought of home. Had she only stayed there, this day of dread could have been avoided. But then she thought of her family and her pets, and wondered if the twister had made its way to them. She hoped that her family was safe from its wrath. She took a few deep breaths and started walking.

*****

After a twenty-minute hike through broken glass, rubble, and hinge-less doors, they reached the other end of the school, which was the only safe exit. Mr. Thompson swivelled around to face the group. "I need you all to stay here. I'm going outside first to see what it looks like. When I call you, I want you all to come out one by one, carefully."

The other teachers nodded in compliance. The students obeyed.

Gently, he pushed the door open. A thin slice of sunlight infiltrated the space indicating that the storm was indeed over. The clouds had cleared and the winds had died. All that was left was the aftermath.

A path to the outside had been cleared by the storm. There were no hanging wires, power lines, downed branches or other dangerous obstacles that obstructed their escape. Mr. Thompson stepped back in and said, "Okay, one by one. No pushing, no shoving. Let's go."

In a single file, each student and teacher made their way outside. Each one gasped as they stepped onto the ground. Although the area surrounding the door had been cleared, looking around they could now see the extent of the damage. Half the school was missing.

Jenna cupped her hands over her mouth when she saw the building. "Oh my God!"

Brick walls had completely disappeared, leaving a fluttering trail of papers in its wake.

Strewn across the ground were shoes, maps, musical equipment, athletic gear. Books lay open in the trees, hanging from the branches, while chairs and desks lay broken on the ground.

Jenna walked further from the door as the remaining members of the group came outside. As she stared at the void that was once her school, something distracted her. On the ground, near where she was standing, was a toppled desk. Beneath it was something that didn't belong. It looked soft and cushy. A stuffed animal was squished beneath the wood. Jenna stood for a moment trying to place it; she had seen it before. And then it hit her—she had seen it inside the school, inside the storm shelter. It was a toy lamb.

Reaching over, she picked it up. Her body shivered. The lamb had been in the arms of the young girl inside the school. The girl that no one else had seen because she didn't exist to anyone else. Jenna felt the fabric beneath her fingers. It was real. The toy was real.

Unearthly questions filled Jenna's mind until her thoughts were silenced by a familiar noise. Her head jerked up when she heard the sound. A terrible, awful sound.

Pacing behind the oak tree was the predatory menace that stalked Jenna's dreams. The living soul of the Siamese Mummy. One quick look and Jenna knew that it wasn't a dream. This cat was real. It was the size of a large lion, with a tan-coloured body and stunning black points on its nose, ears, paws and tail. It watched Jenna, glaring at her as it moved.

Jenna shook her head. "No—it can't be you! It just can't be!"

The animal opened its powerful jaws and released a terrifying roar.

Jenna covered her ears and closed her eyes. The toy dropped from her arms as she backed away. When she opened her eyes, the little blonde girl was standing next to the cat. The cat was now still.

"No—" Jenna gasped.

The girl's pale pink fingers gently stroked the feline's head as it sat, poised in position. It looked as though it was protecting her.

Jenna waved away the unforgettable sight. If the cat was real, then so was the girl. And that terrified her even more. She turned away for just a moment to see if anyone was looking, but no one was. Everyone else was staring at the damage done to the building.

Looking back, Jenna shrieked and nearly jumped out of her shoes when she saw the little girl standing directly in front of her with the toy lamb in her arms. Jenna was drawn to her eyes. They had a sad, empty feel to them.

With her little arms, the girl reached out to Jenna and handed her the lamb. "Thank you for finding Mia," she said. "Would you like to take her?"

Jenna declined the gift and took a step back. The girl was scaring her.

"You mustn't be afraid, not of me. Still, you should heed my warning. Rebuild the wall, up and down, down and up. Not side to side, side to side. Terror lives everywhere, from here to there, not there to here."

"What do you mean? What does that mean?" Jenna said. "Please—tell me who you are!"

The girl gave a crooked smile. "Take Mia. You need her more than I do."

Jenna shook her head. "No...I can't."

The cat roared once again, reminding Jenna of her proximity to danger. The most fearful element in her life was that cat and she was not about to go anywhere near it. Yet, the child seemed to trust it. Why?

With only inches in between them, Jenna could feel the pull of the girl as her spirit began to depart. "Please—tell me who you are! I need to know!" Jenna yelled out.

There was a slight twinkle in the girl's eyes when she looked at Jenna. Then with deliberate steps, she turned and walked back to the Siamese cat. Now standing beneath the tree, she giggled. "I think you already know."

THEY ALL FALL DOWN

Emergency vehicles circled the school, blocking off paths, setting up dividers and barricades. Red and white flashing lights pulsated brightly as work crews scrambled about.

Sounds of crumbling debris mixed with frantic shouts and post-traumatic stress coated the air with tension. And the sun was now setting, which only compounded the fear. Darkness added a dangerous element to storm recovery, and everyone there knew it.

Earlier, when the emergency vehicles had arrived, each student and teacher had undergone a brief medical examination. Afterwards, they were questioned about the storm. One by one they told their story of how they escaped the destruction, and how Mr. Thompson was their shining light to survival. He became the hero of the event.

By the way things were handled it was assumed that everyone had made it out of the building. But embroiled in such turmoil, even the hero had forgotten things. And once the crews had arrived, each person was pulled in a different direction. Keeping track of all those involved in the storm quickly became an afterthought.

Jenna watched Mr. Thompson as he spoke to the Fire Chief. She could hear him describing what had happened inside the storm room. Although his words were jagged and sharp, his demeanour was not. He appeared grounded and modest, the pinnacle of calm, just as he was inside the building.

Looking around at all the people hurrying to and from, Jenna took a deep breath. This was all new to her. A crazed scene unlike any she had seen before. It was completely different to the panic she experienced during the tornado at home. And to add to the stress, she hadn't seen Jason since their talk after school.

On the road behind them, frightened family members were still arriving in their cars. Teens and teachers alike rushed into the arms of mothers and fathers, husbands and wives.

Jenna scanned the road for her family but saw no one yet. No parents, no Grandma Abby. And she wanted them here, right now. After seeing the Siamese cat and the little girl, she wanted out. Home was where she needed to be.

Mr. Thompson was still talking to the Fire Chief. He was now describing what had happened after the storm passed. Jenna remained close to his side, knowing very well that she would be safe if she stayed near him.

"Jenna...Jenna..." she heard a voice. Looking over, she saw Mr. Thompson talking to her. "Are you okay?"

She nodded. "Yeah...I'm fine." Her voice was steady but her mind was unfocused because she was too busy searching for her family. That, and she was lying through her teeth. She was worried about Jason.

Seconds later, Jenna heard someone calling her name. She spun around and saw Jason approaching. With a smile on her face, she ran up and threw her arms around him. "Oh my God—where were you? I was so worried!" She leaned back and saw a white bandage on his forehead. "Your head—what happened?"

"It's okay, I'm all right," he said, downplaying his injury. "A few of us got trapped in the gym and couldn't get to the storm room. But it's okay—look I'm fine."

"Oh, thank God! How did you get hurt?"

"I got hit with a soccer ball." He laughed. "Pretty embarrassing but it could've been worse. The paramedics took me into the ambulance for a while but I'm all right now."

Jenna stood silently for a moment, gazing into his soft hazel eyes. Something inside her was changing. Her affection for Jason was growing. "You scared me, you know. I couldn't find you."

"It's all right, I'm here now. And the cut—it's just a small war wound. Doesn't even hurt."

He acted tough and macho but Jenna knew he was scared like the rest of them. She could see it in his eyes.

"Did you get checked out yet?" he said.

"Yeah, I did. I'm fine." Although Jason was Jenna's best friend, she didn't want to tell him anything about the Siamese cat or the little girl. She gently touched his cheek. "I'm really glad you're okay. I wanted to tell you…" She drifted off.

Jason stared at her. "Tell me what?" he said.

Jenna's eyes were drawn to an old man standing behind Jason, not far from where they were. He hovered near one of the police cars, watching all the people move around him. When he turned in Jenna's direction, their eyes met. Neither one looked away.

"What did you want to tell me?" Jason said.

"Hey, look over there. That man…who is he?"

Jason turned his head. "I don't know, probably someone's family. I don't recognize him."

Jenna thought for a moment. She had seen the man before. From the style of clothing he was wearing, she assumed he was in his sixties or seventies. He was dressed all in brown from his shirt to his shoes. Overtop his clothing he wore a beige trench coat that was open. His back was slightly hunched and he leaned to one side, placing his weight onto the silver cane he carried. He looked professional, academic. But he wasn't a teacher at their high school.

"I think I know him," Jenna said. "I think I saw him at the museum." She averted her gaze for only a moment to ponder, but when she looked back, he was gone.

A loud, thundering crash suddenly tore through the night air. Raised voices shouted all around, "The building is collapsing!"

The Fire Chief screamed, "EVERYONE—GET BACK!" Policemen, firemen and all other rescue teams jumped into action as they pushed people out of the way of danger. All eyes were now on the school as brick by brick the building tumbled to the ground.

"Oh my God!" Jenna gasped. She watched in horror as the school disintegrated.

Shrieks and screams flew through the air as people ran in all directions. Jason grabbed Jenna's arm and pulled her away. Stopping at a safe distance, she tucked her head into his shoulder and peered out from behind his sleeve. "The school!"

"It's okay, it's okay…" Jason repeated the words over and over again.

A terrifying hush fell over the crowd.

Jenna stared at the rubble. "I can't believe it's gone!" The dust filtered down from the sky. In amongst the concrete smoke, Jenna thought that she saw the outline of a body. The figure was coming in and out of view so she couldn't quite tell if it was real or not. And with her track record, she didn't want to say anything. Then she saw the backdrop of the history room behind it. "How is that possible? The history room—it's still standing!"

The room itself was in perfect order. No papers had been moved. No desks or tables had been disturbed. Everything was still in its place, like it had been glued down with an industrial-strength adhesive. All of the walls stood, except for the outermost one. Part of it had collapsed, which provided an opening from the outside.

"Oh—wow!" Jason said, completely astounded.

"That's impossible!" Mr. Thompson shouted.

Jenna lowered her head and began rubbing her eyes. Jason placed his hand on her back to console her. "It's okay."

"No, no, it's my eyes. They're itchy." With the tips of her fingers she scratched them. Jenna felt the onset of an allergic reaction. Her eyes filled with water and she sneezed multiple times.

"Wait, are you allergic to something?" Jason said.

She lifted her head. "No, I don't think so."

"Are you sure?" he said.

The itchiness then began to fade. "Okay, that was weird." Wiping away what was left of her symptoms, she glanced back at the school. And that's when she saw her—the little girl standing amongst the debris. The black dress she wore stood out from the red brick as she held a small bundle of white flowers in her right hand. Sitting in her left hand was a small, green grasshopper. The image was bizarre, and yet somehow familiar.

Although the girl was alone in front of the history room, Jenna was still nervous. She quickly surveyed the grounds, searching for the Siamese cat, but couldn't find it. Still, she had a feeling that it was somewhere nearby.

The girl looked at Jenna and nodded as if to tell her something. Everything around them soon began to slow down as if time itself was stopping. The girl's lips began to move. "Look and see, look and see," she said. Each word was clear and concise, there was no mistaking its meaning. She then turned and walked into the room behind her.

Disappearing through the broken wall, she reappeared on the other side in perfect form.

Jenna watched in amazement as the girl pointed to something on the floor. "Look and see, look and see," she said again. This time it was clear. Jenna saw the outline of a body; the same one she had dismissed only moments earlier, thinking it was a hallucination. The girl gave a confirming nod.

Now understanding the situation, Jenna screamed, "There's a body in there!"

Everyone immediately looked at the history room. Jason took a few steps closer to the building. "I don't see anyone. Are you sure?"

"I'm positive—trust me! There's a body in there!" she hollered. "There's a body in the history room!"

"Okay, no one move!" the Fire Chief yelled. "Someone might still be inside, we need to go in. Everyone else, stay where you are!"

Five firemen, including the Chief, gathered and moved towards the crumbled building. Steadily, they headed for the history room. Each one stepped over the outer layer of broken brick as they came upon a body lying on the ground. Jenna saw the men bending down, tending to it.

"We need a medic!" one of the firemen shouted.

Three paramedics inside the back of an ambulance jumped out. With a gurney in tow, they rushed towards the firemen.

Minutes passed as each worried bystander looked on, wondering who the person inside the building was. Grunts and screeches soon came as the gurney was lifted over the rubble. At first sight of the body, everyone was silent. But when someone yelled out, "It's Mrs. Wallace!" the silence was replaced with guttural gasps of shock and dismay.

Jenna stood, frozen in place, unsure of what to say, if anything at all. Jason reached over and wrapped his arms around her.

Just as the paramedics and fire crew neared the ambulance, a booming crash came from the building. With all eyes on the school, everyone watched in alarm as the history room collapsed to the ground. Pieces of brick, wood, concrete and tiling fell in all directions. Every part of the school was now gone; every inch of it now destroyed.

Jenna saw the little girl standing amongst the remains of the room. She wore a smile that was no longer frightening.

Jenna stood awestruck in Jason's arms. Whoever or whatever this little girl was, she clearly wasn't evil. She had just saved Mrs. Wallace.

With tears of gratitude clouding her eyes, Jenna nodded and whispered to the little girl, "Thank you."

A COMMON THREAD

With a mug of hot tomato soup in her hands, Jenna stood on the back porch of her house staring out at the cornfield. Although the stalks were barely visible in the dark, she knew exactly what they looked like; she could picture them in her mind as if it were daytime.

It was now just after midnight and the air was silent. There was no breeze, not even a slight wind. Jenna's focus was solely on the cornstalks; each one seemed to look back at her. In the dark, they resembled treelike mannequins, expressionless and cold. Daunting as they seemed, Jenna wanted to see them. She wanted to conquer her fear of the field, especially since it had stolen her trust.

Overcoming this hurdle was a new development; she had the tornado to thank for that. After surviving the storm and the destruction of the school without injury, she considered herself incredibly lucky. Fortunately, nothing else in the city had been touched by the tornado. No homes, no buildings. Nothing. Just the school. Although Jenna thought it was odd that the storm was so isolated, she'd heard stories before of similar instances. What she had been through, hit her like a thunderbolt on the drive home from the school. Her realization of the magnitude of the event had left her with a momentous feeling of appreciation. Her only worry was for her teacher, Mrs. Wallace. Jenna's heart broke just thinking about her, especially since Mrs. Wallace was the one who had pushed Jenna and the other student out of harm's way when the ceiling light fell. She had Mrs. Wallace to thank for protecting her, and she prayed now that her teacher would be all right.

Although still physically shaken, Jenna felt that the other obstacles in her life seemed less dreadful. This feeling of unbelievable good fortune compelled her to confront her biggest fear of all: her own mind. And that was why she'd come outside.

Jenna looked out at the dark field. Right now, everything was peaceful. The ground, the sky, the air—all was quiet. She closed her eyes and relished the serenity of the evening. With every breath she exhaled, she released the demons of the day.

Her thoughts strayed to the last time she'd stood in the backyard alone, when something had happened, something horrible. She remembered seeing a light coming towards her but then everything turned black. Hours later, she'd woken up in the hospital with her family around her. Picturing herself back in the intensive care unit, she could feel her body tossing and turning on the bed. Although she didn't remember everything that had happened there, she did recall certain events, most of which made no sense whatsoever. She had experienced several bizarre scenarios: cemetery walks, guiding bumblebees, mummified nurses, invisible ghosts searching for—

"How's the soup?" a voice came from behind.

Jenna jumped. Spinning around, she saw her grandmother walking towards her with a sweater in her arms. "Boy, Grandma—you've got to work on this 'sneaking up on your family' trait. You startled me."

Her grandmother winked and took the mug from her hands. "It's all right. Put this on, it's chilly out here."

Jenna pulled the sweater over her head. "Thanks." She reached for her mug of soup, but her grandmother pulled it close.

"Why don't I heat this for you? It's getting cold. Besides, I'm making some more for your parents inside."

"It's okay, I like it cold." Jenna watched her grandmother carefully. Her actions seemed a little off. It was as if she was hinting at something, and Jenna knew exactly what that was. Back at the school, when her family had come for her, she'd slipped up and accidentally mentioned the little girl. Ever since then, she had sensed a shift in her grandmother's behaviour. There was a peculiar look in her eyes.

Her grandmother handed the mug back and gave a kindly smile. "I know that your parents and I already talked to you about everything that happened today, Jenna, and maybe you don't want to talk about it anymore. I understand that. But I don't think that this is the time to shut us out."

Jenna took a sip of her soup and then turned to face the cornfield.

"There's something I'd like to know," her grandmother said, stepping towards her. "You said something at the school today, something unusual."

"I did?" Jenna said, staring out at the field.

"Yes, you said something about a little girl."

Jenna had anticipated her grandmother's questions but now that they were upon her, she felt trapped into giving a truthful answer. She didn't want to lie but she didn't want to be honest either, for the fear that she might be considered a total loon.

"Yes, I thought I saw a little girl at the school, but I didn't. I mean, no one else saw her...just me. I think it was an illusion or something. You know, it was probably my imagination running wild during everything that was going on."

"I see. But you said that she showed you the body inside the school, and then your teacher was rescued. That's quite specific."

"You know, I couldn't really tell anyway because my eyes were itchy and I was sneezing. I wasn't seeing straight."

Her grandmother angled her head ever so slightly. "Why would you have a reaction like that?"

Jenna was surprised by the disturbed look on her grandmother's face. She seemed bothered somehow. "I don't know, it's never happened before, at least not here."

"Were you allergic to something?"

These were not the questions Jenna had expected. They seemed unimportant, not to mention a little off the map. "Well, maybe, but I don't see how. The only time I ever had an allergic reaction to something was when I visited you in Salem. And that was a long time ago."

"Remind me of what happened then," her grandmother said.

Jenna was somewhat spooked by her grandmother's line of questioning. What did allergies have to do with anything?

"Well, Mom, Dad, me and Scott came to see you in Salem—I was ten years old. During our visit, Dad and I went hiking through Kingsman Heights and I got a small rash on my leg, some sneezing, too. We thought it was poison oak, but then found out it was from a little white flower growing on the trail. It was only one time, and we never told you guys because Dad got bit by that spider after and had to go to emergency. That obviously took priority over everything else. My rash disappeared anyway. And besides, I haven't had a problem since."

"I remember the spider incident," her grandmother said. "Your father suffered greatly."

"Yeah, which is why I never said anything about my rash. I hadn't even thought of it until now. I remember looking up the flower though, to see what it was. Geez...what was the name of it?" Jenna wracked her brain trying to come up with an answer. "It was thorn-something..."

"Frosted Hawthorn?" her grandmother guessed. Her tone was grim.

Jenna was stunned by her response. "Yes, that's it. How did you know that?"

Her grandmother said nothing more. She simply shook her head and backed away. The concerned look on her face gave Jenna shivers.

"No, really—how did you know that? I never told anyone about that, not even Mom."

With small, guarded steps her grandmother moved towards the back door. "Not now, Jenna. Time is of the essence."

"Grandma—wait! What's going on? Is Hawthorn poisonous or something?"

Her grandmother threw open the back door and raced into the house.

Feeling completely bewildered, Jenna rushed towards the door to follow her. She had never seen her grandmother act so crazy. Not once. Not ever. Grandma Abby was the epitome of grace and charm; always collected, always controlled. But something about their conversation had pushed her into a frenzied state, and Jenna wanted to know why.

As she opened the door, something darted behind her in the backyard. Quickly, she turned to look. Beneath the light of the porch bulb, she saw only incandescent beams and darkness. Pausing a moment, she scanned the yard. Nothing was there. She told herself it was probably a racoon, hoping to believe it. But in the back of her mind, she knew that it was probably something else, something bigger. The tornado at the school, the arrival of the little girl, the bulge in the history room walls—it wasn't just a coincidence. And the storm wasn't just a natural disaster either. There was some magical force behind all of it; Jenna could feel it in her veins.

It wasn't until she sneezed, however, that she sensed something else was afoot. Something was nearby. But neither ghost nor goblin could break her attention this time. Her focus was now directed towards her grandmother.

As Jenna disappeared into the house, two eyes came alive in the darkness. With a body cloaked in night colour, it moved through the yard unseen and unheard. There it remained, patiently waiting for the perfect moment to reveal itself.

CONNECTING TRAINS

Jenna ran past her parents as she dashed through the kitchen towards the stairs.

"Hey—slow down for a second," her father called out from his chair. "What's the hurry? Your grandmother just flew by here, too. Is everything okay?"

Jenna stopped and walked back into the room. "Yeah, everything's fine." She was playing it cool; she didn't want her parents to know about the strange conversation she'd had with her grandmother outside.

Her father peered over at her mother who was sitting at the table eating a bowl of soup. Jenna noticed the subtle glance they gave each other.

"It's understandable with everything you've been through, to have all sorts of emotions," he said. "We get that. We just want to be sure that you're all right." Although his tone was serious, his appearance was strangely mellow.

"I know, Dad, thank you. And I'm fine, really. I know that this last month hasn't been easy on you either but I don't want you to worry about me. I don't know how to explain it exactly, but after everything that happened today, I feel...kind of...at peace. Must be the soup," she joked.

"Well, that's your grandmother. Tonics and tinctures—you never know where they'll end up," her mother said, standing from the table. She walked over and placed one arm on Jenna's shoulder. "You're feeling better though?"

"Yeah, I think so." Part of Jenna wanted to stay and chat; she was happy to see her parents more relaxed.

Staring at the mug of soup in her hands, she thought for a moment. Everyone was now at ease, including her. She looked at her parents; each had a weird, balmy grin on their face. It was unusual, Jenna thought. Their words and concerns were sincere, but their actions were sedate. Then it hit her. *Grandma put something in the soup!*

The sound of breaking glass from upstairs stopped her train of thought. She looked out into the hallway. "What was that?"

"What was *what*?" her father said, sipping his soup.

Another noise came from the upper floor. This one resembled a pounding of sorts, like someone bumping into a door. "That! Didn't you hear it? It's coming from upstairs."

"Oh, it's probably just your grandmother," her mother said, sitting back down at the table. "Maybe she's rearranging furniture or something."

Jenna stared at her parents with a gaping jaw. "Are you serious? At twelve o'clock at night?" She watched them both; each one was getting mellower by the minute. *Why would Grandma put something in the soup?*

Placing her mug on the table, she decided to go fishing for answers. She left the kitchen and marched through the hallway towards the stairs. As she approached the bottom step, she paused to contemplate her next move.

Two meows came from above her while she was deep in thought. Scaling the stairs, she saw Ted and Tony sitting outside her bedroom. Beyond them, her grandmother's door was closed. Jenna could hear movement inside.

Quietly, she began to ascend the stairs. Approximately half way up, she heard her grandmother's voice; it seemed as though she was talking to herself. This wasn't uncommon, her grandmother always talked to herself. She would recite recipes, speak to the pets, and read out loud. It was completely normal. The family was used to it.

Just as Jenna was about to take another step, she heard a second voice inside her grandmother's room. This surprised her. She halted all movement and stood on the stairs, listening to the conversation behind the closed door. Although the second voice was muffled, it seemed similar to her grandmother's. *Who else would be in there at this hour?*

Trying to place the voice, she silently inched her way up the remaining stairs. She tiptoed past the cats, hoping they would remain still. With big, round eyes, they watched her, curiously.

Arriving at her grandmother's door, she stopped and leaned in, resting her ear against the wood. Her initial suspicions were correct—someone else was in the room. Jenna then wondered why her parents hadn't said anything downstairs. Surely they would've noticed if her grandmother had a visitor. They must have answered the door to let them in. Maybe her grandmother was listening to a record or a tape of some sort. Jenna nodded to herself, thinking that that was the most logical answer. Still, she remained by the door.

The muffled voice continued speaking. Jenna tried to decrypt the sentences but most of what was said was indistinguishable. Then, she heard something. Not so much a clear voice but rather words that were coming into focus. Jenna's back straightened when she realized what was being said. The hairs on her neck and arms began to rise. Her feet couldn't move; they were fastened to the carpet. It was as if she was meant to be there and nowhere else at that very moment. She heard the unknown voice talking about the tornado, and more specifically, Mrs. Wallace. But what really disturbed Jenna was that her grandmother seemed angry. Her tone was sharp and filled with rage. She was scolding someone; at least that's what it sounded like.

Jenna's thoughts were interrupted when she felt a bump against her leg. Looking down, she saw Ted pressing his head against her ankle, trying to get her attention. She knew that if she didn't pet him soon, he would start meowing, which would broadcast the fact that she was standing near the door.

When she didn't respond to Ted's cuddly pleading, he nestled in between her legs, sat on his haunches and stared up at her. She whispered down, "Just give me one more minute, Ted, just one more minute." Her stalling didn't work. Ted began to meow.

As his cries began to fill the hallway, something thrust against the door from the other side. Jenna jumped back in surprise. "What the—"

Glass shattered from somewhere inside the room and with it came a scream. Now, Jenna was worried.

"Grandma! Grandma! Are you okay?" She turned the doorknob but the door wouldn't open. It was locked from the inside. "Grandma—are you okay?" she yelled.

She expected to see her parents any minute now rushing up the stairs, but looking down, she saw neither of them. In fact she could still hear them talking in the kitchen. *What the hell is going on around here?*

A strange bursting noise came from within the room. Then, a wisp of smoke escaped from the bottom of the door, making its way towards Jenna's feet.

She reached for Ted and quickly stepped to the side. Lifting him up, she shrieked. Her grandmother was now standing in the doorway.

"Jesus, Grandma! You scared me. What happened in there? Are you okay?"

Her grandmother crossed her arms and tilted her head. "Is there something you'd like, dear?"

Jenna quickly glanced into the room but saw no one else in there. Nor did she see any broken glass or cloudy smoke. Looking down, the carpet was now clear; the smoke had completely dissipated.

"Well, to be honest, I wanted to talk to you about what happened outside. You left so fast. And then I thought I heard a struggle or something in your room. Are you okay?"

"Nothing's wrong, dear. I'm sorry I left in such a hurry; that was rude of me. But I'm all right."

"Can I come in and talk?" Jenna asked.

"Perhaps another time, dear. Besides, you should get some rest. I'll see you in the morning."

She stepped back to close the door.

Jenna put her hand up to stop it. "Wait—" She deliberately lowered Ted into the room as she distracted her grandmother with a question. "What happened outside? You said something about Hawthorn and then you just disappeared."

At the mere mention of the flower, her grandmother looked shocked and concerned. "I can't explain, Jenna. I just can't. Not right now." Tiny tears collected at the corner of her eyes.

Although confused by her response, Jenna had the distinct impression that her grandmother's reaction had something to do with the past. It was the look in her eyes that gave it away. Also, it was now clear that something about the Hawthorn flower was upsetting her.

Ted broke the tension when he meowed from inside the room. He had wandered off to a corner and was now pawing at something on the carpet. The sound of his nails clawing at the fabric gave Jenna an opening to enter the room. She squeezed past the door and headed over to where he was sitting.

Her grandmother closed the door. "You really should go, dear."

Jenna wasn't listening. "Ted—you know you're not supposed to do that. You're such a monkey." She inspected the area around him but saw nothing out of the ordinary. She had expected to see broken glass, signs of a struggle—something that reflected the noise she'd heard. But everything was in its place. She knew that Ted however, wasn't just clawing for good humour, she could tell there was something beneath the carpet that he was trying to get at.

His pseudo nail-sharpening session was interrupted when something in the corner of the room attracted his attention. His lips curled back, his ears flattened and he began hissing at the wall. Something was there; something Jenna couldn't see.

"Come on, you two, it's time for bed—for all of us, actually," her grandmother said, sliding in front of them. She gave Ted a stern look and he backed away immediately.

Shivers ran up and down Jenna's body; it was all coming back to her now. Her grandmother's mysterious secrets, her dismissive responses, her behaviour—it was how she behaved when the Siamese Mummy had taken over her body.

Jenna quickly hoisted Ted up off of the floor. Like a protective shield, she held him in front of her, tight to her chest. Without turning her back, she hustled towards the door, keeping both eyes on her grandmother as she left. A fear she had tried so hard to dismiss was slowly snaking its way into her system.

"There's nothing to be afraid of here, Jenna, I swear to you…"

As Jenna backed away, questions began to flood her mind. One of them overflowed into her mouth. "What are you hiding in here?"

"Nothing, nothing at all."

"Then, why did you spike the soup? Was it so we wouldn't notice something going on?"

"No, dear. That was to help you all, to relax your nerves. You had an upsetting day. Listen to yourself—you're letting the fear back in. You can't let that happen."

The soothing effects from the soup were starting to wear off. And the secrets that Jenna had bottled away were seeping back into her consciousness. Like a rampaging landside, she unleashed all of her insecurities.

"I got hunted by a giant wild cat, saw my mother mummified, and watched as my dad lost his sanity when he blamed himself for all the sick animals at his clinic. Then I found out that my nice old neighbour was a crook *and* a criminal, oh, and yeah—that my grandmother was the soul of an ancient Siamese cat looking for a stolen jewel."

Jenna took a moment to breathe as the tears dribbled down her cheeks. With Ted still pressed against her, she stood by the door. "I read the book, Grandma—*A City Lost*, and it said that history would be rewritten. I believed it."

"I see..." her grandmother started.

"No, you don't get it," Jenna said, sharply. "I saw the book sitting in the museum, sitting in its rightful place, thinking that everything was where it should've been because *I* had saved the day. But then I found out that I *didn't* really save the day. And do you know how I knew that? Because that same Siamese cat followed me home from the museum that day. That's what I was trying to tell you last night. That cat is still out there somewhere—I've seen it. But I guess you would know that, wouldn't you, since you and that cat are one and the same."

Jenna's mouth was completely uninhibited, and with each new sentence, she raised her voice. She didn't bother keeping a lid on her comments or her temper. It was the first time she'd spoken about the Siamese Mummy with anyone, and for her it felt amazing to let it all out.

"And the kicker—Mom and Dad think I'm crazy because I told them that something followed me home from the museum. I haven't been able to live that one down. Don't you see? Everyone around me thinks I've gone insane. These nightmares I've had—are real, everything is real. And yet, I still doubt my own mind. No one knows what I'm going through. I'm completely alone here!"

Her grandmother gave a solemn look and then walked up in front of her. "I believe you."

Jenna shook her head and scoffed. "How could you? It sounds absolutely crazy." She took a deep breath and looked away. After divulging all of her secrets, she felt exhausted, deflated, like a balloon that had lost all its air. That, and sleep deprivation was now taking its toll. Her eyes were becoming heavy.

"Well, it *is* quite a story, my dear, but I'm glad you finally told me everything. You mustn't harbour such heaviness alone. A secret like that should be shared."

Jenna looked back at her. Basically, she had just accused her grandmother of causing all of her problems and yet she didn't seem irritated or upset.

"I'm sorry I said those things, I don't know what came over me. I guess I just wanted to explain myself, after all these weeks of keeping it in. It felt good to say it out loud." She lowered her chin onto Ted's furry head and cuddled him.

"I'm glad you were able to tell me, Jenna. Truly. Now, here's what I know. Imagination and reality go hand in hand. There is always some truth to both, as well as some fantasy. If you can learn to understand that, it will help you move through life a lot easier." Her grandmother reached out and scratched Ted's neck. "See, the cat understands." Ted purred as her fingers slid over his silky coat. "I think we've had a wonderful breakthrough. Your parents will be so pleased."

Jenna nodded her head in agreement. "Thank you for listening to my outburst." Although her grandmother never disputed the remarks she made about feline possession, Jenna didn't want to complicate matters by bringing it up again. Her real grandmother was standing here, right now in front of her. *This* was reality, and that's all she cared about.

"You know, there are so many things I could teach you, Jenna."

Seeing the glint in her grandmother's eyes, Jenna sighed. "I just don't want to be afraid anymore."

A large smile spread across her grandmother's face as if she had expected the answer. "I understand."

"I need help, and someone to talk to about all this. But it can't be Mom or Dad, they wouldn't understand. Scott wouldn't either. And I don't want my friend Jason to know—he can never know."

"Of course. Then I will be your confidante. You and I will keep this between us and only us. This will be our little secret."

Jenna's spirits began to lift. "Thank you." She continued to snuggle with Ted. Having him near was a mitigating tool, much like her grandmother's words. However, something was still bothering Jenna. She remembered the scream, the bursting sound, the broken glass, and the puff of smoke beneath the door. Jenna wondered if she had imagined it all and that perhaps it was a side effect of the soup's ingredients.

"You know, Jenna, I can teach you some things along the way that will help you to become powerful."

"Powerful?"

"Yes, I can teach you magical things."

"What do you mean?" Jenna was well aware of her grandmother's gypsy flare. She was known for her wonderful herbal concoctions, whimsical poetry and rare collection of antiquities. But she had never spoken about magic in the sense of power. "I've never heard you talk like that before."

"Well, don't you think it's about time?" she said with a wink.

"Wait, are you talking about spells...incantations...flying on brooms, that sort of thing?" Jenna laughed. "No offense, Grandma, but I think my life is complicated enough."

"You don't believe in magic?"

"It's not that, it's just that magic isn't—"

"Real?" her grandmother answered for her. "You can believe in mummies coming to life but you can't believe in magic? How do you think that mummified cat came back to life?"

Jenna didn't answer. She didn't want to.

Her grandmother smiled. "I could teach you things, Jenna. Wonderful things. Things that not even your mother knows."

Jenna frowned. "Wait—what did you say?"

"I think you heard me." Her grandmother's stare was intense.

"Are you telling me that my mother knows about magic? How come she never said anything?"

"Your mother lives in the world of reality and has renounced any such practice. But white magic runs in her veins."

For the moment, Jenna was speechless.

"You asked for my help," her grandmother said, stepping back, "and I will give it to you." Her eyes were filled with a firm look of resolution "I will help you overcome your fears, my dear. And in return, you will help me with mine."

CLOSER THAN YOU THINK

In her darkened bedroom, Jenna tossed and turned beneath the bed sheets. She sat up, re-plumped the pillow and dropped her head back down. Her mind was awake and restless, and wouldn't let her sleep. Her eyes stared at the alarm clock as each minute clicked forward. Sleep was the furthest thing from her mind.

As the minutes passed, the noise she heard began to change. The clicks started to sound like footsteps. Closer and closer to her bedroom door they moved. Each one had a drowsy lag to it, like someone dragging his or her feet down the hallway.

Jenna looked over at the door. "Hello?"

No one answered; instead a shadow appeared at the base of the door. The dim light from the hallway bounced a shapeless image into her room.

"Is someone there?" she called out. Jenna heard the creak of another door opening and that's when the shadow disappeared. Jenna remembered that the dogs were inside. It was most likely Sam, who was prone to wandering the house at night.

Now realizing that she wasn't going to get any sleep anytime soon, she sat straight up in the bed and massaged her temples. It was two-thirty in the morning. She let out a frustrated huff and looked down at the covers. Ted and Tony were sound asleep by her feet. "If only I could sleep through everything like you guys."

Tiny snores came from each one as if to respond.

Jenna looked off towards the window. The sky outside was black and boring, a sight that she now praised. If she never saw another storm in her life, that would be perfectly fine. She yawned and gently moved around the sleeping felines. Feeling the floor beneath her feet, she stood and made her way over to the window.

Peering through the glass, she stared at the cornfield in the distance. The light from her father's veterinary clinic combined with the nearly full moon provided enough visibility for her to see the backyard and the outermost part of the cornfield. Everything out there was quiet, untouched by the storm. She compared the stillness to the events of the previous day, and then began to replay the terrifying walk through the school.

She recalled the history room in her mind's eye, and as she did, an image began to materialize. It looked like the outline of a body. It wasn't Mrs. Wallace's, as she was still walking in line behind all the students. This was before that. Jenna tried hard to focus on the scene in her head. In real time, it was only a glimpse, a mere few seconds that she had looked inside the room before Mrs. Wallace had pushed her out of the path of the falling ceiling fixture. But now, time seemed to slow down and those few seconds were drawn into minutes.

Directing all her thoughts into the room, Jenna watched as the body came into view. It was a woman. Encased in blackness, she stood with her back turned to Jenna, facing the outer wall.

Just as Jenna was starting to lose focus, a second body appeared inside the room. This one was neither human nor benign. It formed a prominent bulge in the wall in front of where the woman was standing. Jenna watched as she raised her arms into the air and chanted out loud. The bulge moved along the wall back and forth in front of the woman.

This was familiar to Jenna. She had seen the bulge inside the history room right after class when she was there alone, before the tornado had hit. It had stalked her. It wanted something from her. The images were all coming back to her now. The little girl had been standing outside the school, beneath the branches of the oak tree. And when the shadowy bulge had caught sight of her, it disappeared back into the wall into a dusty oblivion.

At that very moment, Jenna realized—the little girl had protected her.

The scene right now was reminiscent of that. But now there was a woman inside the history room, and it appeared as though she was talking to the bulge, communicating with it.

That's when Jenna saw the dangling silver locks of the woman standing inside the room.

It was her grandmother.

Now, standing by the bedroom window, Jenna was brought back to the present moment. "Grandma? That's not possible!" She looked around at her bedroom walls but saw nothing out of the ordinary. Never once had Jenna suspected that the walls might harbour a villain. The idea seemed ludicrous even as she thought it, but sadly, she was at a loss for explanations. It then occurred to her; Ted had seen something inside her grandmother's room earlier, something so disturbing that he wanted to attack it.

Although the hour was early, Jenna was desperate to speak with her grandmother. She hated to wake her, but with questions like these, she wouldn't be able to rest until her mind was put at ease. She grabbed her robe and headed for the adjacent room.

Arriving in the hallway, she walked over and placed her hand on the doorknob to her grandmother's room. Opening the door, she peeked her head inside. The room was empty.

"Grandma? Are you here?" she said, pushing the door all the way open. Hearing no response, she flipped the light switch on the wall. Her eyes squinted from the brightness. It was clear that her grandmother wasn't there. She turned the lights off and prepared to leave, but something stopped her. A persistent niggling in her head told her to stay and look around.

With the lights off, she walked over to the corner where Ted had stood earlier and stared at the wall. She pressed her fingers against it. It was flat and lifeless, nothing out of the ordinary. She moved her hands up and down but still felt nothing. *Thank God!* she thought. But as she turned towards the door, she tripped on the carpet. The edge was pulled back.

Jenna bent down to examine it. Ted's incessant clawing earlier told her that something was there. Even with the lights off, she could tell that one of the pieces of floorboard was out of place. With both hands, she lifted up the wood. Placing the board to one side, she found a small glass box sitting inside the hole. It was roughly the size of a shoe. Carefully, she removed it. The box was delicately embossed with little white flowers on all sides. The first thing that popped into Jenna's mind was the Hawthorn flower.

As she rotated it in her hands, she could see the outline of papers and photographs inside. She was tempted to open the box but respected her grandmother too much to snoop through her things. Quietly, she returned the box to its spot and set the wooden board back on top. She unfurled the rug and sat for a moment gazing down at the floor.

Jenna was intrigued with what lay beneath the wood, so much that she didn't notice when the window behind her opened. A gentle breeze wafted into the room.

Jenna turned when she felt her hair move off her shoulders. She stared at the window in surprise. "I didn't open that..." Goosebumps formed on her arms when she entertained the notion that she wasn't alone in the room.

She jumped to her feet, rushed over to the door and flipped the light switch on. Her fears were mollified; the room was vacant. Still, she searched every corner, every wall. Failing to find anything unusual, she began to relax although her eyes were still fixated on the window.

Behind her, a body-less form slid silently beneath the skin of the wall. It meandered around the hanging portraits and wallpaper to where Jenna was standing.

Jenna stared off into the night unaware that the creature was creeping towards her. Cautiously, she walked over to the window. Looking out at the cornfield, she now understood why her grandmother wasn't in bed, asleep. She was standing outside beneath the stars gazing out at the field.

Jenna gave a sigh of relief. The smile that grazed her face however, suddenly disappeared when she saw a young girl walk out of the cornfield. Worm-like shivers began to crawl through her body. "You've got to be kidding me!" Jenna blinked several times to ensure that her vision was not impaired.

But then a strange thing happened. A peculiar feeling wiggled its way into Jenna's body; one that she hadn't felt in quite some time. It stifled her shivers and pushed them back down. The sensation she was experiencing, was courage. Her quest for answers was squelching out the fear that she had. And like one of her grandmother's special herbal tonics, she could feel the strength inside of her rising. Curiosity, trepidation, eagerness and dread all fused into one swirling mass of emotion. The time had come for Jenna to confront her fear.

FOR THOSE WHO LISTEN

Jenna darted through the hallway into the kitchen. When she arrived at the back door, she hesitated, but not out of worry. She was checking to make sure that none of the dogs had followed her. She then opened the door and stepped out into the crisp, black air. She had changed into a pair of jeans and a sweater, and right now she was glad that she had. The night was cool.

Quickly, she closed the door behind her, securing it.

Straight ahead, she saw her grandmother standing near the cornstalks. The little girl was now gone. Jenna raced down the porch stairs and hurried through the moist grass towards the field. She was determined to find out what was going on. When she approached her grandmother, she slowed down. Taking several deep breaths, she walked up behind her while concentrating on her first question.

"You found the box," her grandmother said without turning.

Jenna came to an immediate standstill. Any thoughts of answer seeking were abruptly kicked to the curb.

"Come, and stand beside me," her grandmother said.

Like a dog who'd been reprimanded for being disobedient, Jenna plodded towards her grandmother with her head hung low. She had no idea what to say. Her grandmother's attention was focused on the rows of stalks. Her black nomadic garb fluttered in the night breeze as she stood still like a rock. Jenna hoped that she wasn't mad.

"I'm glad you found it," she said. "It's a secret I buried many years ago."

"I didn't look inside it, I swear..."

"It's okay, Jenna. I'm not angry. I'm quite pleased, actually."

Jenna was stunned by her grandmother's response. "Pleased?"

"Yes, I knew you'd find it someday. The power of the cat's curiosity—it was only a matter of time." With that, she turned to face her. "Jenna, I know that you saw me out here with her."

Jenna was tongue-tied. She didn't like being accused of spying, even though it was true. Also, she wondered how her grandmother knew about her spying since she hadn't seen Jenna in the room. "So, where is she? Why did she leave?"

"That's...not important," her grandmother said. "Not to you, anyway."

Jenna sensed a distinct change in her grandmother's tone. She wasn't evading her question. She was hiding something.

"But I guess it's time for me to tell you who she belongs to."

Jenna's eyes lit up. Was the girl a friend from her grandmother's youth? A witch from a coven? An imaginary friend—

"She was my sister," her grandmother said. "Her name was Alaina."

"Whoa—*what?*" Jenna said. In all of her crazy deductions, she had not expected that one. She'd heard about her grandmother's older sister, Adella, even though the family rarely spoke of her. But this was the first time she had ever heard of a third sister.

"She was my younger sister, my angel. We were inseparable."

Jenna was dumbfounded. She was left with even more questions now. "I don't understand. If she's your sister...then why do *I* keep seeing her? And why was she at the school with the Siamese cat?"

Her grandmother looked as though she was trying to find both the simplest and gentlest way to impart the information. "She's a messenger, Jenna. She needed you to get to me. Those were images you needed to see, that would help get your attention. They weren't real."

Jenna disagreed. To her, they certainly seemed real. Tactile even. She could still feel the softness of the toy lamb on her fingers. "Could've fooled me."

Her grandmother nodded. "Alaina's quite powerful that way."

This hidden detail of her grandmother's life shone a different light on her. It was as if Jenna was seeing her for the first time. "Why didn't she just come to you directly?"

"Because you needed her, too, just like she needs you."

Jenna's head was starting to hurt. Her grandmother's words were moving in a circle, around and around with no real substance in the center. "You sound like her. That's the kind of thing she said when I saw her. This and that, that and this. Up and down, down and up. It's confusing. What do you mean she needs me?"

Her grandmother sighed. "Alaina was visible to you because there is a threat on the horizon. And you are a link. That's the reason she's here."

Jenna wasn't too sure how to broach the subject but she went for it anyway. "Is she dead? Or am I just seeing her as a child for some reason?" She paused for a moment, thinking about how rude it probably sounded. "It's just that I've never heard you talk about her before. I've never heard Mom talk about her either. Is she some sort of ghost?"

Her grandmother began to cry.

"Oh, God—I'm so sorry, Grandma. I didn't mean to upset you."

"You haven't upset me, Jenna. It's only natural for you to be inquisitive. I want you to know about her."

The night wind started to settle as her grandmother lifted her chin and began telling the story of Alaina. "She was six years old, and wanted ruby slippers. I remember it like it was yesterday."

"Ruby slippers?" Jenna said.

"Yes, from *The Wizard of Oz*. It was her favourite movie." The way her grandmother spoke, the sparkle in her eyes; it was clear that she was still tied to the past. "Mama bought her red patent shoes. It was the last gift Alaina ever received."

Jenna finally had her answer. Alaina was no longer living.

"We all looked the same when we were small," her grandmother explained. "Blonde ringlets, all of us. And everyone thought that Adella and I were twins, we were so similar in appearance. Adella was the oldest; she and Alaina were separated by several years. Being the middle child, I loved and cherished both of them equally, but Alaina and I were very close. I protected her because she was the baby."

"Grandma, this is the most you've ever said about Adella. How come?"

"Oh, Jenna, I wish I could tell you everything. There is so much to know, so much. Where to start is the question." She cleared the tears from her face. "Adella, like me, practiced magic when she was young. Being the eldest, she was the one who brought me into the family coven. We have a long line of white magic in our bloodlines; Adella was simply the one to introduce me to it. Our mother practiced also, as did hers and so on and so on. I learned from all of them and carried that knowledge with me through life."

"Family is so important, isn't it?" Jenna said.

"So is blood, my dear. So is blood."

Jenna crossed her arms. "I always thought they were the same thing."

"Not always, dear, but you'll soon find that out."

Jenna didn't like the sound of that. There was a moment of silence where neither of them spoke. It seemed as though her grandmother was reloading, regrouping.

"For many years Adella and I practiced our craft together," she started. "We honed our skills and polished our spells, until one day something changed. Adella was...different."

"Different? How?"

"She displayed an interest in dark magic," her grandmother said.

"Oh...I see." Jenna was starting to understand why Adella's name was rarely spoken.

"There was a forest near the edge of town where we lived in Salem. We were forbidden to play in the forest; we were told that dark forces resided there. Adella ventured there alone one night. She was just young then, and she had us so worried. Our family searched and searched for her. She returned to us the following night, but she was different. You see, somewhere in the forest, something had reached out to her. Something that was after our family tree—our magic. It took Adella under its wing and she became its apprentice."

Jenna snickered. "Wow—that sounds like something right out of a fairy tale."

"This is no laughing matter," her grandmother scolded her. "This power is very real, very dangerous."

"Oh, of course, I didn't mean it like that. I'm sorry, Grandma." Jenna could see the fear in her grandmother's eyes. She was completely serious. "So, who did this to Adella? What kind of thing are you talking about?"

Her grandmother's eyes came alive in the darkness. "The Sandshadow."

Jenna's mind jumped into overdrive. The shadow in the history room. Her visions in the hospital—it was all coming back to her. "The talisman!"

A burst of air nearly knocked her off her feet, bringing her back to where she was standing. The wind howled around her as it grew in strength but Jenna held her ground. "I remember!" she said with resolution. "Something came to me inside the hospital. A ghost, a shapeless shadow. I remember it now. It crawled up my legs and sat on me. It wanted the talisman..."

"The Mummy's talisman?" her grandmother said.

"Yes, but that can't be. It disappeared after I put the pieces together. It doesn't exist anymore...or if it does, it's with the Mummy."

Her grandmother's response was unsettling, as was her contorted expression. "You might have changed history, Jenna, but that talisman still exists. And it must not be with the Mummy if the Sandshadow is after you, which means that the jewel is closer than you think. Are you certain you don't know where it is?"

"I'm positive. I have no idea!"

"Then that is why Alaina has come—to warn us."

"I liked it better when she was just a messenger," Jenna grumbled.

Her grandmother turned towards the cornstalks. "The warning is a message, just not one that you'd like to hear. I've anticipated this for many years now. The Sandshadow has arrived, and my sister, Adella, has returned."

The emotional fortitude that had led Jenna outside was slowly withering from her system. "So, what happens now?"

"I'm not sure," her grandmother said. "The path that lies ahead of us is uncertain. But I do know that this is a fight I wouldn't wish upon anyone."

Jenna's heart just about flipped when she heard that. Seeing her grandmother's suspicions all out in the open undermined her sense of security. It didn't help that the softness of the air had been replaced with wind-driven turmoil. Jenna was now well aware that another storm was on the horizon. This one however, was much closer to home.

RIPPLE EFFECT

Together they stood, grandmother and granddaughter side by side, looking up at the cornfield. It wasn't quite what Jenna had expected when she'd agreed to help her grandmother. As crazy as it seemed, in her head she had envisioned them both hovering over a black, smouldering cauldron, cackling and reciting spells. Crooked feathers and ravens' feet, eye of newt and bat wings—that sort of thing. That was the calling card of witches, or at least what Jenna knew from folklore. Maybe her grandmother did own a cauldron, but if anything, it was used for herbal remedies and spicy teas. Feathers were used for decoration in her hair, and as for ravens' feet—they remained on the ravens that lived outside the house.

Jenna watched her now, as she stood with her eyes closed, focused on the cornfield. She wondered what her grandmother was doing.

"We're going into the field, Jenna," she said, without looking at her.

Jenna immediately took a step back. The last time she had entered the field, she was ambushed by the Siamese Mummy. The cat had cornered her, distracted her, while a pit of swirling sand sucked her beneath the cornfield. Where she had landed, was horrifying. She'd found her mother, her neighbour, Dr. Osiris, and many other people who'd gone missing from the area. Each and every one of them had been mummified alive. Walking corpses is what they had become. They'd been brought to a darkened structure with pillars and amber globes. It was the Temple of King Odon—King of the Siamese Mummy. Jenna's cornfield was the portal to his temple, which had once existed in the ancient city of Menao, Siam.

Jenna had seen the temple once before when she was lured by the Siamese cat through the cornfield on a previous journey. The cornstalks had opened up into a massive white desert with a sapphire pyramid in the distance—also King Odon's temple. Just a different view of it.

But in Jenna's down-under cornfield adventure, the structure had appeared more cave-like, more primitive. And the treatment she had received exemplified that. Although she hadn't been taken hostage like the others, she'd been tortured by means of captivity. Captured by a vengeful mob of mummies, Jenna had been shoved into a sarcophagus to die. Like a mad woman, she'd pounded and clawed at the stone coffin trying to escape it. It wasn't until she took her last breath, that she was released from her grave. Somehow, she had woken up, injured but alive, back inside the cornfield. She had momentarily contemplated the reasons behind her harrowing catch and release experience, but following that, she ran from the cornfield with the intent of never going back inside it, ever again.

Now, standing in front of the outermost layer of corn, Jenna shook her head. "I'm not going in there," she said.

Her grandmother remained silent and stationary.

Jenna backed away. "You'll have to go in there alone."

"Stop right there!" her grandmother said, her eyes still closed. "You need my help and I need yours. That was our arrangement. You agreed. Jenna, this is part of that arrangement. You will come with me into the field. Your fears and mine are tied together. Severing that tie would do neither of us any good." She opened her eyes and placed an object in Jenna's hand. "Take this."

Jenna looked down at the flashlight resting in her palm. "I can't—you don't understand!" As she turned to leave, her grandmother grabbed her arm, forcefully. Jenna stared in surprise.

"I cannot let you go back," her grandmother said. "There is only one path—and that is forward!"

Jenna pulled her arm away. "No—I'm not going in there!"

In an instant, her grandmother began to recite a spell. "Courage to fly, heart of might, soar with me into the night!" With one hand lifted, she twisted her fingers in front of Jenna's face.

Jenna looked on with complete disillusion. Her grandmother had never done magic on her before, but here she was, putting a spell on her. It was unexpected and beyond abnormal. But before Jenna could do or say anything, she felt a tiny tickle inside her gut. Her nerves began to relax. She felt more tame and agreeable.

"You will come with me, as planned," her grandmother commanded.

Jenna nodded. "Can you promise me that nothing bad will happen in there?"

"No, my dear. I cannot promise you that. But I will tell you that nothing in life worth having comes easy. It takes courage to believe in oneself. I believe in you, but do *you* believe in you? How hard are you willing to fight, to defeat your own fears? That is the question."

Jenna stood quietly, and said nothing.

Her grandmother smiled. "Come, we must start this journey. Close your eyes."

Jenna obliged. She closed her eyes and took a moment to soak in the night air. When she opened them, her grandmother was gone.

"Grandma?"

The wind billowed past her but there was no verbal response.

"Okay, I get it. You're trying to teach me a lesson. Be strong, stop being a wimp. I appreciate your wisdom and all—" Jenna stopped to listen. There was a whisper in the air. It was coming from inside the field. She turned on the flashlight and pointed it past the cornstalks. "Hello?"

She took a step closer to the field. The sounds of nature came alive around her. Rustling leaves, swaying stalks, blustering loops of gusting breezes. Then, beneath the blanket of the moon, Jenna heard her grandmother's voice. It wasn't strained, it wasn't harsh. It was calm, inviting—she was calling for her.

Jenna felt like a puppet, with not much will of her own. Most of her wanted to leave. In fact, mentally she was already back in bed, safely tucked beneath the covers. But the part of her that kept both feet in place was telling her to follow her grandmother and do as she was told.

Whether it was the wind playing tricks or real voices calling out, Jenna didn't have a clue. But the words played over in her mind, 'That was our arrangement, that was our arrangement', and she finally understood. This was her duty, her obligation. The pebble was thrown, and the rings of resolution were rippling towards her. There was no way she could avoid them.

"Okay—I'm coming in." She pointed the flashlight, formed a determined fist with her other hand, took several deep breaths and marched onward into the field.

WELCOME BACK

The smell of sweet green foliage was all that Jenna could register. She was surrounded by large, brawny leaves and stalks. Everything around her was dark except for the area that was lit by the flashlight. Mostly, she kept the light pointed at the ground. Jenna was not going to be caught unawares, not like before.

She'd been walking nearly ten minutes now with no sign from her grandmother when a sudden rustling of leaves up ahead made her stop. She had nothing to protect herself with except the flashlight. She considered hiding behind some of the cornstalks in an attempt to blend in, but then realized that whatever was in the field most likely had better eyesight than her, since it was in the dark. The thought did cross her mind that perhaps the noise was her grandmother. At least that gave her something to hope for.

As she stood in place deciding what to do, something dashed through the leaves directly ahead of her.

Startled, her hands began to shake. Grandmother or no grandmother, she was about to race full throttle back to the house.

"Jennnnnaaaaaaaa..." she heard from only a few feet away. The voice just about gave her a heart attack.

Jenna's not here right now, she thought of saying. She remembered seeing all the mummies inside the cave beneath the cornfield when she was pulled through the ground. This field was a frightening place, and yet here she was again, inside the field at her grandmother's request.

"Jennnnaaaaaaaa...." something echoed into the night. "Look and see...look and see..."

Seconds later another voice stood out amongst the wind. "Ssshhhh.... she can hear you."

Terrifying as it was, Jenna was once again prompted like a puppet to move forward, towards the sounds. The voices became clear as Jenna stopped to listen. When she pushed the leaves aside, her eyes grew wide with wonder. The area was lit with a dim light and resembled a room inside a house. Three young girls were sitting at a children's table playing with dolls and drinking tea. Together they laughed and sipped their drinks from their delicate china cups. One of the girls had a royal, life-like doll that sat prim and proper on a chair of its own. One had a scarecrow that was made of wool and straw, and sat on the table. And one held a small, toy lamb in her arms.

Jenna knew immediately that these were the sisters three. Grandma Abby, Adella and Alaina. Their resemblance was unquestionable. All three had curly blonde locks with chubby, smiling faces. And with their short, hemmed, matching black dresses, there was no mistaking their family relation. Jenna identified Alaina as the little girl with the lamb. By their size, she assumed that Adella was the sister with the scarecrow and that Grandma Abby was the one feeding tea to her baby doll. As a silent spectator, Jenna watched the scene play out before her.

"She can't hear me, she's not listening," Adella said with a smirk.

"She *is* listening," said Abigail, looking down at her baby sister. "You *are* listening, aren't you?"

Alaina gave a cheeky grin and pointed at her older sisters. "No, to you and you, but yes to me and Mia." She rested her chin on the lamb and hugged it tight. "She and I, you and me, forever we will be."

Adella crossed her arms and frowned. "Riddles and rhymes, that's all you say. When will you learn to talk properly?" She leaned over and lifted a teacup to the scarecrow's mouth. "Don't you think she should talk like us, Abby?"

Abigail gave a kindly smile. "Don't you want to talk like us, dear sister?"

Alaina shook her head. "No, Mama says I don't have to."

A look of compassion spread across Abigail's face. "There, Adella, you have your answer. So shall it be. Now, it's time for a spell!"

At this point, Jenna noticed a small, black mixing bowl with steam rising out of it perched in the middle of the table. Adella stood from her seat and tossed a piece of twine, some tiny red berries and a small cutting of black ribbon into the bowl.

"The holly berries are for love, the ribbon is for safety and the twine ties us together. It will be our oath to one another. Let us keep it," Adella said.

Abigail, looking no older than nine or ten, nodded her head up and down. "Let us keep it," she said. She then reached for Alaina's hand. "You will not understand this yet, dear sister, but this oath will bind us together, through happy and troubled times. Take my hand."

Alaina placed her lamb on the chair as she stood and reached out both hands for her sisters. Around the tiny table they stood, arms locked in position, reciting the words of their childhood vow. Many times throughout the chanting, Abigail peered down at their baby sister as she twisted and turned like a youthful devil. The look between them however, was crystal clear; it was obvious that they adored one another. Alaina's innocence was what stood out the most for Jenna, but not far behind it was the unmistakable affinity that Abigail had for her.

The ritual was brought to a halt when Alaina buckled over in pain. She wheezed and coughed as Abigail leaned over to help her. Adella however, seemed unbothered by the incident.

"It's just the curse, Abby, the curse," Adella said.

"No, Adella, it's not the curse. It's more than that—our sister is sick. Get Mama!"

Jenna watched intently, but the scene that she'd been privy to was coming to an end. The characters and background slowly disappeared out of view. Standing now in the wake of the flashlight beam, was her grandmother.

"Alaina was nearly six when we took that oath. I was nine and Adella was eleven. She was the sweetest thing, our little sister, Alaina. It wasn't long after that, that we lost her."

"What happened?" Jenna asked.

Her grandmother was silent for a moment. "She died of polio. It was something we could not protect her from."

Jenna was shocked. "Grandma, I'm so sorry. I had no idea."

"We buried her with Hawthorn flowers. They were her favourite kind." Her grandmother's eyes were filled with a dry pain; a solemn look devoid of tears.

"That's why you got upset when I told you about my allergic reaction."

She nodded. "Hawthorn is a bittersweet memory for me. All my memories of Alaina are. It was a long time ago, but some days it doesn't seem so. We were just children with wild imaginations and the freedom to experiment. That was the kind of family I was born into, Jenna."

"But then Adella changed that, didn't she?"

Her grandmother scowled at her. "Be careful what you say, my dear. Family is still family."

"I didn't mean to upset you, Grandma, it's just from what you told me, I figured that Adella had something to do with what happened afterwards."

"You must understand, Jenna, that for years Adella remained a loving sister to me. We grew together and respected our family, but when dark magic entered her world, our lives were changed forever. Her spirit was encumbered with a poison that no one could touch."

Her words were powerful and passionate but somewhat outlandish like something right out of *Sleepy Hollow*, Jenna thought.

"When Adella embraced the dark arts, she invited the creatures that fed on it."

"You mean...the Sandshadow," Jenna said.

"Yes, and it took all my strength *and* my mother's to send the shadow back to the blackness it came from. But even with all our combined power we could not destroy it. We could only seal it in a shell from which it could not escape."

"What happened to Adella after that?" Growing up, Jenna had only heard brief stories of the older sister and had never met her.

"She was cast out from our family. She disappeared from our lives."

"Oh, that's awful," Jenna said.

"Yes. Yes it was."

Jenna finally began to see the big picture. Her grandmother had lost one sister to sickness, and the other to darkness. She was the last standing white witch in the family. It was now obvious to Jenna, why she herself, had been brought into the fold. Her grandmother truly needed her.

"But wait...you said that you sealed the Sandshadow so it couldn't escape. But it *did* escape, it came after me in the hospital when I was sick."

Her grandmother shook her head. "No, Jenna, it did not escape. It was released."

"By who?"

"Adella. My sister has come back."

Jenna took a deep breath and stared into her grandmother's emerald eyes. Knowing very well that her role in the story was about to change, she straightened her spine and pursed her lips. "What is it you need me to do?"

FAMILY TIES

"Stay close," her grandmother said, as she moved effortlessly through the stalks. "We're not far."

Jenna pointed her flashlight in all directions as she followed in her footsteps. "Far from what?"

"Our destination, of course."

"Oh, right, more riddles." Jenna rolled her eyes. Her grandmother's answers were once again short and cryptic. "I do have one question. I had a vision tonight of someone inside the history room at my school. It was after the had tornado hit, we were all walking through the hallway."

"I told you, Jenna. Those images weren't real, they were just messages."

"I know, but I thought the vision I saw was of you."

Her grandmother came to a standstill. She stopped so quickly that Jenna nearly ran into her. Without looking back, she said, "Did the person look just like me?"

"Yes. She had long, silver hair and was dressed like you. She was facing the wall where a large bulge was moving."

"Jenna, are you sure?"

"Yes, definitely. Oh God—it was Adella, wasn't it?"

Her grandmother turned to face her. "Adella is more powerful than anyone in my family. With years of darkness growing inside of her, she alone would have the power to release the Sandshadow. Just like the devastation she brought forth at your school."

Jenna felt a sudden twinge of anger. "No—that can't be!"

Her grandmother stepped in closer. "That's how strong she is, my dear."

Jenna was appalled. "That tornado almost killed my teacher! There's no magical power in the world that could do that!"

"You couldn't be more wrong, my sweet, Jenna. Now, let that be a lesson for you."

Jenna didn't like this side of her grandmother. She was argumentative, dismissive. Stern. And not once did she consider Jenna's feelings.

"If Adella did something so vicious as to hurt innocent people, then I hope I never meet her, because there's no telling what I'll do."

Her grandmother glared at her. "Choose your words wisely—you never know who's listening."

"What?" Jenna said.

"Adella is still my sister, Jenna. Do not disparage her."

"Are you kidding me? Why are you defending her?" Jenna was completely thrown by her grandmother's loyalty to Adella.

"You are young, you don't understand." She released a heavy sigh and turned her back. "Come, now. We must carry on."

Jenna reluctantly followed behind. She had so many questions buzzing around in her head but her grandmother no longer wanted to discuss her family ties. Instead, she began to walk faster through the field.

"Wait—why are we rushing?" Jenna said.

"We have less time than I thought."

Jenna picked up her pace to keep up with her. Her grandmother was moving so fast that it looked like she was floating over the ground.

Moments later, her grandmother began to slow down. She walked through another row of corn before coming to a full stop on the other side. Jenna hustled behind her, so as not to lose sight. When she brushed past the last row of stalks, she stopped. The field had opened up into a large, white, sandy desert. In the distance was a beautiful pyramid, deep sapphire in colour. It sparkled in the night beneath the stars and the clear black sky.

Jenna took one look and shouted, "No way! The answer to our problem is out there?"

"Yes," her grandmother said with delight. "I believe you recognize it."

"You could say that—it's King Odon's temple!"

Jenna couldn't believe her eyes. It seemed like only yesterday that the Siamese cat had lured her into the desert towards the temple.

"Come, we must hurry," her grandmother said. "The clock is ticking!"

JOURNEY TO THE TEMPLE OF THE KING

The soft sand spread beneath Jenna's feet as she headed for the twinkling structure. It was truly a stunning site to see. Although she had fearful memories of events that took place inside the pyramid, she couldn't deny its beauty. Nor could she deny the peacefulness of the landscape surrounding it. She envisioned scenes from *Arabian Nights*, with camels and men moving beneath the stars on clandestine journeys through time. Jenna pictured herself walking in their footsteps as she too waded through the desert sands.

"I don't believe this," she muttered.

Up ahead, her grandmother moved swiftly in the night. Her stride was fast; she was now further ahead than Jenna was, closer to the pyramid. Jenna was lagging behind. They had been walking a long while and without a snippet of conversation. In fact, neither of them had spoken a single word after leaving the cornfield behind them. Jenna looked back now, but the field had disappeared completely out of view.

"Typical," she said beneath her breath. "My only sanctuary out here is that damn field. And now that's gone."

Although the path they'd taken had led them far into the desert, her grandmother wasn't slowing down. Her speed was consistent, her pace was steadfast. It was Jenna who felt tuckered.

Jenna stopped and leaned over to take a breath. For a moment she wondered why her grandmother hadn't waited for her. She'd seemed almost anxious to distance herself once they'd left the field.

When she looked up, her grandmother was standing by the pyramid watching her. "Come, hurry!"

Jenna's response was delayed when she saw the enormity of the building, and all the sensations that went with it. Much like the cornfield, the temple was not a place that Jenna wanted to revisit. It took a ton of strength and will power for her to even think about moving on now. The very first time she'd entered the pyramid, she was trapped and hunted by mummified pillars that came to life after lightning—inside the pyramid—had awoken them. Her eardrums had bled from the shock of the lightning strike. And then the building had sealed her in. It was enough to make Jenna go crazy.

Needless to say, she was hesitant to go anywhere near the temple now. The cornfield she had conquered with the help of her grandmother. The temple—not a chance.

"I'm just going to wait here!" she yelled.

"Are you sure?" her grandmother said.

At that moment, something tweaked inside Jenna's head. It wasn't in her grandmother's book of etiquette to leave others behind. Especially not with all the persuasive action she took to get Jenna to come along in the first place. Jenna sensed that something was wrong.

The winds began to rise, picking up sand and carrying it towards her. Jenna squinted through the moonlit darkness; something was out there. When she looked back at her grandmother, she shivered. The crooked smile on her face was distressing.

"What's going on?" Jenna shouted.

The old woman said nothing. She stood beneath the moon watching her granddaughter panic.

Jenna could feel the fear rising within her. Her intuition was telling her that something very bad was about to happen. Then her grandmother crossed her arms and winked. At that moment Jenna knew—the woman standing by the pyramid was not her grandmother.

"Who are you?" she yelled.

The old woman said nothing.

"Where's my grandmother?"

Nothing. No answer.

There was no denying that Jenna had once again been foolishly coaxed out into the desert. Her eyes grew wide, her breath came in large heaving gasps. She wanted to faint and have it all be done with.

"The dream is over, the dream is over, the dream is over..." But it was no dream.

The winds whirled past her, lifting up handfuls of sand in its wake. Jenna was on high alert. Her feet were ready to bolt. In what direction, she wasn't sure yet. Backwards, sideways, whatever. Towards the field was where she wanted to go, if she could only find it.

Beneath the guiding light of the moon, she saw something approaching. Scrunching her eyes, she tried to make out what it was.

With horror, she realized that a thick blanket of sandy earth was rushing towards her. It was the size of a drive-in movie screen. She couldn't take her eyes off the monstrous wall of bulging sand. It writhed within itself like something was trying to breakout from inside it.

"The Sandshadow!" she cried. As the words left her lips, an opening appeared in the misshapen menace. Out sprang an army of whirling snakes, spiralling towards her like a deformed helix. The snakes bore black and silver stripes, and their heads were hooded. Jenna had never seen anything so frightening in her life.

She stumbled back as the bulge closed in. Her mind and feet weren't reacting fast enough; the Sandshadow was gaining on her.

As it rippled over the ground, the Sandshadow released its venomous extensions. The snakes landed in the soft earth and quickly slithered towards her.

Absolutely terrified at what she was seeing, Jenna turned and ran. She sprinted as fast as she could away from the mass of hunters behind her. Without looking back, she sped in the direction of the absent cornfield. She ran and ran without as much as a wince, a gasp or a cry.

A moment of reprieve came when she turned and saw nothing behind her. With her heart beating erratically, she spun around in all directions, forcing the flashlight onto every inch of earth. Seeing nothing but sand all around her, she clenched her chest. "Oh, thank God!"

Everything had disappeared. No Sandshadow, no snakes. Just silence.

She hunched over to release the pressure that was building inside. With her arms against her legs she inhaled big gulps of air.

As she took another deep breath, something slithered behind her. The smile disappeared from her face when she heard the noise.

Straightening her back, she froze. Instant tears formed in her eyes when she realized that she'd been ensnared within a triangle of poisonous hisses. Three silver-headed coiling monsters appeared at first, surrounding her. They were giants, all of them, seven feet at least. Jenna stared at their scaly bodies; each one was as thick as a horse's leg. She had never been so scared in her life.

Tears streamed down her face as their forked tongues lashed out towards her. "Leave me alone!" she screamed. "Get away from me!"

She kicked at the closest snake. The animal quickly dodged to one side, then returned and towered above her. Jenna looked straight up at it. The cold, black, lifeless look in its eyes craved to punish her. The other snakes hissed and lunged at her.

Jenna whipped the flashlight back and forth. She felt the weight of it smashing against her attackers. "NO!" she howled. She became completely unhinged and began to thrash about madly with her arms and legs.

Then, from the darkness around them, a bellowing roar was heard. Behind the snakes, Jenna saw the Siamese cat leaping into the air. It broke through the triumvirate of serpents and starting snapping at their necks. It grabbed one and quickly bit down. Jenna heard the crunching of bones, and then saw the animal lying limp in the cat's mouth. She looked on with horror, wondering if she was next. But the cat continued to attack the snakes.

Feeling overwhelmed with both fear and unprecedented gratitude she turned and battled the remaining snakes that surrounded them. Jenna wasn't alone in the fight. She had an ally, and a completely unexpected one at that. Together they fought to triumph over the devils of the desert. The cat was a ferocious opponent, intimidating and fearless.

Blood flew through the air. Jenna cringed at the sights and sounds, as the cat fought with such indomitable will. She was amazed by its courage. But while she was watching the cat, one of the snakes struck, sinking its fangs into her arm. It then quickly wrapped its entire body around her neck and shoulders, forcing her to the ground. It pressed its teeth deep into her muscle and squeezed.

Jenna howled in agony as she struggled to free herself from its grip, but the animal tightened its hold on her neck.

The cat turned at the sounds. Without a moment's pause, it lunged at the snake with its teeth and claws extended.

Jenna felt the world getting dim. She was nearly unconscious when the snake's hold began to loosen. It was still fighting hard to take her life, but the cat was trying to stop it. Jenna pushed at its coils while gasping for air. She could feel its scales still clinging to her neck. A sharp snapping sound then came, and its hold loosened all together. Jenna felt the entire weight of the animal as it collapsed on top of her.

The cat reached over and with its jaws, threw the dead snake to the ground. It then turned back towards Jenna and stood over her.

She tilted her head to one side and looked up at it. Her breathing was slow and shallow; she couldn't speak. She could barely keep her eyes open.

Behind the cat, more snakes were approaching. Jenna saw them slithering towards it. She moved her lips in an attempt to warn the cat, but nothing came out. She felt stripped of all her strength and energy. All she could do was watch.

The remaining snakes struck at the cat with fangs exposed. The situation seemed hopeless, and to Jenna, final. They would both perish in the desert.

Through timid breaths, she watched as the cat spun around to take on each of its attackers. It was the last thing she saw before darkness took her vision.

SILENTLY WAITING

Jenna awoke with a sluggish stir to the soft glow of dim amber lighting. It was gentle on her eyes as she opened them. Her body felt tingly, especially her left arm. Lifting her head, she saw that her arm was wrapped in a white bandage. She couldn't understand why or how it got that way.

Where am I? she thought. She was lying on top of a flat, hard surface of some sort. It stood four feet off the ground and resembled a large table.

She laid her head back down and rested a moment while gathering her strength. Her arm was pulsating with a stinging pain. She put all her weight on the other arm and sat up slowly. What was wrong with her arm? She pressed her fingers against it. "Ouch..." There was only one way to find out how bad it was, she decided, and so began to unwrap the covering.

"I wouldn't do that," a voice came from behind her.

Startled by the sound, Jenna quickly turned to see who was talking to her. The voice came from a darkened corner; she couldn't make out who was there. "Who are you?"

The voice did not respond.

Jenna gently lifted herself off of the table. "Where am I?"

"You don't recognize your surroundings?"

Jenna shifted her stance and braced her arm as she looked around. She counted several globe-sized crystal balls inflamed with orange fire. They reminded her of burning logs, just in spherical form. Each one was poised on top of a mummified statue, held up by stiffened arms that reached into the air. She knew exactly where she was.

"King Odon's temple..."

The voice said nothing.

Jenna looked behind her. Standing tall and proud was the mammoth black and white decorated statue of King Odon himself. His giant icy blue eyes glimmered in the fire's light, high above where she was standing. It was just like before; she was inside the sapphire pyramid.

She gazed up further and saw the apex of the shiny glass building. Each of the four sides came down on an angle, which gave a striking beauty to the internal layout. The walls sparkled in the soft lighting. The image that reflected back in Jenna's eyes was utterly stunning, although every part of her remained in battle position.

"Why am I here?"

"To heal." The speaker's voice was calm, deep. A woman's voice. "Maybe you were hesitant to come because of past experiences, but King Odon's temple is a place of healing and safety. If you experienced otherwise, then that was not of his doing."

Jenna pivoted towards the corner. "I was tortured by lightning and trapped here like an animal last time. Of course I didn't want to come back!"

"Then perhaps it's your perception that needs changing."

Jenna's arm was throbbing. "What happened to me? What's wrong with my arm?"

"You don't remember? Then the venom is working faster than we expected."

"Venom—what venom? What are you talking about?"

The voice paused. "What is the last thing you remember?"

Jenna thought for a moment. "I don't know...I think I was walking in a desert." She didn't understand what that had to do with anything and was starting to get frustrated. "Okay, I answered your question, now you need to answer mine. Who are you? I want to know who I'm speaking to."

"Very well," the voice answered.

Jenna watched the corner closely as she waited for the speaker to reveal itself. Although the voice was somewhat familiar, she had no idea who it belonged to. But when the body stepped out of the shadows and into the light, she shrieked.

"Oh my God—it's you!" Jenna stumbled back behind the stone table at first sight of the pointed black ears and large whiskered mouth.

The Siamese cat moved with a graceful but powerful stride. Its size was impressive, slightly bigger than that of a lion's. It stepped towards her and then stopped. "I am Anzhara."

Jenna shuddered. "Oh my God—you can talk!"

"Yes." Her voice was strong, commanding.

This wasn't what Jenna had anticipated, not in the least. For months she had believed that the Siamese cat was the enemy. Now here she was, talking to it.

"This can't be happening—I must be dreaming!"

"No," she said. "You were brought here. We almost lost you in the desert—the Sandshadow nearly took you."

Jenna's legs wobbled as she stood behind the table. "What happened to my arm?"

"The Sandshadow's servants poisoned you. Part of their blood infiltrated yours. If you had died they would have taken you, and in time you would have become one of them. A Blade Viper."

An image flashed in Jenna's mind. For a brief second she remembered a struggle in the sands. "Was I surrounded by snakes?"

"Yes." The cat's tone was benevolent, but Jenna could tell how serious it was.

"You...rescued me?"

Anzhara nodded her head and rested back on her haunches.

"But that means...they're still out there! They could find us here!"

"King Odon's temple is a sanctuary. We are safe here, for now."

"I don't understand," Jenna said. "How did you survive? There were so many snakes out there. And how did you get me here?"

"I had help," Anzhara said.

Jenna stared at her teeth as she spoke. The pyramid's walls now protected her from the enemy outside, but the cat was still a potential threat. "So, what happens now? Are you planning on snacking on my injured arm? Am I just a meal that you brought back here to finish off?"

Anzhara angled her head and glared at Jenna. "Is that truly what you think?"

Jenna watched her carefully. "No...not really, or else you wouldn't have saved me, I guess."

"You're going to have to trust me, Jenna."

Hearing the cat say her name was unnerving; she didn't like that she knew who she was. "That's really funny…I have to trust you. I mean, that's what you're telling me, right? I have to trust *you*?"

Anzhara remained in place as Jenna began to implode.

"You see, up until now, I thought *you* were the enemy. *You* were the one that hunted me all summer and followed me home from the museum. *You're* the reason I'm like this! So, to me it's quite funny that you're telling me I have to trust you, considering all that I've been through."

Anzhara began to walk towards her. "I understand that this is hard for you—"

"Damn straight it is!" Jenna blurted. The cat was only a few feet away. Its panther-like movement gave her the creeps.

As it approached the table, Jenna moved to the other side. "Listen, why don't you let me out of here and I'll go back to my family and you can go back to yours, wherever they are, and we can just go our separate ways and pretend this never happened."

Anzhara kept moving. Her large paws spread over the ground as she strode towards Jenna. "I can't let you leave."

Staring at her claws as they clicked on the ground, Jenna gulped. Anzhara's threatening response had her tongue-tied. And right now, the game of cat and mouse they were playing wasn't helping.

"Why not?" Jenna said.

"Because…you haven't learned your lesson."

"What lesson? The one where I should've stayed at home in bed?" Jenna's fingers felt along the table's cold edges as she carefully stepped around it. "Yeah, I think I got that one."

"No. The lesson where you believe in yourself, so that you can learn to trust again." With that, Anzhara stopped.

Seeing the look in her eyes, gave Jenna a moment to regroup. She hadn't expected the animal's words of wisdom. Jenna planted her feet and stood across from her. "Trust is a fragile thing, you know. And you scared the hell out of me this summer. Am I supposed to believe that the problem was *me* all this time?"

"Yes." Anzhara's tone was confident, aggressive.

"I find that very hard to believe."

"You don't understand then. It wasn't you I was after. I was searching for resolution, for our lost city. You were the key to it all. You found my talisman—the Star of Omandai. King Odon was and remains eternally grateful for your courageous act, as do I."

"Then why did you try to attack me?" Jenna said. "And why did you chase me home from the museum?"

"It wasn't my intention to attack or chase you. I was sent for you as simple as that. You were afraid to see me as anything else."

"You're kidding, right? You had all those people mummified. My *mother* was mummified. And what about all those innocent animals you made sick? You can't tell me that your actions were harmless."

Anzhara lowered her head. "I was sent to do those things but only because of what happened to my people and my city. Your city had to endure the curse." When she lifted her chin, Jenna saw a look of genuine remorse. "I am sorry for all the fear I caused. But I also knew that the curse would be lifted once the talisman was found. I trusted you to help me."

"I'm guessing that's why I'm here, then. You need my help again?"

"Yes," Anzhara said. "And for that we need to trust each other."

In the time they had spoken, Jenna's pulse had slowed from its racing status. She no longer felt the need to hide behind the stone table. With a sigh, she stepped out from behind it and approached the cat. Anzhara did nothing to scare her, she just watched. Jenna stood only a few feet away from her now.

"Okay, listen. I don't know what it is you need me to do but if you promise not to hurt me, I will do my best to try and trust you."

Anzhara bowed her head. "Agreed."

Jenna fiddled with her fingers. "I can't believe that I'm really talking to you. We're actually having a conversation right now. No one's ever gonna believe this."

"There's no need to tell anyone, Jenna. Secrecy protects both of us."

"Okay," Jenna nodded. But there was one question she had not yet asked, and it was something she needed to hear out loud in order to fully comprehend the situation. "Are you my grandmother?"

Anzhara gave an earnest look, as if she had wanted to tell her all along. "Yes. Abigail and I are one. That is my connection to you."

Jenna stepped closer. She examined the cat's eyes, body, ears, paws, tail—everything, to see if any part of her grandmother was visible.

"Her spirit is harnessed within my body, Jenna. It's what led me into the desert to rescue you."

As crazy as it sounded, Jenna believed her. "You really did protect me out there."

"I had to."

Jenna glanced down at the ground. "I should be thanking you for saving my life."

"You're welcome," Anzhara said, graciously.

A little glow flickered inside Jenna's heart. "So, why did you follow me home from the museum?"

"I followed you because my talisman had disappeared. It went missing right after you discovered it. I was never reunited with it. Jenna—if the Sandshadow finds it first, your world will be in danger. It must be returned not to me, but to its origin," Anzhara said, looking up at King Odon's statue.

Jenna followed her gaze, right up to the top of the twenty-foot statue. She now noticed a slight depression in the middle of its neck. It was round and small. Hidden amongst the shadows of the room, Jenna hadn't seen it until now. "What is that space on his neck?"

"That, is the final resting spot of the talisman. The ruby must be brought here and placed onto King Odon's neck. I was destined to return with it here, but then the ruby went missing. Now, you must find it, Jenna, and bring it here. You, alone, must do this."

"But I don't know where it is," she said.

Anzhara's tone was now dire. "The Sandshadow is after you for this one reason. It needs only this ruby to unleash its full power and change our worlds forever. You see, hidden within the talisman is an ancient Siamese magic. If the Sandshadow harnesses this magic, then nothing will stop it from destroying your world or mine. This is what makes you valuable to the Sandshadow. It is a precious task, Jenna, one that you must hold dearly!"

Jenna was shocked and frightened, knowing that the one thing keeping her safe was that ruby. She had no idea where it was, but realizing how pivotal her role was in finding it, she decided to begin her search immediately. "Where do I start?"

"Start with your mind."

"Okay, but wait—what happens if I find the ruby and I'm nowhere near King Odon's statue? What happens then?"

The look on Anzhara's face was grave. Her harrowing green eyes flashed in the night as she spoke. "If you are not near the temple," she said, "then pray that you are alone when you find it."

LESSONS LEARNED

Through the silky light of the amber globes, Anzhara paced around the statues while Jenna stood watching her.

The stinging in Jenna's arm was fading, but not nearly as fast as she would like. She pressed her hand up against the bandage and winced. "I'm telling you—that's the last time I saw the talisman. I was in my bedroom, I put the three broken pieces of the ruby together and then you crashed through my window. When the pieces connected, this wild funnel cloud *inside* my room took everything away. And that was it. When I opened my eyes, I was standing inside the museum as if nothing had happened."

Jenna had spent the last few minutes describing how she'd acquired the Mummy's talisman earlier in the summer. Severed in three pieces, the ruby had been cleverly hidden not only on her property, but also on the necks of her two precious felines, Ted and Tony, tucked within their collars. Places Jenna had never thought to look.

Then came the task of attaching the pieces. Connecting the ruby was a necessary means; the act itself was intended to end the Mummy's curse. But what Jenna really wanted was her old life back. Sadly, that never happened. Although the Mummy's curse had been lifted, its restless soul remained at large, for reasons Jenna didn't know. Until now.

"What did you see in the museum afterwards?" Anzhara said, weaving in and out of the statues.

"Nothing. The glass display case that held your mummified body was gone. A staff member told me that it was never there, and that some of King Tutankhamun's artifacts were en route to occupy the space. Everything reverted back to the way it was originally. Or so I thought."

"What about the book?"

Jenna shook her head. The book, *A City Lost*, was a thorn in her side and she didn't want to talk about it. It was the story of how the Mummy came to be. The book had been stolen from the museum by someone Jenna had known and respected—the former curator, Dr. Osiris. In the end, it had been returned to its rightful place but the story had changed. Jenna had become a part of the book—literally. Pictures of her appeared throughout the pages. And in becoming part of the storyline, she had inadvertently changed it.

And now here she was in the company of the Siamese cat explaining everything. It was a situation she had never even remotely considered.

"The book was back in the Thailand exhibit. Dr. Osiris—an old curator of the museum had stolen it. But after everything was said and done, the book was back on the podium where it was supposed to be."

From across the way, Anzhara turned to face her. "That's when you first saw yourself inside the book."

"Yeah, and then I heard you growling behind me. That's when I became 'Crazy Jenna'," she air-quoted with her fingers. "And well...you know the rest."

For a moment, Anzhara was quiet.

Jenna wondered what she was thinking. Although she felt alive and awake in the moment, there was still a teensy part of her that was reluctant to believe what was happening. Her eyes kept gazing up towards the pinnacle of the pyramid; she couldn't quite shake off her fear of rogue lightning.

"What's wrong?" Anzhara said, now standing directly in front of her.

Jenna jumped back in surprise. "Okay, you've gotta stop sneaking up on me like that..."

"Jenna, you need to be prepared for anything. And right now, I'm the least of your worries. Now, what's wrong?"

"I was just thinking about the last time I was in here, when one of the globes was hit by lightning." She pointed up to the sky. "It came right through the pyramid and brought all these mummified statues to life. Scared me to death..."

"Maybe you learned something that day," Anzhara said.

Jenna smirked. "Yeah, trust me. I learned a lot—like how to run fast."

The two stared at each other for a moment.

"When did you know your grandmother wasn't herself?" Anzhara said.

"I'm not sure. I think it was when we were near the pyramid." Jenna's head was still a little fuzzy with respect to the details of her voyage in the desert.

"It's the poison," Anzhara said. She explained how the Blade Viper's venom was responsible for Jenna's memory loss and that her arm had been treated with a solution to extract the poison. What Jenna didn't know was that her grandmother had appeared inside the pyramid while she was unconscious to withdraw the venom and reverse the affects. After she had bandaged the arm, she reverted to the form of the Siamese cat, so that Jenna would be watched over and protected with diligent care.

Anzhara feared now that a trace element of the snake's poison remained in Jenna's system. That fear however, would remain a secret between Jenna's grandmother and the feline guardian.

"Adella was inside your house."

"What?" Jenna didn't see that coming. She fidgeted in place. "When?"

"This very night," Anzhara said.

Jenna hadn't thought of it until now, but thinking back, she remembered voices in her grandmother's room, a loud banging against the door and the sound of breaking glass. It was slowly coming back to her. "Oh God—was she the one I was talking to?"

"Yes."

"What happened—where did my grandmother go?"

"She banished herself to the pyramid for safety. Adella is dangerously powerful; she has terrible strength over others."

"Wait a minute—how did you know they changed places?" Jenna asked.

Anzhara turned away and began to wander across the floor. "Because we are one, your grandmother and I, remember?"

"Oh, right." Something deep in the recesses of Jenna's mind made her ask the next question. "I have this feeling that something was in the backyard tonight when I was standing on the porch. It was after my grandmother went inside. I didn't see anything but I could feel it. Do you know what it was?"

"It was one of the Sandshadow's servants; it was following you. Wherever Adella is, they are not far behind."

Jenna shivered. "They were watching me?" Being stalked by the enemy freaked her out even more.

"They have been for a long time," Anzhara said.

"Grandma, I mean, Adella, told me about magic and how she could teach me things. I remember, now. I panicked and spilled the beans on my whole Mummy/museum escapade this summer. I had no idea I was talking to her. God, no wonder she reacted so well—it wasn't Grandma!" Jenna's mind quickly back-peddled to all the things Adella had said inside the bedroom. Lies or truth, Jenna didn't know. "She told me that my mother renounced her magical side. Is that true?"

Anzhara stopped alongside one of the statues. Jenna sensed that her question had hit a nerve.

The expression on her furry face was almost human. To Jenna, it seemed as though part of her grandmother was surfacing.

"Your mother wanted a family more than anything else," Anzhara said, approaching her. "She practiced magic as a young girl."

"She *did*?" Jenna was absolutely stunned by this new piece of information. Her jaw hung open as Anzhara spoke.

"Yes, and she was very good at it, very loyal to the craft."

"This is the first time I've ever heard this. I don't understand—how could she not have told me? I'm her daughter!"

"There are reasons for everything." Anzhara's tone was feathery, much like her grandmother's. If Jenna closed her eyes, she could picture her grandmother speaking to her.

"What are you talking about? What reasons?"

"As I said, your mother wanted a family more than anything. And she didn't want magic to interfere with that. So, she gave up her powers."

The way Anzhara spoke made it seem as though the transition was a simple one, like learning to eat with a fork instead of a spoon. It sounded too easy. And completely ridiculous as well.

"I don't believe it! I've *never* heard her talk about it!"

"And you never will," Anzhara said. "When your mother gave up her powers, all of her memories of the craft were erased from her mind. Not a single one exists within her. It was her decision to do that, she wanted it that way."

Jenna was having a difficult time wrapping her mind around the fact that her mother was a witch. "This is incredible—this is *huge*! But wait...why are you telling me this right now—here of all places?" Jenna began to pace. She was baffled and irritated by the fact that she had to learn the news from a stranger.

"You mustn't be upset by the choices your mother made."

"I'm not mad at her, I'm just mad at the whole situation!" Jenna felt somewhat betrayed by her family, like they didn't trust her enough to tell her.

Anzhara was trying to console her but even more so, she was trying to imply something else. "Your mother's decision was a good one, Jenna. It's what brought you into this world and made you who you are."

"Yeah, I guess." Her frustrated mood began to weaken. "I just wish someone in my family had told me all this."

"Well, I'm telling you now, and you must accept it as that. There are bigger things to think about now. Do I have your attention?"

Jenna looked back at Anzhara with a bit of disdain. "Hey—you were the one that decided to unload all of this on me, not the other way around. What kind of reaction did you expect from me anyway?"

Anzhara stopped and stared at her.

"What?" Jenna smirked. "What are you gonna tell me now? That somewhere down the line I'm related to Zeus?"

Anzhara smiled. "No, simply that all of that magic had to go somewhere..."

TO BE DETERMINED

Jenna's pacing was no longer confined to one small area. Anzhara now stood in place and watched as the raging teen moved throughout the pyramid spewing her thoughts into the air.

"Are you kidding me?" Jenna said, angrily. "I mean...are you *kidding me*? I have *magic* inside of me? Okay—obviously I'm not the only deranged one here!"

Anzhara tried to calm her. "It stands to reason. Follow the family tree..."

Jenna waved her arms about madly as she rambled on. Most of her comments were directionless but every so often she would look back at Anzhara and stare at her as if to point blame.

"This can't be. See—I'm just a normal girl. That's all I've ever been! My grandmother is the magical genius in our family, not me! This has nothing to do with me, not one little bit."

For the majority of Jenna's ranting, Anzhara just let her go.

"You did this to me!" Jenna said, making a beeline towards her. "So take it back! I don't want it. Take back whatever it is you think I have. All I want is a normal life, with my friends, my pets and baseball. That's it—nothing else!"

"Jenna, this is not my place," Anzhara said.

"Sure it is. You're the one who told me, you're the one with all the answers. So do something about it!"

Anzhara shook her head. "I can't. This is beyond my control. But I will tell you, that if you choose to, you can give up your magic just like your mother did."

Jenna didn't have to think. "Good—because I'm going to!"

"May I make a suggestion?"

Jenna scowled. "What?"

"Take one night to sleep on your decision."

"Why? I don't need time to think about it—I'm ready now!"

"Because," Anzhara said, "right now, we must think of connections. We must think of solutions for our problems. Bigger problems—the Sandshadow."

Hearing the logic in her words brought Jenna back to reality. She thought that perhaps her reckless display of verbal spillage was a bit extreme, but she was furious, and for good reason. But Anzhara was right, although she didn't want to admit it.

"Fine," Jenna said with a whimper.

"Now, we must think of the talisman, for that is why we are both here."

Jenna stopped and looked at her. "Wait—what did you mean by connections?"

Anzhara paused. "Jenna, many things in our world tie together. If you took a moment to look at them, you would see where the pieces connect. The Sandshadow is after you because it knows you are connected to the talisman."

Jenna's snarky attitude slowly gave way to reason. "Yeah, the only problem with that scenario is that I don't have the foggiest idea of where the ruby is."

With a furrowed brow, Anzhara looked at her. "Yes, but perhaps you know someone who does."

"I don't think so."

"Perhaps a visit to the recent past would help you fully regain your memory." Anzhara walked over to one of the statues. "Come."

Jenna obliged, although begrudgingly. "That statue isn't going to come alive and grab me, is it?"

"No," she said. "Just come here." Anzhara looked into the crystal globe above the statue. "I want you to stare at the flame inside the glass. The fire inside will pull you gently into the past and warm your mind and body, allowing you to see things that your memory has missed."

Jenna nodded but said nothing.

"It will only be a spiritual visit; your body will remain here, inside the pyramid, where I will guard it," Anzhara assured her.

"Wait a minute—" Jenna scratched her forehead.

Anzhara cut her off. "All you have to do is look at the flame inside the glass. Then let yourself be taken. No one else will see you—you will be invisible to everyone."

"But what if this doesn't work? What if something bad happens to me?"

"Nothing bad will happen, Jenna. I guarantee it. Put your hands on the glass."

Jenna stepped in front of the statue. As she did, her foul mood began to soften. Any lingering doubts she had, slowly disappeared. She felt relaxed now, and surprisingly safe. The amber fire inside the globe was working. Its soothing appearance put Jenna at ease.

Finger by finger she placed her hands on opposite sides of the crystal. Taking a deep breath, she pressed her palms against the glass. It was warm and strangely supple; the material was melting around her skin, drawing her in. Although the initial pull was gradual, she soon felt her body moving quickly through the warm air. Her eyes became heavy, and she closed them. Jenna felt like a kite lightly floating through the clouds above the ground. She was weightless and free as the cottony air blew past her. Any chains she had to the earth were lifted, breaking all bonds of obligation and duty.

Without looking, Jenna could tell she was encased within the crystal.

Anzhara remained next to the statue, guarding Jenna's body as she stood in place.

Inside the crystal, Jenna's eyes opened. Below her, was a long and narrow amber-coloured trail. It sparkled beneath, like a winding sun-kissed river. It was leading somewhere. Jenna thought nothing of it. She hadn't a care in the world. She felt absolutely wonderful and forgot completely about what she was doing or why she was there.

Her path of intoxicating tranquility was soon brought to an end as she felt a strange buzzing on her skin. A sudden jolt tackled her senses and forced her out of her safety bubble. In an instant, the environment surrounding her changed completely. A bizarre zapping noise appeared above her head which made her cower. Looking up, she was startled to see a flurry of tiny lightning strikes coming from the sky. Each one gave off sparks as it collided with her skin. Her body was being electrically prodded on all sides.

Jenna shuddered as each little strike hit her, but after a few seconds, she realized that the zaps didn't really hurt. In fact, the feeling was not completely unpleasant.

Jenna brushed her arms and smiled at the odd sensation. It was like physically being woken up by an alarm clock. "That's so weird..."

Moments after the novelty had worn off, she glanced around. "Oh my God!" She was now standing outside the school as the building crumbled in the wake of the tornado.

Fear began to grow inside of her as she re-visited the scene. Without Anzhara there to guide her, Jenna felt vulnerable. She only hoped that Anzhara was right—that nothing bad would happen to her.

Jenna scanned the area and took note of everything that surrounded her. She couldn't believe what she was seeing. She froze on spot when the most undeniably surreal moment unfolded in front of her. She squinted to get a better look. "Get out!"

In the distance, she saw herself standing next to Jason. "I don't believe it—that's me!" She glanced down at her own body. "Am I a ghost?" Turning in all directions, she watched to see if anyone noticed her. No one did.

Examining the scene, Jenna remembered the chronological order of things. The school had not yet collapsed and her family hadn't arrived. It was the moment where Jason was explaining his injury. Jenna listened and stared at the two of them as they talked. She didn't have to read their lips, she remembered the conversation.

Hoping to learn more from her visit, she searched the entire area. And that's when she saw the old man.

In an instant, all of her memories came tumbling back. The school. The tornado. The little girl. "Alaina!" she exclaimed. Quickly, she surveyed the grounds for the little girl. She then saw her standing near the history room. All the major players were there. It was clear to Jenna that she had come back to this time for a reason, although she didn't yet understand why. Something about the old man however, kept drawing her attention. *What does he have to do with this?*

She looked around to see if anything else piqued her interest.

The scene played out exactly as it did before; not one thing had changed. People scurried about. Shouts and screams were exchanged as emergency crews worked endlessly to calm the hysteria.

With everything that was happening, Jenna felt herself once again drawn to the presence of the old man. She observed her other self looking at the man, and remembered how their eyes had locked in an unwavering stare. *What was it about him that was so interesting?*

Jenna tried to gather as much information as she could. The man was standing alone near a police car. No one walking by seemed to acknowledge him. His clothes were older, perfectly suited to his age. He was leaning over a cane; one that was silver and shaped like a snake. And beneath his fingers, was the shiny hood.

Taking a few steps closer, Jenna focused on the cane. "Oh my God—the Blade Viper!" Her heart began to palpitate; she could feel the questions forming. "Are *you* the reason I came back here?"

The old man turned immediately and looked at her. "My, my—a visitor!"

Jenna was surprised. No one was supposed to see her.

"A feather amongst the leaves," he said, cocking his head. The man seemed confused by her presence, especially since she was standing in two different places at the same time. He quickly glanced from one Jenna to the other. "Two for one!"

His comment ate away at her. "What's that supposed to—" But before she could finish her sentence, her body was yanked backwards, forcing her to double over. "Nooooooo..." she cried. It felt like a large noose was wrapped around her waist.

She looked up and saw the old man getting smaller on the horizon. "I'm not done!" she yelled. "I need to learn more! Let go of me!"

The ground beneath her feet began to shake. Jenna watched as the school collapsed in the distance. Frantic screams flew all around as everyone ran from the building.

That's when the amber trail reappeared beneath her feet and she knew her journey was over. She closed her eyes and covered her ears to muffle the sounds.

Within a matter of seconds, she was standing on solid ground. When she opened her eyes, she saw the amber globe in front of her and Anzhara sitting next to it. The mood inside the pyramid was calm.

"Wait—you have to send me back!" Jenna yelled.

"Why? You were brought back because of something you saw."

"You don't understand! I went back to the school, to the time right before it collapsed, and there was this old man." Jenna's voice was racing. "He saw me. He heard me. I think he's the reason I went back!"

Anzhara seemed puzzled. "No one was supposed to see you."

"Yeah, I know, but he did. This old man…I saw him before and thought nothing of it. But he had this silver cane with the Blade Viper's head on it. Just like the ones I saw in the desert. I remember everything now."

Anzhara looked at the globe. "Blade Viper, you say?"

"Yes, and he stared at me with this disturbed look on his face like I was a criminal or something. Anzhara, you have to send me back. I didn't get to ask him who he was or why he was there."

"That's not necessary," Anzhara said.

"What do you mean, of course it is! Unless…you know who he is?"

"Yes," she said, her voice certain.

"I knew it!" Jenna spewed. "He's one of the Sandshadow's servants, isn't he?"

"On the contrary, Jenna. There's only one being that would be visible during a visit of time-travel."

"Okay, who is he?" Jenna tapped her foot repeatedly while waiting for an answer.

Anzhara smiled. "Your new teacher."

CHANGE OF SETTING

"A *what?*" Jenna said, clearly conveying her disbelief.

"A Veliostriga—a Power Shepherd. They are beings sent to guide nascent witches."

"Oh, we're back to this again." Jenna threw up her arms. "What does that have to do with anything?"

"Everything," Anzhara said. "If you truly saw a Power Shepherd, it means you've come into your powers. I agree—this isn't the ideal time to be encumbered with this, but if the old man is indeed who I think he is, he will have answers for us."

"But how am I supposed to find him?"

"In time you'll know," Anzhara said. "I think there's someone who can help, though."

"Oh, right, and who might that be—my fairy godmother? Why not throw her in there, too. And while we're at it, how do I get my hands on one of those magic lamps?" As if life weren't complicated enough! Jenna definitely didn't want a future full of this magic crap. No way. She stared hard at Anzhara, letting all her feelings show on her face.

Anzhara broke the moment in typical feline fashion; she lifted her paws to lick them. Even after their short time together, Jenna hadn't expected her to act like a real cat.

"What aren't you telling me?" Jenna said.

In between cleanings, Anzhara spoke. "Sshh, I'm preparing myself."

"For what?"

"You'll see," she said, with all the aloofness of a regular cat.

Placing her paws back down, her body slowly began to change. Limb by limb, she morphed into another form until nothing cat-like was left, not even her tail.

"Whoa!" Jenna stood in awe, watching the transition. In her mind, she had made the connection between the Siamese cat and her grandmother, but she hadn't seen the transformation in progress. It was always one body or the other. Now, she had witnessed the actual change.

Jenna rubbed her eyes and blinked. An old woman now stood in place of the cat.

"Grandma?"

"Yes, my dear."

Jenna ran towards her and threw her arms around her neck. "You're okay! Anzhara told me everything." She leaned back. "Grandma—what's my middle name?"

She smiled. "Jean. Your name is Jenna Jean."

"Oh thank God—it *is* you and not Adella." She hugged her again. "I'm so glad you're here!"

Her grandmother took a step back. "You must trust Anzhara. I promise that she will not mislead you. But there is much work to be done and it cannot be done here. If I am to leave the pyramid, it is in the body of Anzhara—only then can I protect you fully from the wrath of the Sandshadow."

Seeing her grandmother standing there brought so many questions to the forefront. "Is it true what she said about Mom? Did she practice witchcraft?"

"Jenna, now is not the time for that." Her grandmother walked away and stood near one of the walls. She raised her hands and whispered into the air.

"Please—I have to know!" Jenna begged her. "Anzhara told me that I have magic inside of me, that I'm a witch, too. She told me about the Power Shepherd."

With that, her grandmother turned. "I know. Your Veliostriga, he's here. You must find him."

"Then it's true..."

"Yes," her grandmother said.

The conversation was suddenly interrupted when the walls of the building began to shake.

"That can't be good!" Jenna glanced all around.

"It's time for you to leave," her grandmother said. The ominous tone of her voice shattered the serenity of the atmosphere. She breezed over the ground towards Jenna.

"What are you doing?" Jenna said, backing away from her.

"Take a deep breath and close your eyes. Do it now," she said.

The last thing Jenna saw was her grandmother's arm reaching for her. Jenna's feet stumbled as she moved. She was drawn to the nails on her grandmother's fingers; they looked sharp and severe as they danced towards her in a menacing manner. She leaned her head and began to recite a spell.

"Grandma—no!" Jenna was frightened that her grandmother was using magic on her. For a moment she thought that Adella had returned. The feel of her grandmother's nails against her chest made her squirm. It hurt, even through her sweater. She was being pushed backwards. "What are you doing?"

Jenna's mind began to shut down; she was losing consciousness. Over and over, her grandmother pushed her, and Jenna took the hits, without as much as a peep.

With one final push, Jenna fell to the ground. She waited for the inevitable landing, but nothing came. She gave up on sight and sound altogether as she closed her eyes and let the fall take her. The air began to whip around her, spinning her body out of control.

Looking up, the last thing she saw was her grandmother's emerald stare, and the wicked smile that went with it.

FROM BENEATH THE SURFACE

Jenna felt a biting prick on her arm. Something nudged her from the side and then stopped. Seconds later, it nudged her again.

With laggard movements, she opened both eyes. To her surprise, she was back in her bedroom.

The alarm clock sat on the bedside table next to her; it was now morning. Across the room, the window was glazed with rain. Thunder rumbled somewhere in the distance.

Jenna looked down as something tugged at her arm. Ted and Tony were sitting on the bed, playing with a piece of bandage that poked out from beneath the covers. Jenna quickly lifted the comforter. She was wearing the same clothes she'd worn the night before. What bothered her was the bandage around her arm.

She could feel the sweat forming on her brow. Any last hopes of a dream-like journey were washed away when she saw the bandage. "It was real…"

The cats playfully pulled at the fabric like it was a toy. It made her grin, but beneath the wrapping was a more serious issue.

She wrapped the remaining bandage around her arm and tucked the end in. Another stinging sensation shot up through her muscle. "Ow!" It reminded her of the event of which it stemmed from. Snakes all around, attacking. Being strangled in the desert beneath the weight of a formidable predator. Jenna closed her eyes and shook away the memory. It was terrifying just thinking about it.

Her thoughts were momentarily side-tracked when she heard voices coming from downstairs. It was a welcome change, and helped keep her tormented thoughts at bay. Jenna opened her eyes and listened.

The cats jumped onto the floor, and with their paws opened the bedroom door. "You guys just read my mind."

As they left the room and headed for the stairs, the voices came within earshot. One was her mother's; the other was someone vaguely familiar. Another woman.

Jenna looked back at the alarm clock. It was eight-thirty. It was early, but she wasn't tired at all. Except for her injury, she felt good, refreshed. She wondered how long she'd been asleep for.

What kind of spell did Grandma put on me?

The room was quiet as Jenna prepared to leave. If it hadn't been, she wouldn't have heard the sound of paper peeling from the wall. It made her look. Not only was the wallpaper torn from one of the corners, it seemed as though something had broken through it. There was a large, starburst-shaped hole in the wall, the size of a dartboard. The outermost part was peeled back like an onion with parts of the wall imbedded into the opening. Something had entered into her room. And Jenna had a pretty good idea what that was—the Sandshadow.

Carefully, she backed away from the wall. It was entirely possible that the Sandshadow was in her room, disguised as something else. Was it still watching her? That was the question. But something didn't add up. In the desert, the Sandshadow was huge. But the bulge she saw moving at the school and the hole in her bedroom wall were not nearly as big. She had a feeling that the answer was a simple one. The Sandshadow was a shape-shifter and could change its size on a whim. It was also possible that one of the Blade Vipers had come into her room.

Jenna grimaced at the thought. Touching her neck, she remembered the cold, reptilian feel of scales against her skin. Just the vision of it gave her shivers.

Assuming that her bedroom wall was one of the enemy's exits, made Jenna realize that the house was no longer safe. Now, only one thought protected her—Anzhara. Her grandmother had said that the cat would guard her. It was comforting to know that she wasn't alone. Help was somewhere nearby. Where, Jenna didn't know. Just as long as it was there.

For anyone else, waking up to such turmoil would have been remedied by simply returning to bed. An easy fix. But Jenna had finally given in, and accepted that this was her fate. It was real and there was no escaping it. The only way she would sleep peacefully again was if she found Anzhara's talisman.

Jenna stared at the wall and then patted her arm gently. Anzhara had told her that the Sandshadow's snakes had almost taken her life. Had it not been for Anzhara, she would have died.

Jenna slowly began to unwrap the bandage. She wanted to see the damage the enemy had inflicted. Reaching the end of the wrapping, she stopped. Two large piercings appeared on the surface of her skin. Looking closely however, Jenna realized how deep they really were. She could feel the impression of the animal's fangs.

She glanced back at the wall and winced. This was no little injury. There was more to it than she had imagined.

Jenna didn't want anyone to know about her injury, so she decided to keep it covered.

The day had started without her, and she needed to get moving. There was much that had to be done. Searching for Anzhara's talisman would be tricky; Jenna really had no idea where to begin. But standing idle was not in her directives, so she turned and darted off towards the bathroom to clean herself up.

The shower head came to life as the water poured from above. Jenna waited a moment for it to warm. She turned back to the sink, rested her hands on either side of it and leaned in to look at the mirror. "What the hell have I gotten myself into?" she said, staring at her reflection.

As steam began to fill the room, Jenna spotted something unusual in the mirror. It was hard to see clearly, but it looked like a small, blue vein. It appeared on her forehead, and was tiny, only a few centimeters long.

"What on Earth?" She wiped the glass clean with one hand, and then looked again. The vein was gone. "Great—now I'm seeing things!" Thinking back, Jenna thought about her attack in the desert, and wondered why there were no other injuries on her body, like bruising or cuts. Her concerns began to fade just like the line from her face, when she turned and stepped into the shower. There were more important issues at hand.

She forgot about the vein altogether as she thought about the challenges ahead. "Can't stop now. Got places to be!"

Jenna's determination was now leading the way.

A NEW PERMUTATION

The familiar sound of the teakettle squealing on the stove brought Jenna's senses to life. She was thirsty and hungry, and needed to fill her stomach. After drying her hair and dressing, it was time to venture downstairs.

The two voices she'd heard earlier were still conversing in the kitchen.

As Jenna entered the room, two women looked up from the kitchen table. "Jenna—you're awake. You remember Maggie?" her mother said.

The woman smiled. "Hi there. I hope we didn't wake you."

Jenna couldn't place the woman. "Nope, the cats woke me. Nice to see you, Maggie."

Her mother saw the confused look on her face and added, "Maggie works at the museum."

"Except I'm hardly ever there," Maggie said. "I'm usually in my office at Brockfield University. So don't feel bad if you don't recognize me. We haven't seen each other in a while."

Her comment put Jenna at ease. "Oh, okay. Sorry—it's early. How are things at the university?"

Jenna's mother stood and walked over to the stove. "Maggie's been quite busy there." She poured the hot water into the teapot and then came and sat back down at the table.

"Yes, it's been hectic, but it's nice to get back into the swing of things after the summer break," Maggie said.

"And you work at the museum...no wonder you're busy." Jenna strolled up to the counter and removed the lid from the teapot. She breathed in the delicious smell of strawberry tea. With her back to the kitchen table, she waited for the tea to steep.

"So, tell me more about the appraisal," her mother said to Maggie.

Jenna glanced back at the table. Maggie looked professional in her ivory shirt, black slacks and glasses. Jenna assumed that she was on her way to work.

Maggie started. "Well, there I was examining the jewel, when the man just started pacing. He seemed really nervous, which was surprising since he practically begged me for the assessment."

"That is strange. So what did you tell him?" Jenna's mother asked.

"I told him that the piece wasn't from around here, but because its condition was so impeccable, it was probably owned by a collector."

"How did the man get it?"

"I don't know, he wouldn't say. He was there only twenty minutes and then his mood changed. He seemed rushed—like he was in a hurry to leave. And he said that time was running out; it was all very weird."

Jenna walked over to one of the cupboards and grabbed three mugs. With her back still turned, she barely listened as Maggie described her encounter. She placed the mugs down next to the teapot and rested her elbows on the counter. She was thinking about the wall inside her bedroom. It was scary to think that the Sandshadow or possibly one of its scaly minions was creeping through the walls of the house, especially since Jenna wasn't the only one living there. Her parents, the pets—all of them could be in danger. But now knowing the extent of her grandmother's powers, she would have put a safety spell or magical barrier on the house to protect those living within. Something like that.

Sitting at the table, Jenna's mother sounded normal. The effects of her grandmother's soup had clearly worn off. Ted and Tony seemed fine. Maggie was visiting and nothing unusual was happening there. Maybe the house really was protected. Even if the enemy was hiding inside, it might not be able to hurt anyone. Jenna was hoping that that was the case.

What she thought of now, was the degree to which her grandmother toiled with magic. Jenna no longer saw her as just a gentle Wiccan who concocted tinctures for pleasure.

As she began to pour the tea into the mugs, she heard Maggie say, "Then just like that, the old man took his ruby and left."

Jenna dropped the teapot on the counter and turned on her heels. "What did you say?"

The two women jumped at her reaction. "Jenna, are you all right?" her mother said.

Jenna looked at both of them. "Ah...yeah." She laughed to diffuse the awkwardness. "Sorry, I didn't mean to scare you. Silly me, I'm such a klutz. Just out of curiosity, though, did you say...ruby?"

Maggie nodded. "Sometimes I get people outside the university looking for appraisals. Like this woman who came in with a Klimt painting—"

Jenna stopped her. "Sorry, but could you go back to the ruby part? It seems like such an interesting story and I missed the part about why the old man was there."

"Jenna—are you sure you're okay?" her mother said. "You've had a rough couple of days. Maybe you should take some tea with you and go lie down."

"Oh my goodness," Maggie said, shaking her head. "Here I am talking about work, and I didn't even ask how you were. Your mom told me about your hospital visit and then what happened at your school. I'm so sorry."

Jenna shrugged and smiled. "So I got attacked and my school was destroyed by a tornado. These things happen. But a strange man with a mysterious ruby—now *that's* interesting."

"Jenna!" her mother said, now very concerned. "What is going on with you?"

"Mom, I'm fine. Really." Jenna peered back at Maggie. "So, what exactly did this ruby look like?"

"That's it! I think you should go upstairs and rest," her mother said.

"But I want to hear about the ruby..."

The front doorbell rang as she spoke but Jenna ignored it. She wanted to know more about Maggie's encounter with the old man. In her head, it wasn't just a coincidence that he'd shown up in her office with a ruby, not if it was the man she was thinking of.

"Maybe you should get the door, Jenna," her mother said.

Jenna breezed over her request. "I'm sure it's no one, Mom. Probably someone selling something."

Her mother looked mystified. "That doesn't sound like you at all. Usually you're running over bodies to get to the door. Go see who it is," she insisted.

Jenna didn't want to, but did so to appease her mother. "Fine." She scurried out of the room and made her way towards the door. Looking through the window on the side, she sighed. It was her friend, Jason.

"Hey there," he said, as she opened the door. "How are you?"

"Good," Jenna said. "You?"

"I'm good. I just wanted to stop by and see how you were."

Although Jenna was grateful for the check-in, she wanted to get back to Maggie. "Oh, that's nice. Well, thanks for stopping by." She practically closed the door on his face.

"Hi Jason," her mother yelled from the kitchen. "Come on in."

"Thanks, Mrs. Matthews," he said, sliding through the opening. "At least your mother is happy to see me."

His smile was cheeky; he gave the impression that there was an ulterior motive for his visit. Jenna wondered what it was. *Good grief! How am I supposed to get any detective work done with these interruptions?* she thought. "Okay, well, I guess you can stay," she said, reluctantly.

He closed the door behind him and followed her through the hallway. "So, you're feeling okay?" he said.

"I'm fine," she said, walking into the kitchen. Her tone was dismissive as they entered the room. Together, they stood by the counter while Jenna gave the introductions. "Maggie, this is Jason. Jason... Maggie. So, Maggie, you were saying..."

"Jenna, you don't have to be rude," her mother said. "Jason, there's a pot of tea there if you'd like to grab a cup."

Making himself at home, he reached for a glass from the cupboard and poured himself some water from the tap. "Water's fine, thanks."

Maggie smiled. "Nice to meet you, Jason."

"Likewise," he said.

Jenna's mind was elsewhere. She wanted to end the pleasantries and move on. "So, Maggie, you were saying about the old man..."

"Oh, well, the jewel he brought in was an ancient ruby—extremely rare and valuable. It was small, about the size of a golf ball. It wasn't set in a necklace; it was just the jewel itself. Authentic, really beautiful—with Siamese and Egyptian engravings on it."

Goosebumps formed along Jenna's arms beneath her long-sleeved shirt. She couldn't believe what she was hearing. "The Mummy's talisman..." she said aloud.

All eyes were now on Jenna.

"How did you know that?" Maggie said, staring at her.

"Um...we just learned about it in history class."

Jason shook his head. "No we didn't."

Jenna scowled and elbowed him in the stomach.

"That's not something they teach you in school," Maggie said. "I know because I had to research it after the man left my office, and even then I couldn't find any information about it."

"Not even in the book at the museum?" Jenna said. Her words came out so fast that she didn't have a chance to screen them. She covered her mouth after realizing what she had said.

"What book?" her mother chimed in. "There's no book like that in the museum." Being the present curator of the Lionhead Museum, she was well aware of every relic, every fossil, and every artifact that entered through its doors.

Jenna skated past her mother's question. She shook her head and said, "You know what—I think you're right, Mom. I think I need to lie down before I say anything else that makes me look like a nut."

"I think that's a good idea," her mother said. "Take some tea with you."

Jenna nodded politely and smiled to herself. Her mom bought the act. But before she left the room, there was one last thing she wanted to know. "Just out of sheer interest...where exactly is the ruby now?"

Maggie shrugged. "I don't know. The man took it with him when he left—and boy did he leave in a hurry. He grabbed the ruby out of my hands and ran. What startled me the most, though, were his eyes. They turned this terrible shade of yellow, almost like a reptile. I thought something was wrong with him, like he was sick. In fact, his whole demeanour was strange. At one point I considered calling the police thinking that maybe he had stolen the ruby. But something about him made me hesitate. For some reason, I felt like it was more important for me to come here and tell you about it."

"Really?" Jenna's mother said, surprised. "Why?"

"Because he mentioned that he knew you," Maggie said. "It's why I agreed to examine the jewel in the first place."

Jenna's mother looked puzzled. "I don't know anyone like that. Are you sure it was me that he was talking about?"

"Definitely. He said Barbara Matthews from the Lionhead Museum."

Jenna looked on in astonishment. "You're his messenger!" she exclaimed.

"What?" Maggie said.

Realizing once again that she had spoken out loud, Jenna cringed. She then scrambled to cover her tracks. "Boy—you're right! That's a strange story. Very odd behaviour. Weird people in this world." She laughed awkwardly. "Anyhoo, it was nice seeing you again, Maggie."

"You, too," Maggie said, looking politely concerned.

Jenna grabbed Jason by the arm. "We both have to go now."

"What are you talking about?" Jason said, as Jenna dragged him into the hallway.

She lowered her voice and hustled him to the front door. "I'm sorry, but there's somewhere I have to go."

"Oh, you mean the school?" he said with a wink.

Jenna glared at him, not truly understanding the reason behind his morning visit. "How did you know that?" she whispered.

His gaze was deceiving. "Just a wild guess," he said.

She pinched his arm. It was a tactic she commonly reverted to from time to time when he took a joke too far.

"Ouch! Okay, okay," he said. "A little birdie told me."

"What? *Who?*"

Jason stood at the door with a sly expression on his face, indicating that he knew something he wasn't supposed to. "I think you need me right now," he said.

Although Jenna was slightly hesitant to make the next move, she did so anyway. "Okay, fine," she said, quietly. "We have to go upstairs. There's something I need to tell you."

A CHANGE UNDERWAY

"I know it sounds ridiculous but it's true...it all happened to me this summer. No word of a lie," Jenna said.

Jenna had spent the last twenty minutes burning a trail in the carpet as she revealed the secrets of her life to Jason. Most of them had been stored away for safekeeping but after the talk they'd had downstairs, many of those secrets were now out in the open for him to judge. She was hoping that he wouldn't, though, considering how close a friend he was.

The emotional drive that enabled her to spill her guts was also what kept her from standing in one place.

"So—say something!" she said, pacing in front of him.

Jason sat, cool as a cucumber, on the edge of her bed listening to her. "What do you want me to say?"

"Oh, I don't know, just say something. Anything. Give me something to go on, here."

"I don't know what to say, Jenna. I mean, I believe you and all..."

"No, no you don't. I can tell." She had hoped for a better answer. She sighed and sat down on the bed next to him. "I wouldn't believe me either. It sounds crazy."

Jason wrapped his arm around her shoulder. The tight squeeze he gave her, made her blush. She wanted to get up and walk away, and yet she also wanted to be near him.

"Is this why I haven't seen you in a while?" he said.

She nodded. "I couldn't leave the house. I felt like this was my only safe place." She stood from the bed, walked towards the wall and stared at the gash. She pressed her hand up against it. For her, everything was real.

She was afraid to look back at Jason now. She'd told him almost everything that she knew, including the part about her magical bloodlines. Perhaps it was more than he could handle.

Their conversation was rekindled when Jason said something totally unexpected. "So, who's the little girl?"

Jenna turned around quickly. She was completely thrown by his question. "What did you say?"

"The little girl...who is she?" he said.

"Wait—you saw her?" Jenna couldn't believe what she was hearing.

"Yeah, I saw her at the school."

"I thought I was the only one! Why didn't you tell me?" she said.

"Because I thought I was hallucinating. I mean, why would a little girl be standing amongst the debris of our school? It's insane."

Jenna crossed the floor and stood in front of him. "It's okay to admit it. It's what led me here."

"All right, then. Who is she?" he said.

Alaina was one of the topics they had not yet covered. "She's...um...family."

"Family?"

"Yeah, from the past." Jenna looked away as she told him, thinking that her explanations had taken them far beyond the reaches of planet Jupiter.

Instead, Jason came at her with another question. "Does this have something to do with your grandmother?"

"You could say that." Jenna was relieved to hear that he was still on board. "Look—there's more to explain but I don't have time to sit here and tell you—"

"Wait," he said, standing from the bed. "There's something on your face."

Jason reached out to touch her cheek but Jenna swatted his hand away. "What are you doing?" she said.

"There's a weird silvery line on your face...it kinda looks like a vein," he said.

Jenna remembered her reflection in the bathroom mirror. "Oh, it's nothing. I saw it earlier on my forehead."

"It isn't on your forehead. It's on your cheek," he said.

Jenna walked over to the large oval mirror hanging on the bedroom wall. "What is that?" she said, examining the small silver line below her left eye. Just seeing it made her panic. She touched her face and looked back at him. "I don't know what it is."

"Does it hurt?" he said, walking up behind her.

"No, but it's freaking me out!"

"Okay, calm down. Maybe we should go show your mom," he said.

Jenna hissed at him. Turning back to the mirror, she sneered. "That's a terrible idea."

"Whoa—did you just hiss at me? Cause you've never done that before. Boy—you must really be mad," he joked.

"No, I'm not mad. Actually, I don't know why I did that."

"Hey, look—it's disappearing." He pointed at the mirror.

Jenna stared at her reflection. Sure enough, the line was fading. She looked down at her arm; the pain was disappearing also. Gently, she pressed her fingers against the bandage hidden beneath her shirt.

"So, what's the plan now, Miss Hiss?" Jason smiled from behind.

As the pain subsided, Jenna's mind and body grew strong again. She spun around to face him. "You said that you could help me. So, if you're willing and able, then let's go. I'll explain the rest on the way to the school."

Jenna glanced down at the rest of her body. Everything appeared normal on the outside. But something on the inside felt different. A cool, shimmering sensation began to wind its way through her system. Starting from the ground up, the feeling worked its way through her toes, moved along her legs, continued up through her torso and headed for the tips of her fingers and her head. She lifted both arms out to the sides and stood like Wonder Woman in awe of herself. She embraced the feeling with all of her senses. Switching stances, she posed in front of the mirror to take it all in.

"Hey, you still with me over there?" Jason said.

Totally absorbed in the moment, Jenna had forgotten that he was there. She dropped her arms by her sides and laughed. "Oh, right. Definitely. Of course."

"Well, I know I'm probably going to be condemned for trying to separate you from your mirror, but a few seconds ago you seemed pretty psyched about going to the school. Are you sure you want to go back there?"

Jenna leaned her head to one side. "You better believe it! That's where the answers are."

"Are you sure you're feeling okay?" he said. "You don't seem like yourself."

Jenna marched over to where he was standing and poked him in the stomach. "Yes! See—I'm fine."

"Okay, okay," he said. "Sorry."

"But you're right," Jenna said. "We should get going. Why don't you go on ahead, I'll be down in a minute."

Jason headed for the bedroom door. "You're the boss."

Jenna watched as he left the room. Looking back at the mirror, she smiled. "Yes, I am. And don't you ever forget it."

TREASURE SEEKERS

The school was a bit of a trek from Jenna's house but she was up for the hike. It was Jason who was slowing her down. And they would've taken a car but Jenna didn't want to arouse any suspicions about where they were going. So, she lied and told her mother that she and Jason were going over to a friend's house, which was nearby.

The only problem was the weather. Although the temperature was warm, the rain was constant, and hadn't let up. Before they'd left, Jenna's mother had insisted that they bring jackets and umbrellas. Jenna complied, to avoid any arguments, and right now she was glad that she had.

A flash of lightning lit the sky ahead of them, appearing like a ladder coming down from the clouds. Thunder shook the ground shortly after.

"Are you sure this is the best time to be doing this?" Jason said. Droplets of water dribbled from his nose as he hurried to keep up.

"Trust me—this is the perfect time!" Jenna knew that the storm would keep all the work crews away from the school. No one would be out in this weather, which meant that no one would be there to tell them to leave.

With the school now in their line of sight, Jenna took a deep breath to ease her nerves. Although it was her idea to return there, it was merely out of duty. If she hadn't overheard Maggie's conversation in the kitchen, this new direction wouldn't even be an afterthought. But she remembered what Anzhara had said, 'In time, you'll know'. And she was absolutely right. Jenna knew. The school was the answer, and right now—timing was everything.

The chain-linked fence that surrounded the football field behind the school was the first thing that they saw from the street. Beyond it, was the wreckage from the toppled building. Both were stunned at the emptiness of the space as they made their way towards the property.

"It looks like the crews haven't cleaned up much yet," Jason said, wiping his face. "The weather isn't helping, I guess."

Jenna stood with her hands clinging to the fence. "I can't believe the school is actually gone. It just doesn't seem real." She searched the area for anything abnormal. Through the falling rain, she saw no signs of anything out of the ordinary. "We have to get closer."

"I don't know if that's a good idea," Jason said. "There's a lot of debris. It might not be safe to walk around. They've got the entire area cordoned off."

Jenna wasn't listening. She was already on the other side of the fence, heading towards the school.

"Jenna—wait!"

"What?" she said, looking back at him.

Jason quickly ducked through a small opening in the fence. "At least wait for me."

Jenna continued on, she wasn't wasting any time. "Come on—we've gotta go!"

Up ahead, she saw the door to the storm room lying on the ground. Everything had collapsed around it. All the brick, metal, glass and wood had merged together into heaping piles of scholastic garbage. There wasn't much to identify.

The smell is what concerned her the most. There was a stagnant stench of wet destruction. As she looked around, she felt a slight tinge of pain in her heart, but not for herself—for the school. It was bad enough that the building had been torn apart, but to see it drowning in the aftermath was even worse.

Jenna stared at the mess. She mentally mapped out where all the rooms would have been. Taking careful steps, she trekked alongside the invisible exterior until she came upon the spot that she desired.

Behind her, Jason was looking at what was left of the geography room. He picked up a large atlas and watched as several sheets of paper fell from it. "Wow—not even the books made it."

Jenna turned her attention to the place where she was standing. "This was the history room."

Jason meandered through the debris and stood beside her. "The last room to fall," he said.

"This was my favourite room—I loved this room," Jenna said. "I had big dreams in here and now it's nothing." She saw one of the chalkboards lying beneath the rubble and wanted to get closer. Slowly, she stepped onto the ruins.

"Be careful," Jason said. "You don't know what's under there."

"I will," she said, reassuring him. The rain had finally let up, now it was only a trickle. She closed her umbrella and used it as a walking stick, as her feet waded through the debris. She heard Jason following behind doing the same.

Upon reaching the chalkboard, she knelt down. Carefully, she brushed away all that was covering it. "Look—"

"What is it?"

"It's a newspaper clipping," she said. Jenna picked up the paper and then opened the umbrella to shield it from what was left of the rain. The print nearly dribbled off the page. She leaned over and grabbed another.

"That's not surprising," Jason said, with an unenthusiastic headshake. "I'm sure Mrs. Wallace kept a lot of articles in her desk."

"This wasn't in her desk. It was attached to this chalkboard." Jenna looked back at him as she dangled the paper from her fingers. "And it's from 1939."

"1939? What's that doing here?" he said. "We didn't have anything like that hanging up."

"Maybe not when *you* were in the room," Jenna said with a grin.

"Okay, so what does it say?"

"It's an article about *The Wizard of Oz*. It's an advertisement for the movie, and the date is August, 1939." Jenna thought for a moment. "Ruby slippers..."

Jason looked confused. "Ruby slippers? What are you talking about?"

"Well, my grandmother, or Adella rather, told me that Alaina's favourite movie was *The Wizard of Oz*."

"And?"

Jenna didn't answer. She was too deeply imbedded in the subject. Leaning over, she found more pieces of newsprint buried beneath a desk. She pushed the desk aside and reached for them. "This one's about a bridge collapsing in Niagara Falls in 1938. And this one's about a racehorse in 1935. None of these are recent, but I've seen them all before."

For the next few minutes, Jenna ignored Jason as she carefully searched for any clippings that weren't soaked or destroyed. Collecting several along the way, she realized that all of them had dates ranging from 1933 to 1939; the years that Alaina existed in the world. It eventually began to sink in, as to why she saw her while inside the school. Alaina truly was a messenger, from her school in Salem to Jenna's school in Wichita. Then it registered—the history room was a portal through time—just like her cornfield.

Jason waited patiently for Jenna to gather all the information she needed. "What else are you looking for?"

"I'm not sure. I thought it would be more obvious, or at least, easier. Clues about a stolen ruby, something like that. But I haven't found anything yet." When she glanced back at Jason, she was startled to see a large shadow standing behind him. "Jason—look out!" she screamed.

Jason turned in surprise. Cloaked in darkness, the shadow lifted its arms and waved a cane into the air. The rain came to a sudden stop.

But when Jenna saw the silver viper head atop of the cane, she knew exactly who it was.

RESOUNDING THOUGHTS

"It's you!" Jenna yelled to the old man who now stood in their presence.

"The feeling is mutual," he returned. He spoke in a light-hearted manner. "But now I have you all to myself, since your twin is neither here nor there." The edges of his mouth curled up into a large Grinch-like smile, and with both eyes he winked.

Jason and Jenna stood next to each other watching the old man. He wore a beige trench coat that covered almost everything except the brown slacks and shoes that peeked out from the bottom. What really stood out in Jenna's mind, was his hair. It reached down past his ears and shimmered in the night. The bright white colour of his locks illuminated him.

Looking down, Jenna saw the silver cane that he carried. It was beautifully detailed. The arc of the Blade Viper's head was designed so majestically. In that instant, she wanted to touch it.

The old man grinned when he saw her eyeing the cane. "The viper is a proud and venomous animal, one that should not be tinkered with. Don't you agree?"

Jenna nodded, silently. It was as if he knew what she was thinking.

"What is your name, my dear?"

She answered without hesitating. "Jenna."

"Of course it is." He giggled at her.

Although his appearance was older, his demeanour was somewhat child-like. His mannerisms were flighty; giving the impression that he was slightly cuckoo.

"And who is this strapping young lad?" he said, peering at Jason.

"I think the more important question is, who are you?" Jason replied.

The old man took a few steps forward. He came to a stop in front of Jason and examined him. He then lifted his cane and tapped Jason lightly on the legs. "Strong boy, you are. A worrier, I think. Or protective perhaps—we'll have to see."

The man stepped sideways towards Jenna but she backed away when he got near. His presence, although somehow alluring, also made her nervous. She felt even more nervous when he leaned in and sniffed her.

"What are you doing?" she said, dodging behind Jason.

The old man followed her. "I know something you don't," he smiled.

Jason turned and used himself as a shield to block him from her. His young, six-foot stature towered over him. "What is it you want, old man?"

"Oh, you're a feisty one," he said. He took a moment to size Jason up. "You *are* protective; a valuable quality that is. I think you might be of use to me."

Jason scoffed. "What is that supposed to mean?"

Jenna remained behind Jason. From there, she listened. She now let Jason do all the talking.

"It's best you come along, too," the old man said to him. "We could use someone with your passion, especially when it comes to your girl over there."

"We're not going anywhere with you," Jason said. "I don't know what it is you want, but this game you're playing, it ends here."

The old man snickered and angled his head. "It's for certain, then. You *must* come as well."

"Look—" Jason started.

Jenna could hear the tension rising in his voice. She reached for Jason's hand. The last thing she wanted was a needless display of macho hierarchy. She wrapped her fingers around his, then came around and stood by his side. "Why do you want us to come with you?"

"Because," the old man said, "you are not protected here. I would tell you the risks, but this is not the safest place to do so."

The two teens glanced at one another. Both were at a loss for words.

"Your grandmother would want this, Jenna," the old man said. "Your rightful path awaits."

Jason whispered, "I think we should get out of here. This guy isn't playing with a full deck, if you catch my drift."

But the old man's comment had ensnared her. "You know my grandmother?"

"Of course, and Anzhara, too."

Jenna paused. "What do you mean by, my rightful path awaits?"

"If you come with me, I will tell you," he said.

That's when she noticed the old man's eyes. Surrounding the brilliant blue were silver circles, something Jenna had never seen before. His icy stare was cold, yet inviting. Slowly, her feet began to move in his direction.

Jason grabbed her arm. "Jenna—what are you doing? Think for a minute, you don't know this guy."

Without looking back, she said, "He knows Anzhara, Jason. And he knows my grandmother!"

"Look—I'm not leaving you alone with him!" Jason said.

"Excellent, then," the old man said. He clapped his hands in excitement just as a child would in receiving a toy. "Two is better than one!"

"Jenna—this isn't right." Jason urged her to stop.

A strike of lightning lit the sky, and as it did, the old man smiled. Jenna saw the elongated fangs inside his mouth. Her heart skipped a beat and she shrieked.

The old man seemed pleased by her reaction. He took her by the hand and immediately pulled her towards him.

"Let go of her!" Jason yelled. He jumped in between them.

"Too late!" the old man laughed. He snapped his fingers and in an instant, all three disappeared out of sight.

BEYOND THE REACHES

Her eyes were open but Jenna couldn't tell where she was. "Where… are we?" she stammered. She coughed in a thin layer of dust as the air settled around them.

"I think we're underground," Jason said, staring up at the rocks, leaves and thick patches of grass that clung to the ceiling.

Jenna looked up. Seeing the world hanging above her like that caused a hiccup in her spatial interpretation. For a moment, she couldn't tell whether she was standing upside down or right side up. "This is really weird. I feel like I'm in Wonderland or something."

"Or something is right," Jason added.

Feeling an absence in the room, Jenna spun around hoping not to be surprised. "Where's the old man?"

There was no answer. He wasn't there.

Jenna looked for a door, a window—any sort of opening that would allow them to escape. She rubbed the arms of her jacket to keep herself warm. The air was cool and dank, which accompanied the rotting smell of earth. Her eyes began to adjust to the darkness but still she could barely see anything. The only light that was visible came from a display of buzzing flashes across the way, and a small fire in the center of the space that seemed to be moving.

"What is that?" she said, staring at the flames as they rose into the air.

"Looks like a floating campfire," Jason said.

Together, they moved towards it. The fire was hovering a few feet off the ground with nothing beneath it. As they approached the flames,

Jenna noticed the change in colour. "That's strange. First it was orange, now it's green, pink...yellow. How's it changing?"

"I don't know," Jason said.

The closer they got, the more they saw. Dangling above the fire was a small, black cauldron. Its handle hung from the hands of an ivory-coloured statue that stood beside it.

"Is that what I think it is?" Jenna said, staring at the body of the statue. It looked like a mummified human corpse. She gazed up at it. "Please say that's not real."

Jason walked up in front of it. The statue was nearly a foot taller than him. "No, it's not real, but it's really life-like," he said.

Jenna surveyed the entire space. When she looked up, she saw something else along the ceiling that was out of the ordinary. A large, thick tree root clung to the earth above her head. But it wasn't just the root that intrigued her, it was the way it grew. With its sharp angles and turns, it resembled that of a rectangle. It was bizarre and completely out of place.

"There's something really familiar about this place, in an upside down sort of way," she said.

"Jenna...I don't like this," Jason said.

Jenna's mind was focused on the root.

"Hey—are you listening to me?" Jason called again.

"What?" she said, peering over at him.

Jason pointed to the cauldron. "Take a whiff."

Jenna walked over to where he was standing and leaned in. The smell of burning wood and sour milk hit her like a fast train. The putrid scent almost brought tears to her eyes. Quickly, she covered her nose. "Oh—that's foul!"

"You're not kidding," he said. "Where the hell are we?"

"You're in my cave, of course," a voice appeared behind them.

Both Jenna and Jason jumped.

Standing behind them, was the old man. His hands fiddled together in a manner that suggested he was up to no good. "That's where snakes usually live," he said, smiling at them.

"This is my home. And yours, too, for the meantime."

His actions portrayed someone who'd been alone for quite some time. It was apparent by the cobwebs and musty setting, that visitors weren't even a question.

"*Your* home?" Jenna said. "Who are you?"

"Oh my, what silliness. I haven't told you. You must forgive me—it's been a while since I've had a student." The old man shimmied up to her. "My name is Locklynn." He stretched out his arm.

Jenna stared at it. Strange markings appeared on the back of his hand, like serpent scales.

"I won't hurt you," he said, waiting for her to shake it. "Even though you should be scared."

Jenna shuddered. "You're a snake—just like the Sandshadow's servants. I don't know what to think. Anzhara told me to trust you but how can I when you have skin like a reptile."

"Yes, yes I do. But that doesn't mean I'm bad," he said. "It doesn't mean I'm good either."

Jenna took a step back, as did Jason.

Locklynn flashed his teeth, showing the sharp points of his fangs. "But right now, none of that matters because you are in my home." The giddiness in his voice was slowly replaced with a timid cackling. "And I must keep you here. For a little while, anyhow."

"Anzhara told me that you're my new teacher. How am I supposed to trust you when I can't even tell if you're good or not?" Jenna said.

Locklynn laughed. He pulled back his hand and inspected it. "You can't trust me. Not ever. But I will teach you, that is a guarantee." He then shuffled past them.

"Well, that sounds promising," Jason joked, eyeing the old man as he moved.

"Come, my new friends," Locklynn said. "Come and see what I have for you." He leaned over the cauldron. Billows of smoke emptied into the air as the fire crackled beneath it.

With synchronized steps, Jenna and Jason walked together. "We've got no choice but to listen to him," she whispered.

Jason nodded. "Let's just stick together."

Through the thin pillars of fire, Jenna spotted something on the walls. Long, lanky, tapered ropes appeared all around them, stuck to the walls. Looking closer, she saw that they were roots, most likely stemming from the same place as the one above her head. Browned leaves lay scattered all over the roots like they were glued in position. Again, it seemed completely out of place.

"Are we by chance...underneath a tree?" Jenna asked.

"We certainly are," Locklynn said, with a twinkle in his eye. "It's the oldest oak in these parts."

"These parts? Where exactly are we?" Jason said.

"We are someplace beyond the reach of the Sandshadow," Locklynn said in a more serious tone. "That is all you need to know." He wafted in the cauldron brew as he spoke.

The terrible scent from moment's earlier had dissipated. The smell no longer bothered Jenna. Instead, the odorous liquid now took on a pleasant hint of rose hip.

All three stood around the cauldron. Locklynn bent down and spread his hands over the fire. In a whimsical display of magic, he lifted the embers into the air and scattered them all around. The darkness gave way to a soft yellow lighting, giving the entire space a beautiful twilight dusting.

Jenna was amazed but didn't want to say it. What was even more impressive was the size of the cave they were in.

In one area, there were several large golden birdcages but no birds. A small horde of fireflies flew back and forth between the bars of the cages, lighting the area with tiny flashes as they travelled.

Looking around, Jenna smiled. There were all sorts of animals inside the cave, some that she recognized and some that she'd never seen before. Her mood began to lift when she saw other living things; it made the cave seem less desolate.

"Do you believe this?" she said.

Jason didn't answer.

She looked around but didn't see him. "Jason?"

"Over here," he said, from the far side of the cave. "You gotta come and see this."

With cautious steps, Jenna walked over to where he was crouched down. He was staring into a shallow, round, turquoise pool of water. "It's a pond," he said.

"Inside a cave? That's strange." Jenna bent down beside him and gazed into the water. She watched as several small purple blobs swam beneath their reflections, each one the size of a plum. "What are those?"

One of the blobs rose to the surface and sat bobbing in the water, looking at her. More of them soon followed. Jenna counted seventeen altogether. One by one, they moved closer to where she was sitting.

"They're little octopuses! Oh my God—they're adorable! I've never seen one up close before."

"Looks like they like you," Jason said.

In three uniformed lines, they swam to the pond's edge like a bunch of little purple troops. Jenna stared at their tiny tentacles as they floated in front of her. She wanted to reach out and touch them, but decided it was safer not to. "I wonder what they're doing?"

As the animals reached the wall of the pond, they broke formation. Each one swam around the other as they tried to get closer to Jenna. Their tentacles slapped against the rocky edges of the pond, like they were trying to climb it.

Jenna sat, enticed by their behaviour. "They're so cute." Her fascination finally took over and she stretched out her hand to touch one.

A sudden ripple appeared in the water as her fingers neared the first animal. In an instant, the swarm of purple swimmers dispersed in all directions beneath the surface. In the reflection of the water, Jenna saw Locklynn standing behind her.

Quickly, she rose to her feet. Jason however, remained in place. He seemed mesmerized by the pond, and was now quiet.

"Be careful," Locklynn said. "Not everything in here is harmless."

"What does that mean?" Jenna glanced back at the water. "Are they poisonous or something?"

Locklynn ignored her and stared at the pond.

All of the little octopuses were now gone, submerged and out of sight. But skimming on top of the water in their wake, were several lily pads of all shapes and sizes. Perched on top of them were tiny blue and black-striped frogs, all of which were the size of a walnut.

This time, Jenna kept her hands to herself. She watched as one of the frogs jumped from pad to pad, closer to where she was standing. Its long, pink tongue extended outward when it came to a stop by the pond's edge. It then leapt onto the rocky wall as Jenna took an immediate step back. It was coming out of the pond.

Within seconds, the frog jumped onto her jeans. Jenna screamed, thinking that it, too, was poisonous. The thumb-sized animal remained attached to her, and then slowly changed colour to match her jeans. "Get it off, get it off!" she yelled.

Locklynn snagged the little amphibian. "Don't be afraid of this one. He's just curious." He cupped his hands around the frog and lifted it up for her to see. Again, its colour changed to match his hands. It was now skin-toned, with a slightly silvery finish. "Would you like to hold him?"

Jenna hesitated, but then nodded out of intrigue. Locklynn placed the frog onto her hands.

"Wow, it's so light," she said.

The frog let out a tiny 'ribbit' and then jumped back into the pond.

"Here comes Teek," Locklynn said, as the frog disappeared beneath the water.

"Who's Teek?" Jenna asked.

A large bubble emerged from the water before Locklynn could answer. Seconds later, a head popped up with a mottled green shell not far behind it.

"That's Teek," Locklynn said.

Jenna was in awe when she caught sight of the enormous turtle. "Holy crow—he's huge!"

"Teek is the last of his breed. He's a Mantooth tortoise. He'll be five feet by the time he's eighty."

"How old is he now?"

"Seventy-five. And wise beyond his years."

His statement forced Jenna to ask, "How old are *you*?"

Locklynn winked in return. "My age is irrelevant." With that, he headed back to the cauldron.

Jenna was starting to get a feel for Locklynn's behaviour, and how good he was at evading certain questions. He seemed reclusive, yet approachable. Devilish, yet kind-hearted. Both Anzhara and her grandmother trusted him, but to what extent? Jenna wondered. Was this the reptilian equivalent to fairies and witches? Good serpents versus bad serpents? Had he spawned from evil but converted to good? He was a Veliostriga, a Power Shepherd, but what exactly did that mean? Jenna was not yet sure. In that moment, she made the decision to find out.

"I was told that you were my Power Shepherd. I guess I was under the impression that you'd be human, or human-ish."

Locklynn scurried about the cave moving things about. For a moment, he turned his back and kept to himself.

Jenna wasn't sure if he'd heard her, so she elaborated. "I wasn't trying to be rude, I just didn't think that my teacher would be related to my enemy."

That stopped him. With his shoulders hunched, he let out a huff. His manner then turned creepy. "Why would you say something like that?"

Jenna didn't reply. Her insensitive remark had sparked a reaction, one that she hadn't expected.

With his head turned to the side, but his eyes still on her, Locklynn slithered across the cave. Something limp now dangled from his one hand. In the other was a large, serrated knife.

Jenna moved towards Jason for support. He was still focused on the pond, staring at the animals in the water. He'd been quiet for a rather long time. She tapped him on his shoulder several times trying to get his attention. "Jason—" she whispered.

There was no response as Locklynn headed for her. As he approached, Jenna blurted out an apology. "Okay—look, I'm sorry! I didn't mean it!"

"Boy, you're an odd species," Locklynn said. "I haven't quite figured you out." Again, his behaviour seemed shifty. "Give me your hand," he said. His eyes were now an eerie mustard colour.

Jenna tried to step back but the heels of her sneakers were hitting the edge of the pond. Locklynn gave an elfin smile and grabbed her hand. He then placed a lifeless brown gecko into her palm.

"Ugh, ick. Is it dead?" The chilly feel of the animal's slimy body against her skin made her cringe. Little droplets of red began to pool in her hand. "This is gross, get it off me!"

Locklynn closed her hand tightly around the animal.

"What are you doing?" she said, pulling her hand back.

"This is a test, Jenna. Look at me."

First, she glanced at Jason. Something about him was different; he wasn't moving. He seemed frozen in position with his outstretched hand touching one of the frogs on the lily pad. "Jason—Jason!" she yelled.

"He's not part of the test, Jenna. Now, pay attention!" Locklynn scolded her. "Look at me!"

Jenna felt herself being drawn back to the yellow of Locklynn's eyes. It was startling, like something right out of a horror movie. She wanted to run, but Locklynn had her hand. She just about fainted when a forked tongue sprang from his mouth.

"Let me go!" she screamed.

"Look at me!" he yelled at her.

A fire began to burn inside of her. A rage she had not felt before suddenly erupted, and in the reflection of the yellow she saw her own eyes turn an alien shade of silver. She lashed out at him with her other hand and struck with full force. He blocked her strike with his cane and when he did, a brilliant white light appeared overhead.

With the gecko tightly clutched in her hand, Jenna felt the anger inside of her suddenly retreat. She cowered beneath the beams of the light. It hurt her eyes to look at it. "Stop it!" she shrieked.

Locklynn lowered his cane and the light disappeared altogether. He watched Jenna carefully as she sat crouched on the floor, shaking.

"Why did you do that?" she cried.

Locklynn leaned over and ran his fingers beneath her chin. His nails dug into her neck as he brought Jenna to her feet. "Look in my eyes," he said.

Jenna did as she was told. She stared silently, wondering what had just happened.

Locklynn's eyes had returned to their natural shade of blue and a kind smile now spread across his face. He pointed to her hand. "You have the strength of a good witch," he said. "Look at what your magic has done."

Jenna peered down as something wiggled between her fingers. She opened her hand and saw a little green gecko moving around. Its tiny suction-cupped toes pressed against her skin. "It's alive!"

Locklynn bowed his head. "You have the power to bring back life. That is your gift."

Jenna was speechless. She couldn't believe what she was seeing. "I did that?"

Locklynn nodded as he reached out and took the gecko from her. Placing it in his hand, he hurried over to another part of the cave and released it. "Your power is new. In time, it will grow."

Jenna followed him across the cave. "Then it's true. I *am* a witch." A tear trickled down her cheek as she thought of the ramifications. "I can heal the dead?"

What would seem like a blessing to most, was not what Jenna desired. All she could think of was the downside of her new power. Would the rest of her life be this frightening? Would she forever now be in harm's way? Whether it was just the gravity of the moment or

Locklynn's terrifying witch trial, Jenna finally gave way to her emotions and cried.

Locklynn said nothing. He headed over to the cauldron and recited some sort of spell while Jenna wept. "You will be fine," he said. "This will not destroy you."

Jenna wiped her eyes. "How do you know? This wasn't supposed to be my life."

"Your expectations have been derailed, that is true. But the path that leads you into the future is not always the right one."

The vagueness of his statement seemed obscure to Jenna. It had no meaning other than fantastical rationalizations. It caused her temper to flare.

"How would *you* know? You're not even human!" She didn't care now if her comment was hurtful. "This isn't a life worth dreaming of. This isn't remotely what I wanted. I just want to be normal!"

"Ahh, but you aren't." Locklynn wagged his finger at her. "You see, there is something very wrong now."

Jenna nodded. "I know—the Sandshadow." With the sleeve of her jacket, she wiped the remaining tears from her face.

Locklynn shook his head. "You think *that* is what's wrong?"

"Of course—what else?" Jenna sniffled.

"We have problems greater than that, my dear. Problems right here in this cave."

Jenna looked back at Jason; he was still stiff like a statue, propped up in position. "What did you do to my friend?"

When she turned back, Locklynn was standing in front of her, holding the serrated knife in his hand. His pointed teeth sparkled in the glow of the metal. She didn't even have a chance to scream before he sliced the blade across her forearm. Blood spurted out from beneath her jacket, but mixed with it were silver flecks of wiggling larvae. Jenna howled as parts of her spilled onto the ground. She looked at Locklynn with absolute pain and terror in her eyes.

He flashed a sinister grin and raised the knife again. "You see, the problem my dear, is you!"

A VICIOUS TRIUMPH

The knife came down and struck Jenna's arms with force. She wailed in agony with each piercing stab. Dropping to her knees, she felt the cold earth beneath her. Locklynn was on a rampage; there was no stopping him. He was too fast, and Jenna had been completely blindsided.

Her wails soon turned into moans as the last bit of strength left her body. She slumped onto the ground and looked up at him. He struck once more, gliding the blade across her forearms as she held them protectively above her head. His expression was lifeless as he cut into her. He leaned his head to one side as if the job he was doing was easy.

Jenna sat, breathing in shallow breaths. The only word she could muster was "Why?"

With that, Locklynn stopped. He bent down with the knife poised and ready in his hand. Jenna was sure that he would finish her off right then and there. Her arms went limp and dropped to her sides. She stared at the blood that flowed from them.

"Your hands, your arms—" Locklynn said, "your magic stems from there. I had to cut you off before you did something terrible."

His words didn't make any sense and Jenna was losing focus. As she let her body relax onto the ground, she saw hundreds of small silver flecks moving towards her as if they were trying to get back in.

Then, with a momentous bellow, Locklynn lifted himself from the ground and shouted, "Be gone!"

A stunning golden light materialized around Jenna's body, illuminating her in the darkened cave. She closed her eyes to block out the painful rays. A strange sizzling noise rose up around her, like the sound of eggs frying on a pan. One by one, the silver specks exploded into miniature flames. The golden light which lasted merely a minute, departed above her, leaving a fading trail of yellow behind it.

Then all was quiet in the cave.

ANSWERS, PLEASE!

A curious feeling of relief and emptiness took over Jenna's senses. Carefully, she sat up. The squirming pieces of silver larvae were gone. Being so focused on the disappearance of the alien flecks, it took her a moment to realize what had happened. She pulled back the sleeves of her jacket and shirt and held her arms straight out in front of her.

"Oh my God!" she cried. The cuts were gone, the wounds were sealed. No blood was dripping from her body. Her strength and vitality had returned.

She looked past her arms and saw Locklynn standing over her. His face was devoid of anger and malice. He held the knife in one hand, and Jenna could see that it was completely clean. He then snapped his fingers and the knife disappeared out of sight. Stretching out his hand, he offered to help her up.

"You are clean," he said.

Jenna refused his assistance. She stood and backed away from him. "You tried to kill me! Don't you dare come near me!"

"Don't be silly, my dear. I would never do such a thing. You were riddled with the enemy's poison, I had to cleanse you." Locklynn slowly stepped towards her. He seemed confused by her actions. "I was helping you—can't you see that?"

"Helping me? You stabbed me, sliced me—cut me open! You watched my blood pour onto the ground and yet you kept cutting!"

"I had to," he said.

Jenna wasn't too sure what to think. She heard Locklynn loud and clear, and was starting to believe him, but trusting him was another issue altogether. "What was that silver stuff anyway? And how did it get inside of me?"

"You were infected by the Sandshadow. You were bitten," he said, taking another step closer.

Jenna watched his feet as he moved, but she was distracted by his words. He'd repeated something that Anzhara had said. Something about how the Sandshadow's servants had poisoned her. Jenna could almost hear the comforting softness of Anzhara's voice as if she, too, was in the cave.

There was a presence now that Jenna could feel, she was sure of it. Someone else was there with them. She scanned the darkened area but couldn't see anyone other than Locklynn and Jason. Jason—

"Jason!" she shouted. A terrible guilt grew inside of her. With everything that had just happened, she'd completely forgotten that her friend was there. She saw that he was still frozen in position beside the pond.

His body came to life as she rushed across the cave towards him. "Those frogs are…" he started. "Whoa—what just happened?"

Jenna ran up and helped him to his feet. "Are you okay?"

"Yeah, I'm fine, although I feel a little…stiff."

"That's an understatement!" Jenna sighed. "Are you okay, though?"

"I'm fine, really. Man—something smells like burnt rubber in here."

Locklynn made his way over to them. "Jenna was infected. The enemy had to be eradicated from her system. This was her trial, not yours," he said to Jason. He then looked at Jenna. "You must believe me—harm was not my intent."

"I don't understand…what's going on here?" Jason said. "Did I miss something?"

Jenna shook her head. She didn't want to make eye contact with Locklynn. She didn't trust him even if his intentions were genuine.

"I was guided to you, Jenna, so that I could help you," Locklynn said.

"Why?" she snapped. "So that I could be hacked up into little pieces? Stay away from me!"

Locklynn seemed honestly hurt by the comment. He lowered his head and shuffled away. "I only wanted to help. That's all I wanted. I *am* good. I *am* good. I *am* good," he told himself over and over.

"What the hell is going on here?" Jason asked. "What happened?"

"If you don't believe my sincerity," Locklynn said, "then perhaps there's someone else you'll listen to."

Jenna whispered to Jason, "I just don't trust him, okay?"

"You should, you must," another voice came from across the cave. The speaker was hidden behind the shadow of a large birdcage that hung from a tall, golden stand. The empty cage gently swung back and forth.

Jenna knew the voice immediately. "Alaina?"

The riddles and rhymes of the speaker came through loud and clear.

"Yes and no. No and yes. It's who I am but not to you." The red patent shoes stepped out from the shadows, revealing the little girl Jenna had come to know. She appeared in human form rather than a ghostly figure.

"Ahh, Jenna…is that who I think it is?" Jason stammered.

Jenna nodded in return. "You're Alaina. My ancestor, my great-aunt. I know who you are."

The girl's blonde ringlets moved back and forth as she walked with a small, yellow bird perched on her arm. The colour stood out against her black, velvet dress. "This is my favourite bird, I used to have one when I was little. Pretty bird. Pretty bird." She petted it gently.

Jason stood with his mouth wide open. Jenna, on the other hand, was more intrigued than ever. Alaina was her relative, someone she trusted.

The bird chirped a few times and then fell silent.

"I know all about you," Jenna said, walking up to the girl.

Alaina seemed unfazed by the statement and continued to pet the winged animal. "Pretty bird. Pretty bird. Call to see, call to see. Who is there, you or me?"

Her ramblings gave Jenna a chance to think. A cemetery flashback came to mind. From where she was standing, she examined the roots along the walls of the cave, and then followed their path up to the ceiling. The large rectangular root suddenly stood out from its background.

Jenna looked at both Locklynn and Alaina with shock in her eyes. "This is your grave?"

Alaina didn't answer. Instead, she stroked the bird's neck, repeatedly. "Birds are meant to fly. Leaving is what they do."

Jenna now understood why Anzhara and her grandmother had trusted Locklynn. His cave protected Alaina's grave; he was her guardian. Armed with this knowledge, Jenna's heart began to open to him.

She bent down in front of Alaina. "You can't leave, can you? Earth is your prison."

The little girl nodded as tears stemmed from her eyes. As she cried, the bird lifted its wings and flew into the shadows.

"We can find you a way out," Jenna said. "I will help you."

Alaina smiled back but said nothing.

Jenna wrapped her fingers around Alaina's hands and pressed them together. She could feel how cold they were, her lifeless flesh. "I am your descendent. And if there's a way, I will help you find peace. I promise you."

The silence that followed only lasted a second. Jenna gasped when the ground above and beneath them began to quake. Holding Alaina's hands, she quickly glanced around. Locklynn seemed just as surprised as she was.

"The enemy is waiting," Alaina said. "They will try to get in, but *in* they cannot get." She squeezed Jenna's fingers, which made her look. "They have come for you. Me, they cannot have, but you, they will try to take. Listen to Locklynn, he is the key. A key of silver, an answer in hiding. Anzhara knows."

Jenna tried to remember everything that Alaina was saying, but the rumbling of the cave was drowning her out. "Wait—I don't know what to do! I don't have a plan!"

"Follow your feet, strength will come. Up and down, down and up. Out you go, to and fro."

"I don't understand!" Jenna stared into her crystal blue eyes.

Alaina gently placed an object in Jenna's hands. "Believe in the power of magic, you must." Her image began to fade as she backed away into the shadow of the cave.

"Please—wait!" Jenna called out to her.

"Be strong inside. The beats of your heart will tell you when to strike. Go quickly. Go now," Alaina said, her voice disappearing.

"Alaina—come back!" But there was no use. Jenna could see that she was gone.

The cave shook on all sides. Bits and pieces of dirt and leaves fell from the ceiling as the rocky perimeter crumbled in places. The animals came alive as their panicked calls carried throughout the cave. Locklynn tried to calm them by reciting soothing words in a foreign tongue.

He looked back at Jenna. "They're here for you, not for us. This cave is a sanctuary; its walls will not be breached. But still, you must go."

Jason ran over to where Jenna was kneeling and helped her up. "What's going on? What is he talking about?"

Jenna took the object in her hand and discreetly slipped it into the pocket of her jeans. "Jason, there's something I have to do. It's a family thing and has nothing to do with you or Locklynn."

"What are you talking about?" he said.

"I can't put you in harm's way," she said. "And that's where I need to go." For Jenna, it was all starting to fall into place.

When Alaina's spirit departed, Jenna realized what it was she had to do. Even with all the questions she had, she understood that her family needed her. Just before Alaina had left, she'd placed an object of desire in Jenna's hands. A precious jewel; something Jenna had been looking for. And it was exactly what she needed to carry on.

The road ahead would be a dangerous one; the look in Alaina's eyes clearly conveyed it. And a valiant effort would not necessarily ensure her success but still she had to try. In order to do so, she had to cut her ties.

"Jason—I can't explain. You need to go back, to safety, to your home. This is where our path branches. You can't come with me."

His back straightened as she spoke, and his manner became more intense. "You don't have a choice. I'm coming with you. Look—this is the most bizarre thing that I've ever done and I'm not even sure that it's real. But leaving you alone in this place, well, that's not gonna happen. You're stuck with me, so get used to it!"

"Jason, I can't—" she started.

"Jenna, button it! I'm coming with you and that's that. You can't do whatever you're doing alone. Besides, in movies, there's always a sidekick," he grinned.

His comment made her smile, but the feel of the quaking ground brushed her smile away. "We can't stay here, we have to go. Locklynn doesn't deserve this destruction. I don't want his home to suffer. We have to go now."

Locklynn surprised them both when he appeared directly behind them. "My home is safe. These animals are the reason why the Sandshadow cannot enter. Teek is a Mantooth, with a very deadly weapon—his carapace." He turned and rushed around the cave, gathering items into a bag.

"What's a carapace?" Jason asked.

"His shell," Locklynn said. "It's venomous to the touch. I told you he was wise. And those little creatures in the pond are my Neptunepods. The ninth tentacle is a poison dart, very destructive to nerve cells." He held up a small vial with black liquid inside of it. "You must never come into contact with it, the poison works immediately."

Jenna thought back to the moment when she had nearly touched one of the octopuses.

"Don't worry, my dear," Locklynn said, looking over at her. "They know good from evil." He hustled as he spoke. "My Night Indigos have poison sacs on their toes. They are the most wicked little frogs, but powerful and potent."

"What about that bird, and those buzzing things over there?" Jason asked. "Birds aren't poisonous. That little girl was holding one."

Locklynn cocked his head and looked at him. "That little girl was dead."

Jenna shivered when she remembered how cold Alaina's hands were.

"A Sundrop Eyelet has the ability to befriend anyone living or dead. Its curse is in its song," Locklynn said.

"Really?" Jenna couldn't believe that such a beautiful, bright bird could cause any harm. But then again, nothing she saw in the cave was what it appeared to be.

"The Eyelet's call is to invoke the spirits of the underworld. Its power is deception, and therefore, is never detected. And those over there," Locklynn said, pointing to the flashing bugs, "are Moonstick fireflies. They are simply meant to illuminate the darkness, when the world has become harsh and lifeless."

"Everything has a purpose here, doesn't it?" Jenna said.

"Of course, this is my world." Locklynn spoke like a proud father. "Nothing here is trivial, everything has meaning. Size is only physical. Some of my most beloved enemies have mistaken that. But you'll see."

The enemy was all around. And yet, the object hidden in Jenna's pocket gave her strength and willpower.

"I'm going with you," Locklynn said, now standing beside her. He threw the bag over his shoulder. "This is the way of it."

Jenna heard several bottles and jars clanging together inside the bag. "Locklynn—no. This is your home, you should stay here."

"The three of us must go together," he insisted. "That is the wisest of all decisions. There will be no refusals."

His authoritative tone gave Jenna hope. She actually wanted him to come. His trial by fire had worked its way into her system, and with Alaina's support, Jenna was now beginning to trust him. "Okay," she said. "But we better go now."

"Where *are* we going?" Jason said, looking willing but confused.

"You'll see," Locklynn said with a wink. He then snapped his fingers and all three disappeared from the cave.

HISTORY IN THE MAKING

A rich, white light blasted around Jenna and the others like a flash fire in the darkness. It was cool inside the flames as the air transported them. Then, as fast as it came, the light vanished and the group of three was standing somewhere new.

They'd arrived at a place that Jenna and Jason had come to know. The setting however was not at all what Jenna had expected. She had to rub her eyes to make sure she was seeing straight.

"How is this possible?" she said, amazed by her surroundings.

"Are we…imagining this?" Jason said.

Locklynn stood in between them. All three gazed up at the brick building in front of them. Its structure was strong, not a single part of it was missing. The school that had been converted to a pile of rubble was now erected to its former foundation. Beaconsfield High school stood without fault, mighty yet simplistic.

"How did you do this?" Jenna said. Although it was night-time, there were several lights surrounding the school, illuminating it.

"With tricks and time," Locklynn smiled. He took a step forward and glanced back at her. "Come, it's time for a lesson."

In the dark of night, Jenna watched Locklynn carefully as he strode towards the school with his cane in hand. He adjusted the bag on his shoulder and headed for the front doors. When he reached them, he turned back and called for Jenna to join him.

She balked at his request but seeing how determined he was, she followed. Jason kept close behind her.

As Jenna approached the two large doors, she stopped. "This can't possibly be real!"

Locklynn tapped his cane against the brick. "It's real, my dear. No illusions here."

Jenna placed her hand on one of the door handles. "Wow—this is incredible!"

"It's time," Locklynn said to her.

"For what?" she said.

Locklynn motioned with his hand towards the doors.

"Wait—you want me to go inside? What if the building collapses while I'm in there?"

"The building will not fall, Jenna. It is safe," Locklynn assured her.

Jenna peered through the glass windows on the doors. Nothing was different, the hallways looked the same. Everything was in its place, and intact. "Let me guess—I'm going to discover something in there, right?"

"Your lesson awaits," was all Locklynn said as he pointed to the door.

Behind her, Jason shook his head. "No way—I'm going with you." He took a step forward but Locklynn lifted his cane and stopped him.

"No—this she must do alone."

"The school might not be safe," Jason said. "You can't let her go in there alone."

Locklynn's blue eyes shone brightly in the night. "Trust me, young man, she won't be."

Although his answer was worrisome, she agreed with Locklynn. From here, she had to go it alone. Once again, she had to put her faith in Locklynn.

She gave Jason a tender smile. "It's okay, I'll be fine. You stay here and keep a lookout."

Jason said nothing; his eyes did all the talking. He simply nodded and touched her arm as she left.

"We won't be far," Locklynn said. He lowered the bag from his shoulder and handed her a vial filled with black liquid. "You remember what this does?"

"Yes," Jenna nodded.

"Then use it if you must."

Jenna took the vial of Neptunepod poison and carefully placed it in her jacket pocket. "Okay." With that, she turned and opened the door.

As she stepped inside the school, a strong breeze came from behind her and slammed the door shut. She leapt off the ground, while trying to hold on to what little amount of courage she had left at the moment. She looked back and saw Jason watching her. She gave him a thumb's up and then started heading down the hallway.

Although there were no visible lights inside the school, it seemed to be dimly lit somehow. Jenna didn't care how, she was just happy that it was.

There was no sign of destruction anywhere; the school was in perfect form. Being night-time and all, it had the same feel as if there was a dance in the gym or a theatre performance in the drama room. It really wasn't that unfamiliar. But then she remembered that she was in fact walking in a building that had been destroyed by natural forces.

Pausing for a moment, she told herself, "There's no going back... don't be a coward."

The school was dormant, not a sound was heard. Jenna continued down the hallway. Her hand was pressed against the pocket that held the vial. She felt secure having it, although she was hoping that she wouldn't have to use it.

The halls were quiet as Jenna walked. Eerily quiet. She almost expected someone to jump out at her. "Damn those horror movies!" she cursed. Thankfully, all she could hear was the tread of her own shoes against the floor.

When she came to a junction in the hallway, she quickly looked around to see which way to go. Every direction was dark. There was no sign of life in any of the rooms, and without a coin to flip to help make a decision, she chose to go left.

For no particular reason, her breathing began to accelerate. In an attempt to remain calm, she recited her grandmother's poem in her head. It was working right up until the point when she heard a sharp snapping sound come from behind her. Her body bounced off the floor like a spring. Quickly, she spun around to face the sound. Her skin was coated with goose bumps. The noise had come from one of the rooms she had already passed. To her, it sounded like a ruler being slapped against one of the desks.

A faint light began to flicker inside one of the rooms. Suppressing her fear was not an easy task but Jenna had to do it. She shoved what was left of her gumption into her feet and started slinking towards the room. The light flickered erratically as if one of the fixtures was malfunctioning, but Jenna sensed otherwise. To her, it was a sign. Someone or something was waiting for her inside the room.

Jason and Locklynn were not far away if she truly needed them. They awaited her call for help, if given. That thought propelled her onward; at least she wasn't alone.

She moved cautiously towards the beacon of light. Many thoughts raced through her head including the location of the nearest exit, but the closer she got to the room, the more she wanted to see it. Without thinking, she now understood which room it was.

Jenna was only ten feet from the room when the light disappeared altogether. In the absence of a visual cue, she stopped to listen. A voice of authority now came from inside it as other timid voices spoke in unison. It appeared that Jenna had stumbled upon a class in session. As she tiptoed through the hallway, she could see that the door to the room was open. Arriving at the door, she peered inside, hoping not to be seen.

The room came to life when she looked in. Light shone all around, illuminating the entire space. Printed on the front board, was the name of the school: Hanover Elementary.

As discreet as possible, Jenna glanced around the room. Each wall was covered with pieces of newsprint. It was the school from Salem, Alaina's school. The one Jenna had seen before. Standing at the front of the room was a female teacher dressed in old-fashioned clothing. And sitting at their desks were the children, roughly the ages of six or seven.

The teacher held a long, wooden ruler in her hand as she said aloud, "The deer is brown. The deer is brown."

The children repeated together, "The deer is brown. The deer is brown."

"Very good," the teacher said. "Now, repeat after me, the whale is blue, the whale is blue."

Jenna listened as the children obeyed her command. She watched their little faces while surveying the room. Off in the corner was a student who seemed fascinated by something on her lap. At first sight of the blonde ringlets, Jenna understood whose class it was.

The teacher smacked the ruler against the table at the front of the room, which startled everyone, including Jenna. The sound was terrifying, even to outsiders.

"Alaina—place the object on the table," the teacher demanded.

Little Alaina lifted up a small piece of twine and rested it on the desk. The teacher seemed quite displeased. She walked past a row of students and stood above Alaina in a threatening stance.

"You should be strapped for this. I would be happy to do it, but instead, I shall take your string and dispose of it. That should be enough to stop you."

"No, you mustn't! Adella will be angry—her will not mine. Return it!" she pleaded.

The teacher walked back to her desk at the front of the room and removed a pair of scissors from a drawer. Jenna's heart plummeted. The teacher seemed cruel, but she despised her even more when she saw Alaina's toy lamb sitting in the drawer. The teacher had obviously taken it away from her.

Alaina cried when she saw the scissors. "No—the twine is what binds us! Please do not cut it!" She stood from her seat and let out a grisly scream in front of the entire class. All of the students covered their ears, as did Jenna. The sound was bone-chilling.

Seconds later, when Jenna looked around, the room was empty. No students, no teacher. No newspaper clippings. The room was now dark.

Jenna was left with an overwhelming feeling of contempt. She couldn't believe how much things had changed from the way teachers had behaved. That type of discipline was no longer acceptable. It was considered barbaric.

With the room now quiet, Jenna looked around. Everything inside it had reverted back to its former state, to the present year in which she attended the school. Feeling somewhat secure in her decision to move forward, she stepped into the room. She wasn't aware that someone was watching her.

As she headed into the classroom, something slid beneath her foot. Jenna leaned over and picked it up. It was a newspaper clipping. She lifted it close to her face to read. The article was about a teacher who'd gone missing in Salem, Massachusetts in 1939. Her body was later discovered lying on the train tracks, not far from Hanover Elementary School where she taught. Completely brutalized and disfigured, her cause of death was ruled as crushing, but not from a train. From something else.

"An animal attack—" Jenna read the newsprint out loud. She quickly put two and two together and realized that the woman in the article was the teacher she had just seen. The one who had taken Alaina's twine away. "Oh God!"

Now feeling quite unsafe in the room, Jenna turned to leave. Something on the chalkboard at the front however, made her stop. There was a sentence written in Latin.

"Suos cultores scientia coronat," Jenna read aloud. She thought for a moment and then translated it. "Knowledge crowns those who seek her."

"Very good," a voice came from one of the corners.

Jenna leapt off the floor holding her chest. "Who's there?"

The person's face was cloaked in shadow. "You were always such a good student, Jenna Matthews," the voice said softly. "Your Latin was very strong."

Jenna identified the speaker immediately. "Mrs. Wallace?"

A dim light began to surface in the room. The woman smiled but Jenna could now see that she was hideously disfigured. Her neck was bloated, with broken blood vessels running up and down it. And her body was malformed. Her right arm was dislocated; it draped to one side. Her left collarbone was higher than the right one, and Jenna could clearly see the outline of broken ribs sticking through her blouse.

She just about vomited when she saw the extent of her teacher's injuries. Her mind raced back to the time of the tornado; the paramedics had said that Mrs. Wallace suffered severe crushing. Jenna looked down at the newspaper clipping in her hand and wondered if her teacher's injuries had been caused by something else. Just the thought of it sickened her.

"You mustn't worry about me, Jenna. I am merely sentenced to a life elsewhere."

"I am so sorry!" Jenna said, her eyes filling with tears. She hated the gruesome vision.

Mrs. Wallace dragged herself closer; Jenna could hear the ailing sounds of paralysis. She took a step back. "Are you here to give me a message?"

"I saved you, Jenna. I pushed you out of the way of danger. And how do you repay me? You leave me for dead!"

Tears began to trickle down Jenna's cheeks. She looked away from her teacher. The remorse she had could not outweigh her guilt. "I'm sorry, I really am!"

"You should be—this is your fault!"

"Stop it!" Jenna cried.

"Why, so you can go back to your cozy little bed and avoid any suffering?" She moved across the room, lugging her broken body towards Jenna. The scraping of her shoes along the floor made her cringe. "When will you care? When my coffin is open for you to visit?"

"Stop! I *do* care!" Jenna whimpered. "I didn't know you were left behind!"

Mrs. Wallace stopped in the center of the room. Jenna listened to the sound of blood dripping from her mangled body. "I think it's time to take away your twine, too."

Jenna looked up at her. Her teacher's remark was unnaturally unkind. It wasn't just inappropriate—it was perverse. And for Jenna, it was revealing.

It was time to end this charade. Jenna breathed in deeply. "It wasn't my fault! I didn't know that you had been left behind, or else I would've gone back for you!" Her fingers toiled with the vial inside her pocket.

"Liar!" Mrs. Wallace shouted.

"No—I'm not the liar here!" It hurt Jenna to think about her next move, but the act was necessary. She was sure that Mrs. Wallace's puppeteer was squatting inside of her.

Without waiting another minute, Jenna pulled out the vial and threw the bottle at her teacher. Quickly, she then ducked behind the large desk at the front of the room.

A spark-driven explosion filled the entire area, breaking all the windows and sending shards of glass rocketing in all directions. A giant black dust cloud coated the room as books soared through the air like missiles. Desks and chairs slammed up against the walls, knocking everything down in their path. Jenna couldn't believe the destruction that her little vial of poison had created. The only thing left untouched was the desk that she was hiding behind.

As the black cloud began to settle, she saw nothing in the form of Mrs. Wallace's body. But through the dust, she saw the black gown of Adella. Her grey, curling locks jostled in place as she searched the room.

Jenna was on to her; Adella was a shape shifter. And her plan to fool and attack Jenna in the history room while disguised as her former teacher had gone terribly askew. She'd fed on the guilt that Jenna had, after she'd left her teacher in the wake of the storm. But Jenna had exposed Adella for the monster that she was. The only problem was that the poison in the vial had no affect on Adella whatsoever, and now Jenna was left with one very powerful, angry witch.

Adella's look was fearsome. "You have something of mine," she said. She raised her arms towards Jenna. The desk in front of her slowly lifted off the ground, revealing her hiding spot. Then, with one quick arm motion, Adella thrust the desk against the side of the room. Jenna screamed as it smashed into pieces not far from where she was crouched. Now there was nothing standing in between them. And Jenna was frightened.

Adella raised her right hand. Against Jenna's will, she was brought to her feet. She could feel Adella's magic reaching out to her from across the room. Jenna's body then began to move towards her, and that's when she felt the first stinging sensation in her arm. Without touching her, Adella twisted her fingers and Jenna's arm rotated.

Jenna screamed out in agony, the pain was crippling.

A malevolent smile crept along Adella's face when she saw Jenna's pocket. She had a glazed look of pining in her eyes. "Yessss..."

Jenna braced her arm tightly as she begged the old woman to stop. "Please—I'll give you anything you want!" she wailed.

Adella cackled, loudly. The sound she made was devious which only heightened Jenna's fear—there was no escape for her. Another twist of Adella's wrist and fingers, and Jenna howled in pain. "Stop it—please!" she cried out in desperation.

The holes in her arm were now burning. She could barely stand and yet her body still moved. Now, only inches away from Adella's grasp, Jenna's death seemed imminent.

"Yes, you *will* give me what I want," Adella threatened her. Her green eyes flashed in the darkness.

Jenna sobbed and nodded to her. "Yes." There was no more fight left in her.

Jenna was within reach of the old woman's fingers when a sudden light at the door caused Adella to screech uncontrollably. Locklynn now stood at the entrance with his cane bolstered above him. A bright, golden light shot across the room, covering Adella completely.

The hold over Jenna dwindled and Adella backed away into a corner. The last thing she gave was a warning to Locklynn.

"I am not finished with you yet. Your soul will be mine, a truth that I bind myself to!" As she spoke, her body transformed into a black, ghostly shadow and disappeared through one of the shattered windows.

Jenna's legs buckled and she dropped to the floor like a fly. Locklynn's light faded as he lowered his cane. Seeing Jenna wounded on the ground, he immediately raced over to help her.

"Are you all right?" he said, bending down.

Jenna wiped away tears and then touched her arm gently. "It felt like Adella was breaking my arm. And the snake bite, it stung so much! I thought she was going to kill me, Locklynn."

Carefully, he helped Jenna to her feet. She wobbled for a moment but then regained her balance.

"How do you feel now?" he said.

"My arm really hurts." She wiped away another tear. "Locklynn—thank you for saving me! If you hadn't come in when you did—"

"It's done, Jenna. You are safe now," he assured her.

Jenna's strong foundation had been rocked to the core. Her emotions were scattered, her head was a mess. "I thought I could handle her, I thought I was strong enough. Adella's a stranger, I know that, but she's my relative. And she tortured me, Locklynn. She enjoyed it."

"Jenna, you must understand something," he said. "Adella is no longer of this world. She is a dark being, bound to evil. She may look human to you, but her earthly spirit departed quite some time ago. You must take all your feelings out of the equation if you plan to defeat her. She will not stop to save your life. That is the creature she has become."

Locklynn's words were harsh but Jenna was starting to believe them. Despite her genealogy, Adella wasn't part of their family. Not anymore. To Jenna, she never really was.

"You're right," she said. "But how do I stop her? Adella didn't even touch me and yet she had this power over me, I couldn't even control my own body."

Locklynn, being the wise teacher that he was, had the answer at his fingertips. "My dear, Jenna. Now that is something I can fix."

A CHANGE IS NECESSARY

"You're not going to slice me open again, are you?" Jenna said, with a hint of distress. "I mean, isn't there another way...a nicer, less harmful way to correct this problem?"

"The venom from the viper's bite has been expunged from your system, Jenna. But the wounds are still open and as long as they are, you will have to fight the evil power within yourself every time you're in the presence of the enemy. I cannot close the wounds but I can give you something that will help you to control your own power. Remember what I told you about the gift you possess?"

"Yes," Jenna said, looking down at her hands. She thought about the tiny gecko she'd brought back to life.

"In time, your skill will grow. But until then, I will loan you something."

Locklynn set down his cane and placed his arms above Jenna's. She felt the coolness of his hands and wondered if he was cold-blooded like a snake. Her eyes grew wide when a sparkling white light withdrew from his palms and transferred into hers. Each of Jenna's fingers hummed and glowed as her skin absorbed Locklynn's light.

"I have given you the Oakenstem. It will guide you in times of trouble," Locklynn said, retrieving his cane. "Part of me is now in you."

"The Oakenstem?" Jenna asked, feeling no change. "What's that?"

"It's the strength of the Blade Viper. It's what allows them to have dominion over their prey."

Hearing his answer didn't help clarify things, it only made it worse. "But you cut me open to get rid of what was inside me. And now you've put something back in?"

"I removed what was left of the poison, the infestation, the evil seeds that were growing inside of you," Locklynn explained. "And now I have given you a precious power, a strength that will fight to save your life."

Jenna saw the glimmer of tiny silver lines flowing like blood through her veins. She held up both hands in front of her face to take a closer look. Whatever Locklynn had given her, was starting to shimmer.

"It has never been joined with white magic. But I see a path of virtuosity and impressive might. In your hands, you will have control."

A new thrill took over. Like building blocks starting at the base, Jenna's body filled with a new and improved power. Bravery and certitude now oozed from inside of her as the pain in her arm disappeared. The beats from her heart were slowing but still she felt incredibly energized. In subtle ways, her body was changing. The Blade Viper's strength was merging with her own.

She raised her chin and saw Locklynn beaming with excitement. His attitude changed however when he saw the serious expression on her face. He turned away as if he knew what she was about to say.

"What happened to you?" she asked.

Locklynn started to clam up.

"Please tell me—I want to know!"

The air was thick with an uncomfortable silence.

With his back turned, Locklynn then spoke. "I was taken by the Sandshadow's servants, many moons ago. Captured against my will."

He stared at the classroom wall while Jenna waited for the rest of his story.

"Such evil forces had never been so lucky to harness the power of a Veliostriga. I was the first. They infiltrated my body, and filled my blood with theirs. I was to be a creation that they would control. My free will was stripped, as was my hope of escaping."

Jenna's heart broke just listening to him. "How did you get away?"

"Anzhara," he said, turning to face her. "Anzhara saved me."

It was all starting to come together. Anzhara had saved Locklynn from a life of purgatory. Anzhara was Jenna's grandmother in feline form. Jenna's grandmother was Adella's sister. And Adella was the sister who had summoned the Sandshadow, which had captured Locklynn. The story was coming around full circle.

As delicately as possible, Jenna summarized the situation. "That's why you're part Blade Viper."

"Yes. But not all of my troubles were troublesome. I learned many things while kept captive. Things that were not meant for my eyes."

"Like what?"

"The Sandshadow dwells in the desert. After he was freed from the constraints that bound him, he grew. And now his size can shift or change for hunting at any given time. Just like Adella. But still, the desert is where he waits."

"Why do you call the Sandshadow a *he*?" Jenna asked.

Locklynn sighed. "Because the monster was once a man."

"Oh—wow. I had no idea!"

"He was sentenced to the desert for a terrible crime and eventually became a shell of a man, living out his days in the sand with the desert vipers. But he did not wither. Instead, he grew into a beast, a monster unstoppable, until he broke free from his desert chains. Ultimately, he sought out those who thrived on dark magic. One day, he found a young girl lost in a forest and took her under his wing. They became unified as one, teacher and apprentice, with a love of black magic."

Jenna listened closely. "You're talking about Adella, aren't you?"

"Yes. Their powers were dangerous and eventually the girl fully succumbed to darkness. So the family combined their energy and magic, and stripped the Sandshadow of its power. They imprisoned it, sealed it away, to separate the monster from their daughter. But then something unexpected happened. They lost their daughter completely, to darkness. She disappeared from the family and never returned. Wherever she was, the hate inside her festered. And once she was grown, she was too powerful to stop. The reason she is here now, the reason she released the Sandshadow, is so they could retrieve the Mummy's talisman. That is their sole purpose."

"Adella told me that her family had cast her out, and I believed her. I'm such a fool."

"Adella, the woman, is gone. I'm afraid to say there's no saving her."

"I don't understand," Jenna said. "Where was she all these years?"

Locklynn didn't know. "Somewhere beyond the scope of man. A place where no one knew."

Something about Locklynn's answer triggered a memory. A thought. A description. As almighty as she seemed, Jenna couldn't shake the notion that Adella had a weakness somewhere. She began to pace in front of Locklynn. "You said that the Sandshadow and Adella were unified as one?"

"Yes," he said. "Inseparable."

"Then it's quite possible that when my family trapped him, they also trapped Adella, unknowingly."

Locklynn's interest was piqued. "Go on."

"And if Adella disappeared somewhere during the Sandshadow's absence, then maybe it was because her powers were bound. She might have been growing as a human, but if her magic was caged, then perhaps she was, too."

"Jenna—I think you might have discovered something valuable."

Jenna agreed. She then thought about the Sandshadow's recent release. "So, the question is—if they were both bound all these years, how did Adella get her powers back to release the Sandshadow?"

Jenna continued pacing. Again, something kept eating away at her. A memory. An object. A connection. *Twine!*

"It's the twine, Locklynn—the twine!" she said, triumphantly.

"The sisters three..." he said.

"Yes," Jenna smiled. "It's their connection. 'The twine is what binds us'—that was their childhood oath. I know how Adella freed her powers so that she could release the Sandshadow! She tapped into the other sisters' powers. It's their connection—their magic. Adella's feeding on it! That's why she's stronger than the other two."

Even though Alaina was no longer living, Jenna now understood the underlying issue of why she was here. As long as Adella was consuming her magic, Alaina would not be allowed eternal slumber. "Alaina's the answer. If we give her peace, then we take away their connection, and Adella's hold."

"She has the Sandshadow now, they will be hard to stop. Their kinship is tight." Locklynn's tone was grim as was the expression on his face. For the first time, he looked afraid. "And Adella will not let you release Alaina from this world. Not willingly."

Jenna felt more confident now. "Then we'll have to take away something else." Her fingers touched the ruby inside her pocket. "You said that the Sandshadow is waiting in the desert?"

"Yes, he is both strong and weak there."

"Weak?" Jenna repeated.

Locklynn nodded.

"You know his Achille's heel, don't you?"

"Yessss..." Locklynn hissed.

There wasn't a pinch of doubt that Lockynn wanted revenge for what the Sandshadow had done to him. In the last few minutes, Jenna had watched his emotions range dramatically, from elated to fearful, from solemn to duplicitous. But with the topic of vengeance looming, she knew he would be wizardly-wise and ready to avenge his past.

Thinking only of Locklynn and herself, Jenna hadn't realized until now that their third party was absent.

"Where's Jason?" she asked.

"The circumstances changed; he wasn't safe here. I had to place him elsewhere."

"What do you mean? Where is he?"

"He's safe and out of harm's way. He wanted to run in and help you but I couldn't let him do that. So, I sent him somewhere."

Jenna frowned. "Locklynn—where did you put him?"

"Teek is protecting him," he smiled.

"Locklynn! He's back in the cave? Oh, man, is he gonna be mad!" Jenna began to fidget. "Wait—what do you mean by 'placed'?"

"Well, I had to restrain him first before moving him." Locklynn showed no remorse.

Jenna dropped her head into her hands. "Jesus, Locklynn—you can't just keep freezing people!"

She looked up as he touched her arm. "You mustn't think of that now. Your friend is in a safe place and that is all that matters. I will have him join us when the time is necessary. But you must understand that the Sandshadow will not hesitate to use him as a pawn. How will you fight then, when your friend's life is in danger?"

Jenna hadn't thought of that. "You're right, I'm sorry."

"Allies are wonderful, but can also be used as weapons. That is one war you do not want. Your friend is safe. Yes, we will need him, but until that time comes, his absence will keep us all safe."

"Okay, I get it. So, what do we do now?" Jenna said.

"First, we search for answers. Then, we will turn to an old friend."

"And where do we search for answers?"

"Look around," Locklynn said. "What you need is right in front of you."

PAPER TRAIL

"You're saying that there are clues hidden in this room somewhere?" Jenna said. She surveyed the damage.

"Hidden, maybe, but in plain sight also. Watch carefully." With a tap of Locklynn's cane, everything slowly came back together. Toppled desks and chairs were restored to their proper form as every shard of broken glass simultaneously lifted into the air and then returned to the windows from which they came from. Pencils, papers, chalk and rulers—everything in the room reverted to its original configuration.

Jenna stood in awe of Locklynn's remodeling. "That's amazing!"

Locklynn said nothing as he began to walk around the room. He was focused on the walls.

Jenna went to the front of the room and began rummaging through Mrs. Wallace's desk. She looked up when Locklynn stopped beside one of the walls.

"Here," he said. "Something's missing. I feel that whatever was here at another time was deliberately removed."

The wall had nothing other than a banner on it, advertising a time capsule.

"Another time?" Jenna said. She placed the books and sheets of paper that were in her hands down on the desk and walked over to him.

Locklynn was eyeing the wall with great scrutiny. He raised his cane to show Jenna. "I fear that this emptiness is what we are searching for."

"Are you talking about the newspaper clippings from the classroom I saw in 1939? Alaina's school in Salem?"

"Yes," he said, scratching his chin.

Jenna tried to remember the placement of articles on the wall Locklynn was referring to. The papers weren't placed in chronological order, nor were they grouped together by topic. "There was no order to them," she said. "So let's do multiple choice."

Locklynn wrinkled his brow. "I don't understand."

"It's a test. Multiple choice—process of elimination." Jenna closed her eyes.

Moments went by as she mentally reviewed the headlines and pictures in her head. And then it came to her. "I know which one it is." She looked around the room. Fixated on the desk in the corner, she hurried past all the others to get to it.

Locklynn followed closely behind. "What is it you've found?"

Arriving at the desk, Jenna bent down and reached inside of it. "I have no idea if this is even possible—but if this room is capable of a time warp, then maybe at one point there was a crossover." Her fingers came across something flimsy and thin.

"This is what we're looking for," she said, pulling out a piece of newsprint. She then held it up for Locklynn to see. *'Community Mourns Life of Child'*, it read.

He took the paper from her. "This is it! How did you know?"

Jenna smiled with satisfaction. "This was the desk that Alaina was sitting at when I looked in."

"Well done," Locklynn said. "A lesson learned. There is wisdom in you."

Jenna was humbled by his remark. "Thank you." She looked at the picture that accompanied the newsprint. "Hold on—I know that picture."

"Yes?" Locklynn said.

"I've seen it before, but not here."

"Where did you see it?" he asked.

Jenna grinned. "Home."

PICTURE PERFECT

Travelling with Locklynn was akin to running a race at speeds no one could rival. With the tap of his cane or the snap of his fingers, he could transport anyone or anything from one place to another.

Jenna was now standing in a new place that Locklynn had brought them both to. She was alone in one of the bedrooms of her house, admiring the jewels, ornaments and other such trinkets that surrounded her. The room wasn't hers, but it was one that she needed to visit.

Jenna saw the rocking chair in the corner and pictured her grandmother sitting in it, telling stories before bedtime. It was a magical room, filled with adventure and mystery. The tribal masks along the walls and ancient artifacts poised on the dresser would attest to that. This room was dynamic. It belonged to her grandmother.

Locklynn had transported them to Jenna's house. While she was searching inside, he waited outside near the cornfield, hidden safely out of view. Jenna's parents were next door at the clinic, tending to the overnight animals. The light was on and they were busy working.

The house was lit when Jenna had appeared inside the kitchen, but there wasn't a noise to be heard. All the pets were asleep for the night. Luckily, she hadn't wakened them. She'd tiptoed upstairs to her grandmother's room, going past her own without any thought. And now she stood looking down at the floorboards. What lay beneath them was what drove her there. Stored safely beneath the wood was possibly the next clue to the puzzle.

Jenna knelt down and removed the board. She saw the glass box and smiled. She was happy that no one else had taken it. She lifted the box out of its spot and opened the lid. Going through the contents, she came upon the object that she needed. It was a picture of Alaina. Flipping it over, Jenna read what was written on the back. '*August 1939. Night at the theatre, The Wizard of Oz.*'

Jenna removed the newspaper clipping from her pocket. Sure enough, it was the same picture the newspaper had used for the article.

Her favourite movie, Jenna remembered. *The ruby red slippers.* She read the date again and realized that the picture had been taken only a few months before Alaina's death. It saddened Jenna to think of how her life had been cut short. She would have loved having her in the family. As her focus returned to the inscription, she noticed something else that was written below it. A spell.

> *'Of wing and water, of crystal bite,*
> *To be as one beneath the night*
> *From blood comes Earth,*
> *From jewel to stone,*
> *May the hands of time*
> *Move body to bone.*
> *Nosce te ipsum'*

Written in Latin, Jenna had to translate the last few words. "Know thyself." She then noticed a small glass bottle inside the box. Picking it up, she rotated it beneath the ceiling light. It was filled with a milky white liquid, tiny white seeds, and red-coloured berries. Taped to the bottom was a tiny piece of paper with the words, 'Nosce te ipsum', same as what was written on the photograph.

Acknowledging the correlation, Jenna placed the bottle in another pocket. Her clothes were quickly becoming a sanctuary for all things magical. She closed the box, returned it to the hole and placed the boards back on top.

As she stood, she caught a glimpse of her reflection in the small mirror above her grandmother's dresser. Something was different.

A noise downstairs made her look towards the door, however. It sounded like someone was in the kitchen. She didn't want anyone to know that she was home, so as quietly as possible, she crept over to the mirror. She just about screamed when she saw the length of her canine teeth. They had grown about half an inch, making them noticeably longer than her other teeth.

"Oh no!" She held her mouth open and stared in surprise. She was frightened by her own face.

"Jenna—" a voice appeared by the bedroom door.

"Mom?" Jenna closed her mouth and covered it with one hand as she turned in a panic.

"Jenna, that *is* you. I thought I heard someone up here. Where have you been? You left hours ago with Jason."

"Um…well…we hung out and watched a movie but then we got bored. So we walked home. I thought I'd come up here and see if Grandma was around."

Her mother smiled. "Grandma's not here, she's out with some friends. I thought you knew that. You've been away all day, you should've called. Your father and I were worried."

"I'm sorry, Mom. I guess I just let the time go by." Sweat was starting to drip down her face; she could feel the droplets as they slid.

"Jenna, you've been acting very strange these last few days and it's understandable, considering what you've been through. But your father and I think that you should stay home and rest for a while. Take it easy. It would be better for you."

"I can't." Jenna spoke through her fingers. "Besides, I feel fine. Never better." Jenna did her best to improvise, but she wasn't good at lying.

"Why are you talking like that? Are you hurt?" She walked over to where Jenna was standing.

"NO!" Jenna yelled as her mother closed in. "Don't look at me—I'm hideous!"

"Jenna!" She moved her daughter's hand away. "What is going on?"

Jenna recoiled, ashamed of what she looked like. "I can explain—"

"Explain what? Geez, you scared me, I thought something was really wrong."

Her mother's relief was perplexing. Jenna wondered why her reaction was so relaxed. With a brief turn towards the mirror, she sighed. Her teeth had returned to their normal length.

"What's that you've got in your hand? Is that one of your grandmother's pictures?" Her mother took the photograph from her.

Jenna tried to come up with a plausible answer for going through her grandmother's items. "Grandma said I could look at it. It was her—"

"Sister. I know. She showed me this once."

"You know? How come you didn't tell me about her?" Jenna said.

"There isn't much to tell you. Your grandmother's very private about it."

Jenna didn't want the conversation to end, but seeing as her face was changing and that Locklynn was waiting outside, she had to go. Her mother wouldn't understand anyway. The world of magic had been closed off to her.

"Mom—I have to go."

"But I made dinner…"

"I'll have some when I get back, I promise." She headed for the bedroom door.

"Jenna—stop! Where are you going? It's eleven o'clock at night."

"It is?" Jenna couldn't believe how the time had flown. "I'm just going out to the field. I want to be alone for a while, get some fresh air."

As she neared the door, her mother said, "I don't want you to go. I'm putting my foot down, I want you home tonight. You *need* to stay home tonight."

The comment made Jenna stop dead in her tracks. It wasn't what her mother said that irked her, it was how she said it.

"You know, there are some things you just can't forget," her mother said. "Powers may have been stripped, ties may have been dissolved, but some memories are too strong to erase." Her mother was not acting normal.

"Mom—what's my middle name?"

She looked befuddled. "What?"

"What's my middle name? Tell me!"

"It's Jean…why?"

For a moment, Jenna had thought that Adella was back in the house. Her stomach settled when she realized that that was not the case. On the other hand, it was now clear that a secret had been revealed.

"Some things linger, you see, even though they're not supposed to. So, you pretend. That way, no one asks."

"Mom…what are you saying?"

"I'm saying that I want you home tonight. It's safer."

Jenna was floored. "You mean—you *know?*"

Her mother nodded.

"I don't believe it! Adella said that you wouldn't remember anything."

"Adella is not part of this family anymore, she has chosen the path of black magic. She is dangerous and unwelcome here."

Jenna looked at the clock on the wall. "Mom—you understand then. I have to go. You have to stay here and take care of Dad."

Her mother crossed her arms and shook her head. "I know you think you have to, but I can't let you."

Jenna didn't want to argue, nor did she have time to. "This isn't your choice, Mom. It's mine." She then walked out into the hallway.

Heading into her own bedroom, Jenna quickly gathered some things. She found her backpack sitting in the corner and placed a flashlight and her grandmother's glass bottle inside of it. The jewel Alaina had given her remained safely stashed in the pocket of her jeans.

Her mother entered the room as Jenna took off her jacket and threw it on the bed. "Jenna—you can't leave like this."

Seeing the photograph still clutched in her mother's hand made her hesitate. But then she grabbed a sweater from the dresser and threw the backpack over her shoulder.

"Jenna—you can't go. There's nothing out there but danger. I worry for your safety. You're my daughter! Please listen to me!"

Jenna spun around to face her. "Mom, you know I wouldn't be going if I didn't have to. I'm going to put an end to this family feud. Alaina needs to be at peace. Don't you want her to have that? And Grandma's out there—she needs my help! This monster needs to be stopped and I'm going do it!"

"Jenna—listen to yourself! You sound crazy!"

"I'm not crazy, Mom. This has to be done!"

Her mother grabbed her arm as she tried to leave the room. "I won't let you go, Jenna!"

"You can't stop me," she said, pulling her arm away. "And you don't want to, trust me." Without giving her a chance to respond, Jenna hurried out of the room and ran down the stairs to the kitchen. Behind her, she could hear her mother following.

"Jenna—come back!"

Jenna snatched some granola bars off the counter, then shoved everything into the backpack and raced for the door. She stopped when she saw her mother standing in front of it.

"You can't leave. If you do then you won't come back!" she cried.

Jenna shuddered at the statement. "What do you mean?"

"I've seen what happens. Your future starts and ends in the desert. You won't come home!" Her eyes were glazed with tears.

"Mom—that's impossible! That's not going to happen. I have Grandma and Anzhara on my side. And Locklynn. And Alaina. Mom—I have the power of the Blade Viper inside of me."

Her mother's expression changed immediately. "Blade Viper? How did you get that?" She was stunned by the revelation.

"I have my secrets, too." Jenna pushed past her and opened the door. This time her mother didn't try to stop her.

Jenna saw the light still on in the clinic. She wanted so much to say good-bye to her father but knew that his suspicions would be raised, which would only put him in harm's way. "Please don't tell Dad. He can never know."

Through one of the windows, she saw him tending to a sick Collie. He was the kindest man, and Jenna only wanted to protect him. She whispered good-bye with a tear in her eye and looked back at her mother. "I *will* be back, I promise!"

SHADOW OF THE NIGHT

A strike of lightning powered through the darkness, as Jenna ventured off towards the cornfield. The moon above was hidden behind a strange hand-shaped cloud—appearing like fingers that were blinding it. With the moon covered, the ground was dark; it looked like a roving abyss. Jenna felt comfortable, safe in the night. Not one part of her craved the daylight now. Lightning stemmed from somewhere beyond the cornfield but Jenna wasn't bothered, nor worried. She welcomed the darkness and all that went with it.

She pulled the flashlight out of the backpack and shone it towards the stalks. In the blackness she couldn't see Locklynn anywhere in the yard. As she approached the stalks, a sudden rustling of leaves came from behind them. A hushed voice soon emerged from the field. Jenna listened carefully. Every sound around her was heightened, from the gentle breeze to the motion of the leaves. She heard everything in all directions.

She called out for Locklynn. Seconds later, he stepped out of the field several feet from where she was standing.

"Here!" he yelled, while waving his cane. "Follow me!"

Jenna ran over to where he was standing. "Why here?"

"No reason at the moment. Just a quieter path than the one already taken."

"It's all the same—we're going to the desert."

"Yes, but I've found a less-travelled way. With Adella watching, we need to be wise."

"Hey, why can't you just snap your fingers and take us there?"

Locklynn angled his head in that special teacher's way that made Jenna wish she hadn't asked the question. "This place is sacred, my dear. To appreciate that, you must travel through it. A step-foot journey is just what you need. So, come now, follow me. I know the way."

"All right." Jenna stepped through the first row of corn. The apprehension she'd felt before was gone. She was happy now to be in the field; she felt as if she belonged there amongst the earth and greens. Even more so, she wanted to kneel down and touch the coolness of the ground. Part of her wanted to crawl on it. Keeping on her feet was almost a task in itself. But she could hear Locklynn ahead of her moving away and so she kept to the plan and followed behind.

*****

They'd been walking for nearly twenty minutes, discussing the Sandshadow's origin and history, when Jenna got a hankering for some food. Her stomach growled at her and so she stopped to grab a granola bar from her backpack.

The clouds began to part from the sky, allowing the brightness of the moon to shine down. The night was beautiful, and now quiet. As Jenna rummaged through her backpack, something moved by her feet. She didn't see it, she sensed it.

Suddenly, the granola bar in her hand didn't seem nearly as appetizing. She dropped the snack and sniffed the air where she was standing. Whatever it was, was warm-bodied. It wasn't large in size, it was small. Jenna could feel the heat emanating from it. It was a mouse.

From her vantage point, the animal had an orangey-red glow around it, which made it all the more enticing. An unprecedented feeling began to take over; Jenna wanted to capture the mouse. Its hide was now appealing to her.

"You must stay on track," Locklynn said, appearing in front of her. "The Blade Viper inside of you is getting stronger but you mustn't let it take over."

Coming out of her daze, Jenna realized how she was acting. She felt somewhat ashamed. "I feel so strange, like something's burning inside of me."

"Stay in control, Jenna," was all Locklynn said.

She understood what he meant, and he was absolutely right. No wonder he was a Power Shepherd. His calling was perfectly suited to him.

He gave a noble nod and then motioned for her to follow as he moved briskly through the stalks.

Jenna did her best to leave the mouse behind, although it was difficult since it looked so delicious.

Locklynn watched her carefully. "Jenna, come now," he said.

She did as he asked. Together, beneath the light of the nearly full moon, they walked through the field in silence. Neither said a word. Both were focused, both were driven. Locklynn's thirst for vengeance led the way as Jenna's desire for a family truce followed closely behind. United by a common enemy, the shepherd led his faithful flock of one into the realm of darkness.

DREAMS BE TOLD

"I sense a shift," Locklynn whispered from a few feet ahead.

"Hopefully a good one," Jenna said. With each step, she became more impatient. A seed of indignation had sprouted inside of her. She was angered at the predicament they were in. Locklynn hadn't let her eat or talk or do much of anything. She was needed but not needed now. *This is probably how Jason feels*, she thought. But then she remembered how he was frozen in captivity.

Judging by what Locklynn had said, something up ahead was different. *Finally*, she thought. *We're almost there!* She walked up and stood alongside him.

"Notice anything?" he said, bending down to feel the soil.

Jenna's eyes looked around but her head didn't budge. "The air smells sweet like cherries."

Locklynn didn't seem happy about her answer. "No, not cherries."

"Don't you smell it, too?" she said. "It's beautiful. It reminds me of Jasmine and cherries. I know that scent—I remember Grandma making a tea like that." She took a few steps in the opposite direction from which they'd been travelling.

Locklynn stood quickly and ran in front of her. "Look at me."

Jenna stopped and stared off into the distance. Her head felt light, airy. "I think I see something."

"Jenna—fight the lure!" he said.

She didn't know what that meant. Seconds later, she didn't care. Two tiny patches of white clouds formed over her eyes, covering both irises completely.

Locklynn waved his hands in front of her but they were invisible to Jenna.

"I think I see something," she said again. Her voice was robotic.

There was nothing Locklynn could do. Jenna was in a trance. With every sensory organ on alert, he watched over her as she slipped into a standing coma.

Inside Jenna's head, she was witnessing what looked like a scene from a movie. It was similar to the last one she saw in the cornfield but the players and setting were different.

She saw herself this time, walking in the desert with a large animal by her side. It was Anzhara. Locklynn was behind her and so was Jason. The ground was lit by the moon. The mass of white sand around her was flat and level, but in the distance, Jenna could see dunes rising up. The landscape was enormous; she felt incredibly small just looking at it.

She knew the area well enough. It was the desert she had walked through to get to the sapphire pyramid. But in this scene, the pyramid was gone. It was nowhere in sight. And the dunes were new; Jenna hadn't seen them before. Being as large as they were, she would've remembered them.

The setting was ghostly; the tension was building. Jenna could feel it. With most of the players in place, she wondered where all the villains were. When she glanced around, all she saw was sand. Her friends were now gone, no one accompanied her. Alone in the desert was not a scenario that she liked. She felt vulnerable, exposed and utterly defenseless.

What sounded like a wild animal charging was actually a rush of wind moving through the night. The Sandshadow was on its way. The vision showed Jenna trying to escape but all she could do was stand in place, stuck to the ground. Every limb went numb as the Sandshadow approached. Jenna saw the hooded reptiles squirming inside the monster's mouth. But before they sprang, Jenna heard a familiar voice behind her, which made her turn.

Her mother reached out to touch her but as she did, the snakes broke free from their master and lurched to the ground. As a team, they slithered around her mother to form a tight circle.

Inch by inch, they closed in. Jenna watched from outside the perimeter of snakes, but did nothing to stop their hunt.

The Sandshadow hovered above Jenna, protecting her like a parent or guardian. She was now its disciple. The snakes then opened one end of the circle, leaving a space for Jenna to enter. She understood what they were asking her to do.

Under the command of the enemy, Jenna made her way past the snakes until she was standing directly in front of her mother. She could see her mother's blood pulsing beneath her skin. It was intoxicating. With each beat, Jenna's fangs grew. In the time it took to blink, she lunged at her mother, and with one vicious strike she sank her teeth into her neck.

Her mother's head fell backwards and her body dropped to the ground. Jenna stared without regret. She was pleased with her kill. And so was the Sandshadow.

The group of snakes was no longer menacing; Jenna had become one of them. Standing over her mother's body, she noticed something lying in her hand. A mess of broken glass lay shattered in her palm. Glass, from a bottle.

The vipers hissed and retreated from where Jenna was standing. She wondered why they were acting so strange. Looking at her hands, it became clear. She screamed when she saw her own skin dissolving and blowing away in the wind. From her chest came a sizzling sensation as something blistered and seared from within. The pain was horrific.

When she saw the front of her sweater covered in a smoky white residue, she realized that she had been poisoned.

A timid chirping appeared by her feet. Jenna looked down, wondering what it was. Sitting on the ground beside her was a small grasshopper; similar to the one she had seen in her backyard, the night she was attacked. Its emerald colour stood out amongst the white sand. It was definitely out of place. It sat watching her while rubbing its front legs together.

"I know you," Jenna said, staring at the little animal. Her lips crumbled as she spoke. Time seemed to slow down as her body gradually wasted away.

"Direction is time," the grasshopper said. As its legs moved back and forth, everything came to a stop. The scene she had just been part of began to move in reverse. The skin on her body slowly regenerated as the cloud of white smoke diminished from around her. All the snakes returned to form the ring around Jenna and her mother. The shattered pieces of the broken bottle reconnected as Jenna's mother rose from the ground with the intact bottle in her hand.

The scene rewound itself moment by moment until Jenna was left standing alone in the desert. The grasshopper faded out of view, as did everything else. It was then that she heard her name being called. Closing her eyes, she focused on the voice of the caller.

The two clouds of film lifted from Jenna's eyes and she was left with a feeling of bewilderment. Looking straight ahead, she saw Locklynn speaking to her.

"Jenna!" he cried.

Coming out of her trance, her eyes bounced all over. "Where am I?"

"You're in the cornfield, Jenna, you're safe. I sent Sinnicks to retrieve you."

Still slightly dazed, she rubbed her eyes. "Who's Sinnicks?"

Inside Locklynn's hand, was something small and green. He opened it for Jenna to see.

Her eyes lit up when she saw the grasshopper. "*You're* Sinnicks? You belong to Locklynn?"

"Yes," Locklynn said. "I sent him after you. The Sandshadow was tapping into your mind."

Jenna reached out to touch Sinnicks. "I didn't think you were real. Wait a minute—I saw Alaina holding him at the school when they found Mrs. Wallace. You helped save her," she smiled.

"Sinnicks is a Time-teller; a clock of valuable knowledge," Locklynn said, petting him softly. "He has the power to reverse time."

Jenna pulled back her hand. Sinnicks had warned her about the enemy in the backyard the night she was attacked. Small but strong, he was wise beyond his size.

Thinking back, Jenna now recalled what had happened. She remembered a light rushing upon her, and then the terrifying sounds of bullets mixed with the chimes of a grandfather clock.

Jenna had raised her hands up to protect herself against the intruding light. The sounds of a snake hissing and tearing through her palms now made her grimace. She remembered everything, but at the time of the attack her memory was lost. She had later woken up in the hospital, completely disoriented. But after her grandmother had arrived, the haze that had blocked her progression was cleared from her system just as an evil shadow was chased from her room. Her grandmother was not only her guardian angel but was also the key to her miraculous recovery.

Jenna now stared at her hands; not a single mark from her assailant's assault was visible from that night. Not even a scratch. Her grandmother's magic had indeed healed her. But now there was a different threat; a war was waging inside of Jenna. Gently, she touched the holes on her arm.

"I saw what they wanted me to do, Locklynn. They want me to take my mother's life," Jenna's voice trembled. "They can't make me do that—I won't!"

"That is why I sent Sinnicks after you, to stop that from happening. To reverse the lure. You were drawn into a vision that would have kept you from returning."

Jenna didn't understand. What made sense to Locklynn seemed like nonsense to her. "Locklynn—please promise me that I won't hurt her!"

Locklynn nodded. "I will stop you before that happens."

Jenna's mood changed. She hissed at him, angrily. "Because my mother might not be the only one I want to hurt."

It seemed as though the roles had undergone a reversal. Jenna was not to be trusted, and Locklynn was now the gauge for purity.

Locklynn raised his cane and shone a light on top of her. "I will not let you hurt anyone."

Jenna ducked down, hiding beneath her arms. Like a toad, she squatted on the ground, quivering from the light. "Get that away from me—it's hurting my eyes!"

"I will not allow you to endanger the life of yourself or others—is that understood?" Locklynn commanded.

Jenna nodded several times.

"Very well," he said, lowering the cane. The light dimmed and his voice softened. "I will help you, Jenna. But with the power of the Blade Viper inside of you, you cannot trust me alone to save you. You have to be strong."

Jenna cowered beneath the cornstalks. Looking down at the earth, she simpered. "I will try to be good, but I'm afraid of what's happening to me, Locklynn."

"Look around you," he said.

Jenna gazed up and saw the long, green leaves from the stalks dangling above her. In her state of disarray, they looked almost sympathetic. Each leaf appeared like an appendage, reaching out to her with kindness.

"The field wants to help you," Locklynn said, pointing his cane towards them. Each cornstalk bowed to his cane. "You have friends here."

Jenna was amazed by what she saw. The field looked alive with Locklynn near it, and it painted a completely different picture for her. She didn't know what to say.

"Trust in those around you, my dear, and you will see change."

Jenna sighed. This burden she carried was weighing heavily on both her mind and body. The transformation into enemy physicality was draining the life from her. The holes had not healed and now Locklynn had empowered her with the strength of the Oakenstem to overcome the enemy's control. Was she strong enough to carry them both? Jenna wondered that now.

"I'm sorry, Locklynn, it's just so hard to fight. I feel the thrill of predation seeping through my veins but I don't want to hurt anyone. I really don't."

"I know," he said, helping her up.

Jenna knew that he understood. He was fighting the same battle inside.

He rested his cane against one of the cornstalks and pulled down his collar so that she could see his neck. The markings on his skin mirrored the ones on her arm. She empathized with him. The holes of the invader were Locklynn's branding, and now hers as well. But what Jenna found to be most amazing, was the extent of his resilience. Locklynn was able to overcome the Sandshadow's dominion.

"How did you do it? How did you conquer their power?"

"The Blade Viper may be strong, Jenna, but it wasn't there first. I am a Veliostriga at heart. Understanding that, led me to freedom. You are not a servant unless you allow them to take you. Remember who you truly are, then fight the evil with everything you have! Do you understand?"

She looked at the grasshopper sitting in his hand. "I think so."

"Then tell me, what else did your vision show you?" Locklynn asked.

"I saw a bottle in my mother's hand. It was poison. She crushed it against me and all I could feel was burning. My skin crumbled like ashes from a fire."

"Was your mother dead or alive?" he said.

That part made Jenna sick. "Why does that matter? It was horrible!"

"Listen to me, things are not always as they seem, my dear," he said, stroking Sinnicks.

"Dead—she was dead," Jenna answered.

"But not completely, I think." Locklynn's tone was indecipherable. It sounded hopeful yet displeasing. It struck Jenna in an ill-mannered kind of way.

"But that's not going to happen!" she said. "Neither one of us will let that happen!"

"Of course," he said. "There are ways around everything. But I believe that this bridge would be best crossed if we took preventative steps."

"Locklynn—speak English, please!"

"Something we've already seen holds the answer to your future demise."

"You're talking about the poison in my mother's hand?"

"Yes." The way he spoke made Jenna think that he already had an answer.

"Wait a minute…" She took the backpack off her shoulders and placed it on the ground. Leaning over, she opened the bag and searched for her grandmother's bottle. Finding it, she took it out and examined the cloudy white liquid. Carefully, she removed the lid. Her senses went into overdrive when a familiar smell crawled up her nose. She sneezed several times and then quickly placed the lid back on, making sure that it was tightly sealed.

"Frosted Hawthorn," she said.

"Yes, Alaina was buried with it," Locklynn added.

Jenna wiped her nose with the cuff of her sweater as she tried to fight off another round of sneezes. "Grandma told me that they had placed a bouquet with her body. She was holding it at the school after the tornado had hit. Was it for protection against the Sandshadow?"

"Yes—but only for the vipers. Hawthorn is pure poison to them, which makes us both vulnerable," he said.

"Okay, so neither of us are going to touch it." Jenna stared at the bottle. It was intriguing but repulsive at the same time. Promptly, she returned it to the bag.

"Hawthorn will not destroy the Sandshadow, though. There is only one thing that will do that. Up and down, to and fro, here and there some will go."

Jenna stroked the grasshopper's back as it sat in Locklynn's palm. Its large, oval eyes watched her as she solved the riddle. "It's time, isn't it? And reversal of fortune."

Locklynn smiled. "You're learning fast, my dear."

Thinking of all dimensions, past, present and future, Jenna pulled out the photograph of Alaina. "If time is Sinnicks' specialty, then keep him close, we might need him." Her thoughts then wandered to the ruby resting in her pocket, and slowly a plan began to materialize. Jenna was starting to see a clear-cut future path ahead of her. "Get everyone, actually. We're gonna need all the help we can get!"

KEEPERS FINDERS

Jenna was on a mission. Her pace was steadfast and her footing was firm. Locklynn was now letting her lead. She had learned something from him, another valuable lesson. They were more alike than she had thought and it was a turning point in their relationship.

Together they moved through the field in the direction of the wind. Both wanted closure, but also an ending that would reap the most benefit. And that meant one thing—defeating the Sandshadow. In doing so, it would eliminate the Blade Vipers and take control away from Adella, or at least that's what she was hoping. If they acted quickly enough, they could bind Adella's powers and send her to a place where she could never harm another being.

The solution was to give everyone what they wanted—the Mummy's talisman. The Sandshadow, Adella, the Blade Vipers—they all wanted the talisman. They needed it. But the only one who truly deserved it, was King Odon.

A monumental event that had fallen from the pages of time had once again been brought to Jenna's attention. She recalled the story of the ancient city of Menao in the land of Siam. Both Locklynn and her grandmother had described their versions of the story. Jenna simply had to piece them together.

There sat a magnificent temple. Built to worship the King of the Cats, people would walk miles to honour the feline God known as King Odon. His temple was designed as a pyramid and cut from the deepest blue sapphire. Inside, an enormous statue of King Odon was erected. Mummified corpses were placed throughout the temple as each one held an amber globe to signify their eternal patronage. Inside such hallowed grounds, only those pure of heart were allowed to enter.

Surrounding the city, were King Odon's most powerful feline servants. Nine massive Siamese cats, each slightly larger than a lion, sat protectively around the city's borders. As guardians of Menao, each wore a ruby medallion around its neck that prevented evil from entering. Known as the Stars of Omandai, these rubies held the power of King Odon. Forces of good magic protected the medallions, which in turn protected the city. Neither the cats nor their jewels were to be touched. By anyone.

A white spell was placed on the guardians. Any thief who dared touch a temple cat or its ruby, would endure an afterlife plagued with disease and pain. Their lives would be spent bound in white linens. Tightly constricted. Inescapable.

King Odon's power was not without weakness, however. If one of the rubies were to be taken, the city would be left vulnerable to the evils of dark magic, a fate worse than demise. And only those who worshipped such magic could overtake the guardians of Menao, although none had ever tried.

But on a night that seemed so innocent, the fate of Menao changed forever.

Shadows entered the city.

In an act of vicious greed, one of King Odon's cats was stolen. It took four thieves to capture the animal. The cat fought fiercely to free itself but one of the thieves had power beyond its own. A corruption seeded with evil roots put the animal in a slumbering state. Once the ruby was removed from its neck, the city was doomed at the hands of the intruder. The temple, being the protective conduit between the cat and the city, felt the immediate loss of its guardian. The eight remaining temple cats were turned to stone by incantations read by King Odon's human servants. Their ruby talismans were sealed to their bodies, never to be separated. The cats were wrapped in royal cloth, then separated and taken to different ends of the Earth, their locations never to be disclosed.

With the loss of the first temple cat, black magic infiltrated Menao. Destruction was thrust upon King Odon and the city fell into ruins. Its walls collapsed beneath the weight of such unearthly oppression.

Earthquakes swallowed the land, and the people of Menao were lost to the world.

But before his temple disappeared out of sight, King Odon placed all of his remaining retribution onto the thieves who escaped with his royal cat. His wrath was momentous. Already cursed as they were for stealing the guardian, he forced the destructors to live out their remaining days blind in the sand. The ruby became invisible to them as their vision disappeared. In the desert, they would find no peace, no reward for their act. Water would be their only jewel.

Death came to three of them, at the hands of one of their own. Powerfully dangerous and tormented by crazed intentions, the last standing culprit had severed ties with his thieving brotherhood and ended their suffering in the sands. Unfazed by his own actions, he grew even stronger, wilder in spirit in the absence of life. Solitude brought him nothing but delirium. But still, he survived. He learned to live off the desert in ways that no others could.

As the years passed, he learned to follow the wind. He listened to it, breathed it in, until he, too, found ways to harness it. It became his shield, his shrouded weapon—his natural connection to a world that was now unfamiliar.

Life and death walked next to him as he scourged the land for food. Although blinded, he began to track the movements of the desert viper. Each muscle, each rib, each bone that flowed through the sands, he could sense. He studied the snakes with all that he had until his own strength and power soon overcame them. He hunted without sight and fought many vipers. Each battle had ended in a bloody triumph. He had endured their poison, and the bite did not kill him. Their venom soon became his sustenance; their bodies sustained him through time.

With such little life around him, he became a creature unknown to himself. A cross between King Odon's curse and the blood of the viper, he turned into something unrecognizable. Night and day became one. Time became irrelevant. Enslaved to the sands of which he was imprisoned, the creature became a monster.

The city of Menao became a story, a legend by all accounts. Only one element of the destruction survived—the temple cats, eight of which were never found. The stolen cat was unearthed in 1909 by two archeologists on an expedition in Luxor, Egypt. Its body was found mummified and buried near the Valley of the Kings. Not much was known about the animal as none had survived the devastation of Menao. It was in all respects, a lost city.

It wasn't until the mummified cat went on display for a world tour, that certain events were set into motion. From London to Paris, Jakarta to Rome, the cat remained dormant in slumber. But when the animal reached the shores of North America, something began to stir. It travelled across the States, from city to city. Every place it stopped, people from far and wide would come to see it.

When it arrived at the Lionhead Museum in Wichita, Kansas, lost stories began to surface. Whispers were heard around the city. Tales were told. And the Mummy, whose dormancy had been so quiet, rose from its linen grave to begin its hunt and punish all those who stood in its way.

A young woman who lived on a cornfield, not far from the museum, was unknowingly drawn into the plot. Through fear and isolation, she was enlisted to help find the Mummy's talisman, if only to the end the terrible curse it had inflicted on her city. But Jenna Matthews had found the talisman and in doing so, had changed the paths of all those around her, although they did not know it.

Little did Jenna know just how much she had changed the fate of the Mummy's future, as well as her own.

Jenna felt the ruby now pressing against her pant leg as she brushed past the leaves in the cornfield. A smile spread across her face. A sense of victory was now at hand. The idea of her returning the ruby to its rightful place was not that outlandish. In fact, it was achievable. And more than that, it was necessary.

Walking ahead of Locklynn, she saw something peculiar beneath the ground.

"What is it?" Locklynn said from behind.

"I don't know. I think it's an animal underground." A greenish-blue outline appeared around the animal as it scurried beneath the soil. It was long with a thin, tapered body. "That's weird, there's no orangey-red outline around it like the mouse."

Locklynn passed by her, immediately. "Do not follow it!"

Jenna didn't want to. It wasn't as appealing as the mouse. It didn't have a warm, juicy, tantalizing hide.

Locklynn lifted his cane in front of her. "I feel a trap. Whatever is underfoot, is not warm-bodied."

"You mean it's cold-blooded, like a snake?" She took a step forward.

"No, Jenna. The enemy is near, I can sense it."

Jenna watched the ground closely. The greenish-blue image around the animal slowly turned deep red in colour. "Now, that's something I could eat!"

Still, Locklynn wouldn't let her by. "No!"

Jenna huffed and leered at him. "But I'm hungry and I need to eat." Her stomach growled when she thought of the meaty hide that challenged her. A fiery yellow glaze suddenly coated her eyes as the predator inside of her was awakened. She dropped the backpack and flared her nostrils. "It's dinner-time!"

Jenna ducked beneath Locklynn's cane and raced off in pursuit of her meal.

Sinnicks jumped onto Locklynn's shoulder as he grabbed the backpack and screamed for Jenna to return.

Jenna didn't listen, nor did she look back. She was starving, delusional and in the midst of a hunt. Locklynn ran through the field after her, trying to keep up, but she soon disappeared out of view.

Jenna was fast, she wanted to eat. The fangs dropped from her mouth as she focused on the meal ahead. Locklynn was no longer behind her but she could still hear him rushing past the stalks, calling out her name.

Suddenly, the animal beneath the ground came to a stop. As it did, the earth around it began to quake. Jenna's feet came to a grinding halt when up through the soil sprang one of the Blade Vipers. Its forked tongue lashed out at her and she jumped back, nearly falling. In the blink of an eye, she felt the cold feel of snakeskin winding around her body, squeezing her.

Locklynn broke through the cornstalks behind her and lifted his cane, but it was too late. Jenna and the snake perished in a blast of silver smoke.

Locklynn stood for a moment, astounded that they had taken her so quickly. Without a moment to lose, he snapped his fingers and vanished into the night.

KINDRED SPIRITS

The smoke soon cleared from Jenna's sight and she was finally able to see where she was. The pressure that held her body firmly in place broke away as the mass of bones and muscle disappeared from around her. She buckled over and coughed.

"Locklynn!" she called out.

He didn't respond, he was nowhere in sight.

"Locklynn!" she called again.

Her feet now stood on a mound of white desert sand. From her vantage point, she could see the perfectly sculpted dunes in the distance. Jenna was now in the desert. The sand sparkled beneath the moon's light. Beautiful as it was, it frightened her, for she was alone, just like in her vision.

The Sandshadow had summoned Jenna. Somewhere in the sands, it lay in wait.

Moments passed, but the monster had not yet shown itself. Jenna wondered where it was; she didn't want to be caught unawares. In the distance she thought that she heard her name in the wind. Behind her, a figure began to take form. A powerful body moved swiftly towards her. Its green eyes glowed in the night; it was Anzhara. The feline ran through the sands to reach her, but something was wrong. Anzhara was limping—one of her back legs was injured. She then disappeared out of sight and Jenna was left wondering what had happened to her. Seconds later, Anzhara reappeared at the top of a dune. Jenna was awestruck by her beauty as the cat stood looking down at her from the peak.

Anzhara yelled out to Jenna but her voice was muffled by the growing wind. Jenna saw blood dripping from her leg. *Oh no!*

With tender but deliberate steps, Anzhara descended the dune. But as she did, her body began to fade away like someone blowing sand off a sidewalk. Anzhara was gone.

Jenna prayed that it wasn't a mirage. "Anzhara!" she cried. "Anzhara—where are you?"

"She's not coming back," a voice came from nearby.

Jenna turned and saw her mother standing alone, not more than ten feet away, talking to her.

"That can't be you…"

"I warned you not to leave," her mother said.

Jenna looked away. "You're not real, you're just an illusion."

"No, Jenna. I am real. And I've come to save you from this life you're so desperate to ruin."

Jenna was so focussed on her mother's voice, that she didn't hear the rapture of snakes moving towards them. Filled with bitter intentions, the serpents formed a ring around her mother and taunted her with their venomous fangs.

The ring began to open at one end and Jenna felt herself being welcomed into the group. The scene was playing out just as it did before.

Vile hisses echoed in her head as she took steps towards her mother. The predator inside of her was surfacing. All Jenna saw was the heat-coloured patches of the warm-bodied creature she was about to kill. It was so easy, so simple; the weak little prey that awaited her.

The pulse of her mother's blood got stronger as she approached. Jenna's fangs grew; she moved closer.

The ring of snakes closed, and with no way out, Jenna smiled. "Evil is in the eye of the beholder."

"Jenna, you're not evil," her mother said, softly.

But Jenna was gone. Her demonic counter-part had taken over. The Blade Viper was now speaking for her. "You can't stop me…not now."

"Then I'll make this really easy for you." Her mother leaned her neck to one side, offering herself up willingly.

Jenna hissed in excitement. She blinked as the colour in her eyes changed to a piercing shade of yellow.

Her mother gasped when she saw them, but still she didn't struggle. "I will save you, Jenna Jean," was the last thing she said.

With her teeth aimed at her mother's neck, she instead backed away quickly.

Her mother's hand was reaching for Jenna's pocket.

"No!" A voice screamed from outside the circle. Jenna looked and saw Locklynn and Jason standing side by side, with the vial of white poison ready in Jason's hand. Locklynn lifted his cane into the sky and from it came an enormous umbrella of light. The serpents recoiled from the brightness leaving Jenna and her mother exposed.

Then, from behind them all came a thundering blast.

"It's the Sandshadow!" Locklynn cried. "Throw the potion!" he yelled at Jason.

"Jenna—Oh my God! Your eyes!" Jason screamed.

"Throw it!" Locklynn hollered. "There isn't much time!"

"I can't—it'll kill her!"

The spell Jenna was under began to lift. Her eyes and teeth returned to normal. "Throw the bottle, Jason!" Jenna screamed. "Hurry—before it's too late!"

The snakes began to slither away into the desert in all directions. "No!" Locklynn screamed.

With the bottle in his hand, Jason was suddenly swept off his feet and pulled high into the sky. A giant mass of sand appeared in the night and lifted him even higher. Jenna and Locklynn looked on in horror.

"Locklynn—do something!" Jenna screamed.

Locklynn raised his cane to stop the attack but a thick blanket of sand rushed towards him and knocked him to the ground. There was nothing anyone could do.

With one massive force, Jason was thrown back down to the earth. His screams were silenced when his body plummeted into the ground. Jenna stood in utter shock, tears streaming down her face.

The Sandshadow had arrived.

Locklynn reached for his cane in the sand. He then stood to face the master adversary.

Her eyes filled with tears, Jenna turned around and glared at the woman behind her. "I am going to stop you!"

The woman sneered at her. "Remember who you're speaking to, my dear."

"I don't care who you are!" Jenna snapped. "You're not my mother!"

"You will be punished for your insolence!" the woman said, angrily.

Jenna shook her head. "Not this time!" She didn't wait for a reply. She spun around and dashed through the desert towards Jason's body. "Jason!" she cried out. She searched the sands for him, but he was nowhere in sight.

"He's dead and buried—you will not find him!" her mother called out behind her.

Jenna didn't respond; she kept on running.

"The Sandshadow rules us all. Your death is his life!" her mother shouted.

Jenna ran without stopping, in the direction of where Jason fell. She was desperate to find him. A fall like that would have been fatal, but she didn't want to think about that.

Her tears were stifled when a heavy sound penetrated the air, moving the sand all around her feet. Jenna looked behind her and saw Locklynn fighting the Sandshadow. Ghastly shockwaves bellowed from its mouth as Locklynn shone his light upon it. Looking more like a mouse fighting a lion, they battled each other in the night. Locklynn's magic was no match for the giant monstrosity that loomed above him. It was only a matter of time before Locklynn was overpowered. Jenna had to hurry.

"Join us," Jenna's mother said, appearing now in front of her. "Your power will be unsurpassable."

Jenna came to an immediate halt. "No—never! You may look like my mother but I know that it's you, Adella. And I will never join forces with you, ever!"

"You are not as strong as you think, my dear."

Jenna could no longer look at the woman who spoke to her. "Show your true self. You can't masquerade as my mother anymore. Let me see who I'm fighting!"

"Very well." A black, sparkly sheen appeared around Jenna's mother as her body changed into that of an old woman with long silver hair and glaring green eyes. "We meet again."

"Not for long, Adella." Jenna was confident in her manner. During the transition, she had scooped up a handful of sand. She took it now and threw it in the old woman's face.

Adella screamed and Jenna ran. But when she looked back, Adella was gone. There was no sign of her anywhere. Jenna couldn't waste any time, because in the distance she saw a horde of snakes heading her way.

Searching the sands, she couldn't find Jason anywhere. She knew he was out there somewhere but just couldn't see him. She didn't want to give up on him but she couldn't let Locklynn suffer either. So, she turned and sped through the night towards Locklynn. As she ran full speed towards him, something shiny distracted her. It lay half-buried in the sand in the direction she was running. It was the bottle of Hawthorn poison that Jason had been holding.

Jenna made a beeline for it. When she got within inches of it, she dropped down onto her knees. With both hands, she dug furiously into the sand.

A strained voice came from the ground and Jenna dug even faster. Jason was alive.

"Jason!" she cried. She could hear him coughing. "Jason—hold on!" She was afraid that he was being suffocated.

Frantically, she dug until the tips of her fingers came across something. Feeling for his hand, she then pulled with every bit of strength that she had. The upper half of his body lifted to the surface but his legs were still buried.

Jenna laid his body back down in the sand. She could see that he was too weak to move. She leaned in to listen to his breathing. "Oh, thank God! It's okay, Jason—I'm here!"

A faint whisper came from his lips. "Th…th…"

"Jason—can you hear me? You need to rest."

He shifted his head and nodded slightly.

Jenna placed her finger on the underside of his wrist to check his pulse. "Oh no! Jason—stay with me!" Now she was worried; his pulse was not normal. "Look—I'm right here. I won't leave you." She knew it was a lie, but if it gave him some degree of comfort, she was happy to say it.

A blast of ground-shaking roars sounded across the desert. Jenna rested Jason's hand on his chest. "Listen to me—please don't move!"

She reached for the bottle of hawthorn poison but saw that it was cracked and leaking. Jenna didn't want to touch it, but she could hear Locklynn's voice telling her to be strong and to conquer the Blade Viper that festered inside. She decided that he was right.

There was just one thing left to do. Quickly, she removed the rest of the sand that covered Jason's legs. His right leg was fine but when she saw the state of his left leg, she grimaced. "Oh God!"

His left leg was poised in an unnatural position; the lower leg was broken. Blood was seeping from the knee. There was no way he was walking away from this.

Jenna tried to mask her sadness, but Jason saw right through it. "Go…" he said, coughing.

Jenna didn't want to now. She was afraid to leave him.

Looking up at her, his body quivered. "You…know…you have to."

She took his hand and held it tightly. Silently, she nodded.

The sound of snakes was fast approaching. It was time to say good-bye.

"You're going to be just fine," she said, as the tears erupted from her eyes. "I will come back for you!" She leaned over and gently kissed his lips. It was the first time she had ever kissed him.

Jason shivered on the ground. "Be…carefu…" His body then went limp. As he drifted into unconsciousness, Jenna knew he wouldn't be back.

She placed his hand on his chest and wiped the tears from her eyes. She knew what had to be done. Pulling her sleeve down over her fingers, she carefully removed the bottle of poison from the sand. She cringed and then sneezed over and over when part of the contents soaked through the fabric and touched her.

Scared as she was, Jenna stood and watched the swarm of snakes make their way towards Jason's broken body. It was a sole effort, most likely a death sentence, but she needed to put all the attention on her. With all the courage she could muster, she faced the swarm head on. "That's it, come and get me!"

"You're not alone," a familiar voice suddenly appeared next to her.

Hope filled Jenna with momentary happiness when she looked over and saw Anzhara next to her in the sand, uninjured. "Anzhara—you're here!"

"Yes, and together we will fight." Anzhara's voice was almighty. It was the backbone Jenna needed.

As the clan of snakes closed in, both Jenna and Anzhara prepared for battle in different directions. "I don't know how this is going to end, Anzhara, but I will not give up!"

The feline bowed her head. "Neither will I."

The snakes slithered effortlessly in the sand, moving towards their prey.

"Jenna—you need to get to the pyramid. It's invisible to you now, but when you see the Catstar in the sky, follow it and the pyramid will appear. I know that you have the ruby—Alaina told me. You must protect it at all costs. When you get inside the pyramid, I will meet you there and you can give the talisman to me."

Jenna watched Anzhara carefully. "Okay. Are you sure you're able to fight? Your leg—can you run?"

"Yes, Jenna. Now go! I will stay and help Locklynn." Anzhara looked strong like she always did. With a devout nod, she turned and raced off towards Locklynn.

What Anzhara didn't know was that Jenna had a plan of her own. Just like Alaina had said, the beats of her heart would tell her when to strike. As the snakes approached, Jenna's pulse began to decelerate. That's when she knew it was time to act.

The swarm of vipers began to branch as half of them charged off after Anzhara. For Jenna, that didn't matter. She had a plan for that, too. With the bottle clinging to her fabric-covered palm, she waited for the group of snakes that were heading for her. Doing her best not to let the fear in, she held her ground until she could see the colour of their eyes.

As they approached, Jenna darted off ahead of them, towards Locklynn and Anzhara.

With their fangs primed and ready for laceration, the snakes chased after her. Jenna was pleased that her plan was working, for when she looked back, Jason was left safely alone in the sand.

Jenna's feet were flying; she felt like an Olympic athlete. All or nothing, was what she thought at that very moment. Now, she needed to lure the other group of snakes away from Locklynn and Anzhara.

Nearing them, she called out, "Come and get it—fresh blood right here!"

More ripples shook the ground as the Sandshadow tried to beat down the warriors that stood beneath it. Locklynn's light held back the fearsome predator but Jenna could see that Locklynn's power was weakening.

She soared through the desert, gathering more vipers as she ran. Her plan to distract them was working. When she saw them gaining on her, all bundled together, she turned and threw the glass bottle into the middle of the group. Without thinking, she dove headfirst into the sand and covered her head.

Piercing screams emanated from within the cluster of snakes as a dark cloud coated the area. One by one, they fell on top of each other, into a smoldering pile of decomposing flesh. The sounds they made were grisly. Some struggled to move away from the group but were crippled so badly that they fell not far from the mess.

Silver flares sprang from within the dark cloud that now started to swirl around them. Jenna lifted her head to see what was happening.

The cloud spun faster and faster, lifting the snakes into the air, whipping their bodies around.

"Uh oh!" This part Jenna hadn't anticipated.

The winds twisted violently into a funnel-shaped sand storm. Jenna crawled further away so as not to be taken with it. A frightening flash lit up the sky, momentarily blinding her. Jenna covered her eyes and looked away. Waves of thunder echoed in the night. Jenna couldn't help but look back. Electric sparks flew everywhere as a massive silver fire exploded inside the storm. Jenna screamed and pressed her body against the sand.

She laid there listening to the terrifying sounds, but then the air fell silent. The funnel of serpents had disappeared into the night. She rolled onto her back and rested a moment while holding her chest. She had conquered the Blade Vipers, a great victory indeed. The triumph of her vanquish, however, was not to last.

Sounds of the enemy soon trumpeted across the desert as the Sandshadow roared into the night. Hearing the level of anger, Jenna sat up and looked back at the monster. But what she really saw was the fear in Locklynn's eyes. The look he gave was ominous, and Jenna knew that the Sandshadow's retribution would be fierce. Anzhara also had a strange look in her eyes, as if she hadn't expected Jenna to destroy the snakes.

"Save yourself!" Locklynn screamed.

Jenna shook her head. She had to run back and help them. "NO!"

"Get to the pyramid!" Anzhara yelled. "You must!"

Jenna watched her two guides slowly back away from the Sandshadow. Each step they took was undeniably foreshadowing the evil that was about to be unleashed. All three of them stared with wide eyes as the titan of sand began to spin in front of them, churning the crystal earth into another shape. Jenna felt the force of wind pulling her towards it. She lay flat to the ground while the Sandshadow transformed into something else. The winds howled across the desert. Then, a sound like no other came from the sky. The sound of vengeance.

When Jenna looked up, she shrieked. A gigantic Blade Viper, the size of a whale, now hovered above them all. Its black and silver striped body moved from side to side as it sat on a ring of its own coils. Its muscles rippled in the night beneath the moon's glow.

"Oh…my…GOD!" Jenna nearly fainted when she saw it.

Its fangs dangled down; each one twice her size. Its yellow eyes penetrated the dark night, driving fear through the hearts of all those who looked at it. It was frightening. It was colossal. And it was bloodthirsty. But the part that scared Jenna the most was its hood. Looking more like a cobra, she shuddered at the sight of it. Seeing Locklynn now, Jenna realized that the only good she could offer him…was to run. She knew he would understand her motive.

Without a moment's hesitation, Jenna lifted herself off of the ground and bolted through the desert. She searched the sky for the Catstar that Anzhara had spoken of. Jenna assumed she would know what that was when she saw it. Forcing herself onward, she sprinted through the desert, hoping that at any minute the pyramid would reveal itself. But so far, all she saw was sand.

Glancing back, she saw the monster Blade Viper in pursuit. Her heart leapt into her mouth. She only prayed that she could outrun it. One goal, one masterful motion—that's all it would take, if she could only get to the pyramid.

A slight glimmer in the sky soon appeared above her. Jenna looked up and saw a twinkling constellation in the shape of a cat's eye. "YES!" she yelled. Beneath the star, came a downpour of shimmering light. Within seconds, the pyramid was growing out of the sand like a weed. Jenna was almost there.

A haunting bellow came from behind; the Blade Viper was almost upon her.

Jenna was surprised when Anzhara suddenly appeared next to her, without Locklynn. "Hurry, Jenna—it's coming!"

Jenna was too afraid to ask what had happened to Locklynn. Together, she and Anzhara ran.

Seeing the glowing sheen of the pyramid, gave Jenna everything she had wished for. It meant sanctuary. She was so close now. The sapphire walls came into view, and like a family waiting for a visitor, an opening formed on the side as if to welcome her in.

As Jenna neared the opening, no sounds came from behind her. No roars, no bellows. But this time, Jenna would not be fooled. The Sandshadow was out there somewhere. It was playing with her. And she had no choice but to humour it.

As fast as they could, Jenna and Anzhara leapt through the opening of the pyramid. It immediately disappeared behind them, sealing them in. That's what Jenna was waiting for.

Through the dim amber lighting, Jenna headed for King Odon's statue. Anything was to be expected in here. With an inconspicuous glance, she surveyed the statue until she found the small depression in the center of his neck. She knew what had to be done; she just had to find a way up there.

Something moved behind her and she turned to look. Standing by the entrance, was Anzhara.

"I'm so glad that you're here with me," Jenna sighed. "I never know what to expect in here."

"We won't be safe for long. The Sandshadow will find a way in," Anzhara said.

Jenna believed her. "Especially if it's invited…"

Anzhara didn't respond.

Jenna heard the wind outside, pounding at the walls. "It's here, isn't it?"

"Yes," Anzhara said.

"There's no way out for me, is there?" Jenna walked around one of the mummified statues. "This is where I'm meant to fall."

"You mustn't think like that, Jenna. There are ways around it; we will find one. Is the ruby safe?" Anzhara said, as she paced along the wall.

"Yes," Jenna said, watching her carefully. "I have it."

Thunder rumbled outside sending shockwaves through the pyramid. The walls shook on all sides. It was only a matter of time before the Sandshadow found its way in.

The battlegrounds had shifted, and Jenna was standing right in the heart of it. She remained close to the statue, she felt protected there. Besides, she couldn't make her move, not yet anyway. She touched the ruby in her pocket; it reminded her of what everyone was after.

"I think you should move away from the wall. It's not safe there," Jenna said.

Anzhara continued to pace back and forth.

Thunder echoed all around and the walls shook again. Glass from the apex fell into the pyramid.

"The walls won't hold, Anzhara. That monster is coming in here. Please, move away!"

As Jenna pleaded with Anzhara to move, a blood-curdling scream blasted through the night. Without warning, one of the glass walls exploded inward. Jenna dropped to the ground behind the statue. She screamed when the Sandshadow slithered in through the side of the pyramid. When Jenna looked up she saw Anzhara wrapped in the viper's coils.

"No!" Jenna screamed.

Agonizing wails came from the feline as the snake tightened its hold.

Jenna wanted to stop it, if only to play along. She ran out from behind the statue. "What do you want? I'll give you anything, just stop hurting her!"

The Sandshadow was seething, but upon hearing Jenna's request, it loosened its grip on Anzhara. Jenna sank back towards King Odon's statue. It was time to implement her plan. Slowly, she moved, one foot at a time, not taking her eyes off the snake for a second. Its reptilian stare was gross and unforgiving. There was a bounty on Jenna's head; this monster wanted her dead and gone. But there was one thing standing in its way—and it was the only thing keeping Jenna alive.

Out of the corner of her eye, Jenna spotted a white light travelling through the sands. It gave her encouragement.

She stared at the hooded evil. "Please don't hurt her. If you want someone, take me!" Jenna kept moving backwards, carefully, steadily.

With Anzhara still tucked in its coils, it slithered towards Jenna.

An enormous forked tongue sprang from its mouth, reaching Jenna's body. It slid up and down all sides of her. The smell was nauseating. It was a putrid odor, like rotting meat. Jenna closed her eyes and tried not to react, but the slime on her skin was starting to tingle. She wanted to scratch herself to relieve the itch but was afraid to show any weakness.

As the viper moved in front of her, a stinging scent came from its mouth. The smell of venom.

A puss-like drool dripped from the tips of its fangs and landed on the ground next to her. A tiny cloud formed above the sizzle. Jenna was careful not to step in it. She looked up at the snake's teeth as they dangled above her head. They were enormous and could sever her in half at any moment.

Still, Jenna kept moving back. She stopped when her feet touched something behind her—it was the base of King Odon's statue. With her right hand, she felt for a ledge. She tried not to smile when she came across one.

The snake lowered its head until its eyes aligned with Jenna's. It stared deeply into her soul.

Looking into the snake's eyes, she offered up a trade. "I know what it is you want. Give me Anzhara and I will give you what you need."

The snake hissed with satisfaction. Jenna tried to remain strong but her legs started to wobble. Something was happening. The snake had a mental hold on her. It had ensnared her with its eyes. She stared at it without blinking, and soon felt herself swimming in a sea of yellow. She began to let go of her fighting spirit. Her hand dropped down into her pocket and the snake nodded to her. Jenna played with the ruby and then slowly lifted it.

"That does not belong to you!" a voice shouted from behind.

The snake turned and saw Locklynn with his cane armed and ready.

Now freed from the viper's hold, Jenna shook her head and wiped the slimy film from her face. Her other hand was wrapped around the ruby in her pocket. She had nearly given it up. Coming out of her daze, she looked over at Locklynn.

"Jenna—go!" he screamed.

Jenna turned quickly towards King Odon's statue and started climbing.

A brilliant beam of white light streamed out from Locklynn's cane towards the beast, blinding it, forcing it to retreat. The viper screamed and cowered from the light but with one strike of its thick tail, it lashed out and violently threw Locklynn against one of the walls. Anzhara immediately dropped from its hold.

The light from Locklynn's cane disappeared as he fell to the ground, gasping for air.

Instead of attacking the viper, Anzhara turned towards Locklynn. As she ran, her body morphed into an old woman with poison in her veins.

She grabbed Locklynn by the throat and lifted him off the ground. His legs dangled in the air and his cane fell from his hands. Adella was draining the life out of him. "I warned you," she said.

In the absence of Locklynn's light, the viper returned to the blood it was thirsty for.

"Looking for me?" Jenna yelled from the top of King Odon's statue. She was now standing on his shoulders. In her left hand was the ruby. "I believe *this* is what you're looking for." The jewel sparkled in the amber glow of the pyramid as she held it up for everyone to see.

"NO!" Adella dropped Locklynn and raced towards the statue, enraged that she had been fooled.

The viper gave a harrowing bellow that frightened Jenna to the core. But it was too late; the end was near. The viper's body lifted high into the air and lunged for Jenna, but she was ready for it. She quickly leaned over and placed the ruby onto the neck of King Odon. She felt the near miss of razor sharp teeth reaching for her arm but she immediately withdrew behind the statue to hide. The fangs hit the front of the statue sending shivers up Jenna's body. But the fate of the ruby was sealed. Dazzling streams of blood-red light suddenly shot out from the jewel in all directions, filling the pyramid with a crimson coating.

The viper let out an ear-piercing scream and recoiled from the statue. Jenna was both shocked and frightened when a hulking red paw reached out from the ruby and pulled the snake towards it. She had never seen anything like it in her life. The viper's body began to spin uncontrollably into a whirling funnel of black and silver maniacal madness. A crazed reptilian shrieking reverberated throughout the pyramid. Jenna couldn't escape the sounds.

Sickle claws from the giant red paw lashed out like knives into the spiralling tornado. The frantic sounds of submission and chaos merged as the paw dragged the viper into the ruby.

Adella came to a sudden stop. Upon seeing her master's demise, she quickly disappeared from the pyramid without even trying to help.

Jenna braced herself against the statue, feeling her hair whipping all around her. Beneath her, each of the amber globes burst into pieces as orange glass flew through the air. One by one, each of the mummified statues was ripped from its base. Thousands of white and orange shards whizzed past Jenna's face and body like it was a combat zone. She ducked her head and pressed herself against the back of King Odon's statue to avoid being sliced. And the noise—she couldn't believe the noise. It was mad hysteria. Jenna wanted to cover her ears but that meant releasing her grip on the statue.

The pyramid trembled all around as the remaining walls succumbed to the pressure. As each one fell, the debris was sucked into the whirling cyclone. The menacing stripes flew past Jenna's face and she saw the viper's yellow stare. The animal was still fearsome, regardless of its demise. Feeling the pull of the winds, Jenna came within inches of the enemy's teeth when she was nearly hauled out from her hiding spot. She clung to the statue with all her might.

The winds moved closer to Jenna as the paw retracted into the jewel with the viper, and all of the pyramid in tow. She closed her eyes and tightened her grip. Then, with a flash of red lightning, the paw disappeared. And so did everything else.

UNENDING EXPECTATIONS

The air was still and tranquil—a complete contrast to what had happened only seconds earlier. But the silence had a ghoulish, sinister feel to it. It was unearthly. Jenna sensed that something was not right. The menace might have been defeated, but the night was not over. It all seemed too anticlimactic; it didn't seem possible that the Sandshadow was gone. A foe as powerful as that couldn't be contained for long. That, she was sure of.

Jenna slowly stood from behind the statue. She scoured the open space but Adella was nowhere in sight. That angered Jenna deeply. She wanted to punish Adella for her betrayal.

"Jennaaa…" a ragged voice came from the ground.

Jenna saw Locklynn lying on his stomach. "Oh my God!" She quickly found her footing and climbed down the statue. "Locklynn!"

He lay on the floor, coughing. And then he was silent.

When Jenna neared the base of the statue, she jumped onto the ground and raced towards him. The image was disturbing. Locklynn lay motionless, like he was sleeping. But Jenna feared the worse. She remembered how hard he'd been thrown into the wall, and how Adella had choked the life from him. Seeing him lying still on the ground upset her greatly.

She dropped to her knees beside him and leaned in. "Locklynn—can you hear me?"

Nothing. No response.

Gently, she rolled him onto his back. His eyes were closed and he wasn't breathing. "Oh God!" She reached for his hand. His fingers were cold, and when she couldn't find a pulse, she panicked. Jenna looked for any obvious injuries, but couldn't find any. At that point, she assumed they were all internal.

Locklynn's skin was dull and slightly grey. Jenna didn't know what to do. She waited for a sign; a hiccup, a cough, a blink—anything that would let her know he was okay. But he didn't move.

Jenna sat by his side holding his hand in hers. She could feel the scales on his skin. They were soft now, and shedding, like feathers from a bird. "You can't leave me, Locklynn," she said, her eyes swelling with tears. "I don't know what to do without you."

Locklynn lay still and quiet. His arms, legs, body—everything was now stiff. It was clear to Jenna that he was gone. She glanced around the open space as the wind whistled past her. The pyramid and everything in it was gone. The only thing left standing was King Odon's statue. Jenna looked up at it, feeling morbidly alone. Jason was gone. Anzhara was gone. Her grandmother was nowhere in sight. And now Locklynn had left her.

Surrounded by sand and nothing more, she cursed Adella's name. "How could you do this?" she screamed. "You monster—you killer! He was an innocent man!" The weight of Jenna's emotions finally came crashing down upon her. She hunched over Locklynn's body and cried.

"You helped me become this person that I am now. I need you to teach me. I'm not done learning!" She leaned back and looked at him. "Please don't leave me, Locklynn! Please!" she sobbed.

Tears streamed down her face and landed on Locklynn's hand. As they touched his skin, a soft, glowing silver light appeared around his body. Jenna sat back and watched in amazement as Locklynn began to move. First his feet, then his hands. His fingers wiggled and his nose twitched. Then the scales on his hands grew back. As the silver light faded, his eyes slowly opened.

Jenna couldn't believe what was happening, she was absolutely astounded. But when she saw the twinkle of his brilliant blue stare, she couldn't hold back. "Locklynn!" she cried.

"Jenna?" He looked up at her, confused.

"Yes—it's me, Jenna!" she smiled. "You're alive!"

"Oh? And I wasn't before?" he said, lifting his head.

Jenna didn't know how to answer that. She was just thankful that Locklynn was alive.

Carefully she helped him sit up. "Where are we?" he said.

Jenna was startled by his comment, thinking that perhaps his memory had been lost. But then she realized how different things now looked. They were sitting in the sand with no protective walls around them. The pyramid was gone. And so was the Sandshadow.

"We're in the desert, Locklynn. Don't you remember the fight in the pyramid?"

"Yes, some of it. I was not awake for the rest," he said with a wily grin.

Jenna released a tearful laugh. "Well, that's understandable," she said. She couldn't believe that Locklynn was moving when only a moment ago he was gone.

Locklynn was silent for a moment. "You were crying, why?" he said.

Jenna wiped the tears from her face. "I thought I lost you. For a moment there, I actually did. Locklynn—you died!"

"Died?" Again, he looked confused. "But now, here I am."

"Yes. I don't know what happened, but you came back."

"You brought me back, Jenna. *You* did this," he said with certainty.

Jenna was stunned. Part of her immediately believed it because of the gecko inside Locklynn's cave, but part of her unequivocally denied it. "That's impossible, I couldn't have!"

"I said that your skill would grow, exponentially as it turns out. And for my sake, I couldn't be more thrilled."

Jenna felt like an indecisive weather vane, not knowing which way to go. She could return to a normal life and renounce magic entirely, or she could embrace magic and thrive on powers that reached beyond the grave. It was a far cry from her city life, and either way her future would change. She stared at the sand, now wondering what other surprises awaited her.

"Come, my dear. We need to carry on." Locklynn calmly got to his feet.

With both arms extended, Jenna helped him stand. He placed one arm around her shoulder and leaned in for support. "It's okay, I've got you," she said.

"Ahh...the student is taking over. How admirable." He rocked back and forth, slightly off balance. Once he was steady, he looked up at King Odon's statue.

Jenna followed his stare. "We stopped him, Locklynn—we stopped the Sandshadow!"

"And Adella?"

Jenna shook her head. "She disappeared. She's out there, somewhere."

"Yes, but the power of the talisman has broken their bond. At least for now," he said.

The ruby sparkled beneath the moon's light as it rested in its proper place.

Locklynn coughed and rubbed his neck. "My smart girl—you knew that Adella had shape-shifted into your feline. You knew all along..."

"Yeah, it was her wound that gave it away. I saw Anzhara in the desert and she was hurt. But later when she came to me, I could tell she was different. She told me to keep the ruby, which went against everything that Anzhara had said."

"Very wise, Jenna. Very wise indeed."

"And now the ruby is safe," Jenna said.

"Because of you, my dear," Locklynn said with a wink.

"Actually, if it wasn't for you breaking the viper's spell I was under, neither of us would be here right now." Jenna was overwhelmed with gratitude. "Thank you, Locklynn. You are truly good."

"Well, I—" He nearly choked on his words when Jenna wrapped her arms around him and squeezed.

It was obvious that he'd never been hugged before. "That's a human action, isn't it...embracing someone?" he said.

"Yes." Jenna smiled and leaned back. "You did good, Locklynn. But wait—where's my grandmother? And where's Anzhara?"

"They're both waiting for you in a safe place," he said. "Anzhara was never injured. She was merely a ploy to help you see evil."

"You did this, didn't you? You protected them," Jenna said.

Locklynn smiled in a humble manner. "I had to, for all this to play out." He stumbled in place as he spoke.

Jenna shouldered his arm. "Are you okay?"

"Yes, but I am a shepherd without a staff..."

They both searched the ground for his cane but neither one could find it.

"I think it got sucked into the ruby," Jenna said. "But it's okay, I'll help you."

Locklynn's tone suddenly turned serious. "We must find your friend—"

With everything that had happened, Jenna had completely forgotten about Jason. "Oh God! Locklynn—get us out of here now!"

He nodded, and they huddled together. "Hold on!" he said. Then with a snap of his fingers, they both disappeared beneath the moon's light.

FALLING STARS

Jenna felt herself once again being transported. In the flash of a moment they arrived in another part of the desert, where Jason's body lay quiet in the sand. Together, she and Locklynn knelt down beside him. She lifted Jason's hand; his pulse was nearly non-existent.

"He can't die!" Jenna whimpered. "I can't let him pay for my mistakes. Please tell me you can fix this!"

Using both hands, Locklynn placed them over Jason's leg but nothing happened.

"What's wrong?" Jenna said, her voice shaking.

"I do not know." Again, he placed his hands over Jason's body, but Jason didn't move. "My power has been hindered," he said.

"What do you mean? This is what you do—you put things back together."

"Something is blocking my ability to heal," he said, looking at her.

"Like what?"

"I do not know, Jenna. I do not know."

"Then let me try." Jenna placed her hands over Jason's leg but Locklynn stopped her.

"No! Your gift is to heal the dead," he said. "Your friend is alive. Right now, your power is useless to him."

"Then, what are we supposed to do?" Jenna said, feeling fearful.

"The boy is meant to die," a voice travelled across the sand.

Both Jenna and Locklynn looked up.

Standing in the desert, with her black dress blowing in the wind, was Adella.

Jenna jumped to her feet and stood protectively in front of Jason. "No, he's not. This is all your doing, isn't it? You put some sort of hex or something on him so he couldn't be healed."

Adella smiled. "Your teacher is right, you are learning fast."

"Why are you doing this?" Jenna stared in complete disillusion.

Adella was stoic. Her mannerisms depicted someone without a soul. "You took something of mine, my dear. It is only fair that I return the favour."

Jenna shook her head. "You mean—you did this out of revenge?"

"It was a necessary means," Adella glowered.

Jenna could feel her anger rising. She couldn't believe how cold the old woman's heart was. It was clear to her now who the real monster was.

"Jenna—don't!" Locklynn warned her. But Jenna wasn't listening.

"There's no way you're getting anywhere near him," Jenna said. "I will stop you."

Behind her, Locklynn summoned Sinnicks to the scene. The grasshopper immediately appeared next to Jason's body.

"Find them," Locklynn said, "and bring them here!"

Sinnicks left in a tiny green puff of smoke.

"You cannot stop me," Adella goaded her. "Your courage is admirable but pointless. Your boy will leave this earth, and that is the way of it."

Jenna was combative, willing to fight. "No, he won't. Your gift may be to take life, but mine is to save it. And trust me, I will save my friend!"

"We shall see," Adella said, watching her closely.

Within seconds, Sinnicks reappeared beside Locklynn. Standing next to him, were Anzhara and Alaina.

Jenna turned when she heard a low growl behind her. At first sight of Anzhara's teeth, she smiled. Her reinforcements were here.

"Strength in numbers, I see," Adella sneered. "Hello dear sisters. How nice to have you all here in this moment."

Jenna turned back to face her. "The odds just aren't in your favour tonight, Adella. The power of our family is truly good, you will never conquer that." Magic might have led Jenna to this moment, but her inner strength was shining. "You are nothing but a stranger to us. I, for one, will not hesitate to protect those I love."

Adella's laugh was condescending. "What an interesting thing for someone to say who also is somewhat evil." She wagged her finger at Jenna. "Tsk..tsk."

Jenna took a defensive stance. "I'm not evil!"

"Jenna—stop!" Locklynn begged her. "Do not chase the lure."

"Ahh…but you're not quite human, either," Adella said with a wicked wink.

"I *am* human—more human than you'll ever be!" Jenna yelled.

Adella moved towards her. "You think because you have a magical mix of good and evil raging inside of you, that you can overthrow me?" She chided Jenna. "You are a sad little toy, my dear. That's all you are."

Jenna remained firmly in place as Adella moved forward.

"You are *all* feeble," Adella said, stretching out her arms. With her palms facing the ground, she warned the rest of them. "I am the earth, the very ground you walk on. Your footing is my playground of which I can remove at any time."

Jenna did her best to suppress her fear. She couldn't let the monster win. She glared at the old woman. "Let me make this as clear as I can. My family ties to you never existed. You are nothing more than a pitiful waste of our bloodline. These chains of darkness that you've wrapped yourself in—I hope they drown you in your sleep!"

As she spoke, something soft touched her fingers. Looking down, Jenna saw Alaina holding her hand. "Love is your gift, Jenna, not pain. Do not speak such horrid words."

"Alaina's right," Anzhara said, walking up to her. Her emerald eyes shone beneath the moon. "Remember who you are."

"Yes, Jenna—such sage advice from a sister who abandoned me years ago." Adella sneered. Her comment was filled with contempt. It was a harmful slur against her sibling.

Anzhara faced her head on. As she did, her body transformed into a woman with black gypsy clothing and long silver hair, Jenna's grandmother.

"You were not abandoned, Adella," her grandmother said. "You were sacrificed."

Seeing Abigail in human form infuriated Adella. "Your goodness will not triumph over me, dear sister. Your wisdom will be your defeat."

"We shall see," Jenna's grandmother said.

Locklynn sat alone with Jason in the sand. "The boy is falling," he said.

When they all turned to look at Jason, Adella vanished, leaving a trail of wind in her absence.

Jenna looked back. "Where is she?"

No one answered. No one knew.

A black, shadowy cloud suddenly materialized near Jason's head, Adella was now standing beside him.

Locklynn quickly lifted his hands to form a shield around Jason, but Adella blasted him into the air. He landed on top of Jenna and the others, knocking them all to the ground.

Jenna scurried through the heap to get up. "NO!" she screamed.

Adella bent down and gently stroked Jason's cheek. "Say good-bye now," she smiled.

"Get away from him!" Jenna hollered.

"My dear girl—you have no idea what is inside you. But trust me when I say….you *will* find out. And I will be waiting. Nosce te ipsum!" She threw one hand into the air in a furious motion.

A flash of black smoke exploded around them. In an instant, Adella was gone. And so was Jason.

LET THE DARKNESS DECIDE

Jenna sat in the sand, hunched over and crying. Her plan to protect Jason had gone horribly wrong, and now she had lost him to Adella, a fate worse than dying. There was no stopping the tears.

Alaina crawled over and squeezed Jenna's hand. "The end is not over but the start has begun. The player plays the game, but loses only to win."

Feeling utterly disheartened, Jenna couldn't understand a word she was saying. All that made sense to her now was that the dark witch had prevailed. And all that was good, was now lost.

Another hand reached out to her, and Jenna looked up. "My darling, Jenna," her grandmother said. "The future is not lost, there is more to your boy than you can see. He is safe amongst the danger."

Jenna took her hand and stood. "How? That monster has him!" Tears muddled her vision as she stared at her grandmother. "I let this happen, this is all my fault!"

"No—this was meant to happen, Jenna. This is all part of your journey." Her grandmother's voice was enchanting; it compelled her to listen. "A journey which begins now."

Jenna looked at her suspiciously. "What do you mean?"

"Would I have brought you into the fold for nothing?" she said with a grin.

Jenna peered at all three of her guides. Locklynn watched her as he stroked Sinnicks and whispered to him. Alaina nodded her head up and down as she played in the sand. And her grandmother stood like a pillar of strength, steady in the night with a sly expression on her face.

That's when Jenna had a revelation. "You knew that Locklynn and Alaina had the talisman this entire time, didn't you?" she said to her grandmother.

"Yes," she said. "I had to keep that hidden from you, my dear Jenna. Please believe that. Your life would have been forfeit at the hands of the Sandshadow, had it not been for that secret."

Jenna sighed. She understood why she'd been kept in the dark, and that her search for the talisman was all part of the journey. "I believe you," she said. "But what happens now? What about Jason?"

Locklynn pointed to the area behind where Jenna was standing. "Look and see," he said.

Jenna turned to look. She paused when she saw a large wooden door standing in the desert by itself.

"The decision is yours to make," Locklynn said.

Jenna was stupefied. "What is that?" The door stood alone, with nothing surrounding it but white desert sand. No walls, no roof. No handle.

"It's a path," her grandmother said. "A symbol of your awareness. It begins here."

Jenna couldn't take her eyes off the door. It looked like something right out of a science fiction movie. "What path? What are you talking about?"

"The path to enlightenment," her grandmother explained. "It's your crossing over, my dear. Your future, if you choose to accept it."

Jenna was beginning to understand. "You mean…a life of magic."

Her grandmother nodded.

Jenna glanced down at her hands—they seemed to be humming. A gentle light appeared around them as if they were telling her to move onward.

"Follow your inner light," Locklynn said, "and you will find your future."

"But what about Jason? I need to get him back!"

"And through the door you will find him," her grandmother urged her.

Jenna slowly turned and took her first step towards the unknown. Looking back, she saw all three of her guardians watching her as they remained in place.

"We will never be far from you, Jenna," her grandmother said.

Locklynn and Sinnicks both bowed their heads to her.

Alaina danced around happily while twirling her dress. "She's going to be one, not two or none. The smart little mouse finds the cheese," she said, clapping her hands.

Jenna continued towards the door. As she approached it, she saw three words carved into the wood at the top, much like a school desk at the mercy of a bored student.

'Nosce te ipsum', it read.

"Know thyself," Jenna said aloud. It was what Adella had said to her right before she disappeared.

When Jenna lifted her hand to touch the door, it opened by itself. She took a deep breath and gazed through to the other side. All she saw was black infinite sky. Looking closer, thousands of twinkling stars came into view—it was another universe. Jenna was completely awestruck by the bottomless vision that awaited her. No floor, no ceiling. There was no end to it. Just sparkling prisms of light scattered throughout the darkness. An astronomer's dream.

The scene was beautiful, and gave her a feeling of tranquility.

Bracing for the unknown, Jenna stepped through the door. Where she was headed, she didn't know. But the time had come for her to find out.

~

ABOUT THE AUTHOR

Kara Bartley has been a Niagara Falls resident since the age of six. Her love of animals and life-long fascination with bones led her into the field of paleontology. In 2005, she graduated with a master's degree in Vertebrate Paleontology from the University at Buffalo. Her fictional and non-fictional worlds collided on a dig for fossils in Kansas, where her first book *The Siamese Mummy* was born.

Her novels include *The Unearthlings, Call of Adhara, The Moon in Habock's Mirror, 34* and *The Wolves of Ridley High*.

Kara also owns and operates PALEOTALES, an educational service that combines her love of paleontology and passion for storytelling. Through school and event presentations, Kara ventures into the past with her mix of ancient life and creativity.

ABOUT THE ILLUSTRATOR

Tammy Dunlavey grew up in North East, Pennsylvania with the innate ability to draw. When it came to education, she chose science over art, as science offered her a path untaken.

In August of 2001, Tammy was diagnosed with Multiple sclerosis. In light of her medical challenges, she continued on and received her master's degree in Invertebrate Paleontology from the University at Buffalo.

Although Tammy has returned to her artistic roots as both an artist and illustrator, she finds that paleontology often appears within her creations. Her journey with MS has also played a significant role in her work as her life experiences are wonderfully reflected in her art.

ABOUT THE ILLUSTRATOR

Tammy Dunlavey grew up in North East, Pennsylvania with the innate ability to draw. When it came to education, she chose science over art, as science offered her a path untaken.

In August of 2001, Tammy was diagnosed with Multiple sclerosis. In light of her medical challenges, she continued on and received her master's degree in Invertebrate Paleontology from the University at Buffalo.

Although Tammy has returned to her artistic roots as both an artist and illustrator, she finds that paleontology often appears within her creations. Her journey with MS has also played a significant role in her work as her life experiences are wonderfully reflected in her art.

THE PALEO TWINS

Tammy and I first met at grad school in the fall of 2002. The first thing I remember her saying to me was, "Oh—*she* must be the Vertebrate paleontologist!" From that sarcastic moment on, we were friends. We shared an office in the geology department at the University at Buffalo where Tammy studied Invertebrate paleontology and I studied Vertebrate paleontology. Throughout our studies, we talked and travelled. At school we were given the name, 'Paleo Twins,' and to our delight, it stuck.

I soon found out that my twin had an amazing flare for artistry, whereas I had succumbed to the creativeness of words. It was through school that we met as friends but it was paleontology that brought us together as artists. Our support for one another transcended our education as Tammy and I joined forces as artist and novelist. She is the illustrator behind the words and I am the storyteller behind the pictures.